Sudden Deception

A JILL OLIVER THRILLER

JUDITH PRICE

CONTENTS

To my children & my husband,
thank you for believing in me.

PROLOGUE

"Finish, khalas," he heard a man say in Arabic. "It's after 4 a.m., and it will be light soon."

There it was again—talking. In Arabic.

His left eye was swollen shut. He tried to focus his right eye as he lay in the warm sand. He couldn't see past the lantern's glare, which hung on a pole stuck in the sand beside him. His right eye winced shut when the hard boot cracked another of his ribs. Grains of sand burned his skin like a lit cigarette as they hit his open wounds. Only the release of a breath numbed the pain. A bead of sweat dripped onto his dry tongue, stinging his split, purpled lips on the way down. He licked them anyway.

He could hear no sounds from the brightly lit city of Dubai here in the dark desert. No honking horns or colorfully lit buildings typical of the steel and concrete metropolis. There was no refuge here, no friends in the desert. He could only see silhouettes of men reflecting off the sand and their boots. Even falling in and out of consciousness, he could recognize military-issued special ops boots anywhere. He tried to focus. The talking grew louder, shouting now; he had to think.

Just move, he ordered himself. Now.

He moved his hands ever so slightly. Nothing. They were stuck together at the wrists, bound tight. He couldn't feel his legs—or could he? He shifted as if to shiver. The sharp crystals of sand felt like razors against his raw skin. He was naked. His groin ached, but he couldn't recall why. Then a moment of hope: His legs were not bound.

He searched for cognition.

Move. Survive...

But it was too late. Strong hands gripped his ankles, pulling his body fast; the sharp sand granules ripped his skin. His teeth jarred together each time his chin hit a rock. The large man hauling him across the desert's merciless landscape stopped, and before he could figure out what was happening, he was flipped onto his back. His hands dug hard into the sand underneath him. Thick fingers smelling of gasoline pried open his mouth. He choked as a mitt-full of sand was shoved into his mouth and down his throat.

"We must end this," another man said in Arabic.

He understood Arabic and recognized this man's voice.

Bastard.

He needed to survive. He coughed and spat, trying to breathe, gagging. A bright light swiveled closer and glared into his one open eye, blinding him. For a second, he thought he heard a whisper.

Whoosh! The smell of gasoline sizzled his nostrils. Then the pain began to soften as the light faded into blackness.

CHAPTER ONE

11:12 Zulu Time — Catalina Mountains, Tucson, Arizona.
One week earlier.

Every successful covert operation has four vital elements. Or so the saying goes in most military organizations.

Shoot. Move. Communicate. Survive.

Jill Oliver sighed. Survive. She could do the other three easily. The last one? Well, that was the game, wasn't it?

The soft rumble of the Hemi in the Dodge Charger kept Jill company as she raced along the highway. The clock on the dashboard read 04:12. Blackness stretched across the early morning sky, dotted with stars. Pretty soon, dawn would flow over the eastern mountains like burning lava.

Early mornings were part of her job. Not something she cherished about her duties as a US Marshal—but there it was.

Shoot. Move. Communicate. Survive.

As a terrorist profiler for the Special Operations Group, a division of the US Marshal Service, Jill typically exuded self-confidence. Her long, jet-black hair hung in a tight ponytail, barely touching her lean, muscular shoulders as she swerved the car down the mountain road. But even with the hot, black coffee in her stomach working to awaken her entirely, she wasn't feeling particularly confident. Something felt wrong.

Something about her latest case gnawed at her. It was a critical case. The welfare of what was known as the world's strongest superpower, the US, was at stake—even more so than what had been reported to the public. She knew the truth.

She had been working on the case for some time now. Today, there finally seemed to be a breakthrough. And Jill didn't mind being summoned to Virginia in the middle of the night because lately, her mind would not let her rest.

She had seen proof that Matta Al Jazeera, Al Qaeda's new number one, had purchased uranium at a bargain basement price of $12 million. She'd seen the recent intel report sighting Matta in Brazil. It was all too close to home for her liking, given what else she knew.

It wasn't yet in the news that a former Soviet official, now leader of the Chechen clan on Manhattan Island, had been arrested after a small stockpile of tactical nuclear devices was found buried in a New York state junkyard he owned. This intel proved what the Chief of Military Research and Development had stated in a high-security brief—that nuclear devices had been smuggled into the US and buried at several locations on US soil. The fact that Al Qaeda and a group of Chechens were working together was even more worrisome.

The pile of folders stacked on the front seat seethed with papers pushing past its limits. Jill was dressed in her usual blue windbreaker with US Marshal branded in large, bright yellow letters on the back. Black fatigues hugged her lean quads as her foot pushed ever so slightly, vibrating the 450 horsepower through her body.

Jill loved playing with the fierce power of the bright red car.

Her mobile phone vibrated, then chirped on the black console.

"Oliver here," she snapped into the phone, navigating toward the streetlights in the distance.

"How far away are you?" Tom Walker, her colleague, commanded as if he were her boss.

"'Bout twenty minutes," Jill replied.

"The suspects have been apprehended—two from Yemen and one from Algeria. They fit the profile you wrote and are now headed to Guantanamo Bay. They need you in Virginia to be part of the satellite link. You need to watch the interrogation and determine if these are the men you wrote about in your profile."

Tom knew that Jill knew all of this, but clearly, he was posturing to appear important to someone who must be listening. The politics Jill thought she had left behind at the FBI in Virginia were starting to seep into her current agency... and it was beginning to piss her off.

Tom wanted her job and expected to get her job. He thought that Jill being the only successful female applicant in the missile escort program for SOG was simply a political move. Even after she proved herself during the extensive specialized training in physical tactics, hand-to-hand combat, and weaponry, Tom still anticipated being the lead profiler for the unit. He strutted around like a stunted rooster during training, doubting that Jill would meet the rigorous physical and mental ability standards.

But she had proved him wrong—and he had been nipping at her heels like an angry little Chihuahua ever since.

Jill ended the conversation. The phone clunked as she dropped it onto the black console, and she allowed herself the luxury of enjoying the beauty of Tucson as she drove.

David loves Tucson.

David.

An uneasy feeling pricked Jill's gut. David Brown, a freelance war correspondent for Time magazine, and more importantly, to her at least, her new husband. He was often away for extended periods. But she had been waiting to hear from him for over five days.

Jill's mind struggled to choose between thinking about David or national security; both battled for her attention. David's lack of communication had begun to fuel an unsettling feeling that something was not quite right. She dismissed her intuition and blamed her crime-oriented work for invading her home life. Still, her intuition had always been exceptional—something her Navajo grandmother said was natural.

Jill had learned to harness the gift early in her career. She called it "being in the tunnels." It was proven in her first years at the FBI when the CIA had assisted in setting up an RV—Remote Viewing—department. Jill was one of the program's first and most talented viewers and was a natural. During the Iran hostage crisis, Jill could describe the exact location where hostages were being held without ever being physically there.

Initially set up by the CIA as a clandestine department, the new FBI department was to assist the FBI with defense intelligence. Since 9/11 and with more homegrown terrorists on the rise, the FBI wanted to tap into this type of intelligence research and engage it as a powerful national defense tool. Testing had begun with top-secret, distant targets, often involving life-or-death situations, which is how the good folks at the CIA proved the sometimes-controversial techniques worked.

Nevertheless, getting the department up and running in the FBI was a hard sell. Most of the gray suits at the FBI looked at this intelligence technique as psychobabble, but viewers had produced accurate information that saved lives. There was no crystal ball. It was indisputable: hard, proven science, akin to a modern-day Google using the unconscious resources of the brain's functionality. It has been said that every human has a natural psychic ability, but only a few know how to use it. Jill was one of those few.

"Listen to your instincts," Grams would often say. Grams was right. Relying on her instincts had helped Jill solve many cases. She was confident and secure about her work. But when it came to David, she was unsure. Maybe it was because she was not used to being in love.

Jill had lost her mother to a drunk driver at a young age and had never known her father. Her grandparents had taken her in and taught her about her native heritage. She spent many nights in the desert, maturing into who she was today. They raised her off the reservation, teaching her life skills that could be learned if you were blessed with the genes of a Navajo Indian.

"Some things are better left alone," Grams would remind her.

The Navajo reservation, the largest in North America, had many problems—some of which were why her grandparents left. They chose instead to live in a small three-room trailer just outside of Page, Arizona. Surrounded by rock and desert, they would sit in the back of their cozy home around a fire in the cool evenings. Jill loved to listen to Grandpapa tell her stories of his youth. To Jill, he was a warrior. With his strong hands and worn face, he was a man of honor, an elder.

They said they taught Jill the Sacred Sundance, which white authorities for decades had made illegal—it was witchcraft. It had still been practiced secretly on the reserve at a place called Anna Mae until recently, when the tribal police destroyed the structure in an attempt to stop the ritual. But it was Grams who was ever-present after her death, even today. She was a healer, a sand painter, and a modern-day medicine woman.

After losing Grams, Jill simply wanted to be loved—to be held, cherished, and given all the little things love brings you. Only since she had met David just over a year ago was she able to feel anything, really. Ever since Matthew McGregor and the fateful day, she Remote Viewed and stumbled across him and his location. The events that followed were the main reasons she'd left the FBI. It was that day that changed who she was, as well as who she would become.

Traffic was light as she navigated toward the Tucson military air base. As she drove, Jill knew she would see a mix of cultures, depending on which part of town she was in. There were more poor people than one would have hoped to see. Tucson had a large military base for a city its size. It was customary to see F-16s on maneuvers, blaring over the city's outskirts. Their low-altitude, high-speed flights were fascinating and magical, and the jets' passage would be followed within milliseconds by the rumble of their afterburners.

Jill pulled up to the guardhouse at the gate of the Air Force base, flashed her USMS badge, and waited for the usual queue to move forward. She sat under the large sign that read DAVIS-MONTHAN AIR FORCE BASE until the gate lifted and the faceless guard waved her through with a no-nonsense gesture. Oh, how she missed the pleasant smiles of the pre-9/11 era.

As Jill's car rumbled toward the hangar, her phone vibrated. She had answered before the chirp finished, anticipating David's voice on the other end. They could often predict a call from each other as if they had a magical, private mental communication highway. She pulled the phone to her ear and uttered a sweet "hello." A familiar voice greeted her. But it wasn't David's.

"Jill, it's Jeff McLain, David's editor." Jill felt a slight twinge in her gut. David's work often put him into harm's way, something she had never truly gotten used to feeling any sort of resolve. But somehow, with his charming charisma and calm demeanor, David always had the ability to comfort her.

"Have you heard from David lately?" Jeff asked. The impact of his question reached the bottom of her stomach and tugged at the morning's coffee, pulling it upward toward her throat.

"Ummm... not since Wednesday when he left, 'bout five days ago," she replied. Jill's voice was off-key. "Why?"

"He missed his deadline, and I haven't heard from him either." Jeff's delivery felt a bit too fast to be matter-of-fact.

David worked most deadlines to the last minute, sometimes madly editing before midnight. But the words lingered in her ears, then resonated in her stomach, pushing the coffee further; she swallowed—her only reprieve. A picture of David in front of his computer suddenly entered Jill's mind, then left as fast as it had appeared.

"He went to Doha, right?" Jill expected confirmation. She had not been alarmed when David first told her about his assignment. Jill knew he had been to Doha, Qatar, at least twice. From what he had told her, she knew it was one of the Middle East's safest and most modern cities.

"Yes, and I, well, I'm not too worried, Jill. I just thought I'd double-check with you. There has been some fighting recently in Iraq, but nothing is even close to Doha. It's protected. If anything had affected him, we would have heard something. I've tried contacting our PRO there but have not heard back from him either."

"PRO?" she queried.

"Public Relations Officer; we use them in, ah... more complicated countries. They help our correspondents from time to time. Jill, I am not sure of anything yet. I've put out feelers, so please, don't worry. Get in touch with me if you hear anything, okay?" Jeff gave her his personal mobile number and hung up.

Jill looked at the closed phone and thought of David, but before she could spend time in the tunnels—her gifted intuitive tunnels—she was summoned back to the breaking daylight. She saw Tom, a scrawny shrimp of a man, standing outside the hangar as she parked. She grabbed the folders beside her, tucked them under her arm, slid out of the car, and briskly walked toward him.

Tom was dressed in the same casuals as Jill, with one difference. He always wore his badge on a beaded silver lanyard, complete with the silver circle star, announcing his importance at a glance.

His slight, commanding wave annoyed her. Tom attempted to shout past the sound of the engines. "The FBI, CIA, and NSA are involved in apprehending the suspects—and you know how important those folks think they are."

"Almost as important as you think you are," Jill ruminated without voicing her thoughts.

To Jill's relief, the engines drowned out Tom's squeaky voice as they approached the waiting Learjet. Every breath he took emitted a slight whistling sound, which pricked like a pin under her fingernails.

Walking toward the plane, Jill stopped abruptly. She turned to her right, then around, as if someone had tapped her shoulder. The air smelled of jet fuel, and a lone strand of black hair wisped past her view in the slight breeze. She couldn't see anything suspicious, but she felt it. Something sinister, but she couldn't put her finger on it. Jill often had these feelings when something was wrong or something didn't fit as she raced through the intuition tunnels of her mind. But today, she wasn't in her tunnels; she wasn't trying to do anything but end this case. So why the unsettled feeling? Was it David? Had his non-communication put her off-kilter, or was it Jeff's call? Or was it... no, it couldn't be Matthew McGregor.

Jill didn't know, and she didn't have time to be jumpy or relive her paranoia about McGregor. It couldn't be him—he was tucked away in a cell in the worst prison in California.

Torture was against international and US law, but McGregor didn't care about that. After all, he had planned to kill her anyway. He had particularly enjoyed bludgeoning his other victims to death with an ice pick to the face—thus earning him the media moniker "The Ice Man." If only she had waited for her backup when confirming the location after the viewing. If only that accident had not happened—the one that blocked the road. But as any FBI agent knew, there was no negotiating with Father Time. Jill's tongue wiped her new teeth—the three replacements she'd gotten after McGregor got through with her original ones.

It had been over three years since Eric Wallace and the team rescued her, and she'd rarely had a nightmare since she married David. But she sometimes wondered if she would ever be truly rescued.

Her nightmares usually started with the sketches—the ideograms drawn in that fateful Remote Viewing session. It was a typical RV session that had begun with the group attempting to find a target. In this case, it was the Ice Man. Three women had disappeared, were tortured, then murdered. The FBI's violent crime unit was getting nowhere, so they called upon the FBI RV group to assist them.

In stage one of an RV session, the target was assigned a random number. "Optimum trajectory," the Remote Viewer guru had called it in Jill's training. "OT is the best place for your mind to be before we begin." To get to OT, the viewers were given target numbers. "To achieve optimum trajectory, they placed their pens on the last digit—always the digit one. Lose yourself in them; numb your thoughts." The process was like a radio station signal drawing the Viewer toward the target. All living things are made of energy, and if a Viewer can connect to the target on an energy level, the Viewer can then see the target and its surroundings. In this stage, the Viewer usually sits with a pen and paper to record the viewing. The Viewer needed to be hyper-attentive and zero in on sights and sensations. In the FBI RV department, this was usually achieved through group meditation.

Once the Viewer felt connected to the energy, they would enter stage two and begin to write. First, they would record the sounds and smells. Then the tastes, textures, and feelings. Does the Viewer feel afraid, mad, or sad? Everything was recorded in writing. When they began to see colors and textures, and the viewing became more vivid, the Viewer would enter stage three—that's when they sketched an ideogram. There was no thinking involved, just recordings of what each in the group had viewed.

But Jill didn't have time to think about McGregor or Remote Viewing. She needed to go forward into the future and stay out of her past.

As she shook off the thoughts and continued toward Tom, dark shadows stretched past the hangar, sending chills up her spine.

CHAPTER TWO

The Learjet was headed toward Virginia. Jill took out her Bose headset to block out the chatter from the galley between Tom and that annoying flight attendant, Heather, a youngish woman with dyed blond hair hoisted up into a neat, tight bun. Heather's leathered skin spoke of too much smoking and sunbeds, which pushed her age forward a decade. Jill knew most of Heather's life story. During Heather's flight breaks, she would often navigate toward Jill like a cat in heat, plunk herself down, and endlessly chatter about her life. She thought maybe it was good that she was tied up with Tom.

Concentrate. That was what Jill needed to do. As the plane bumped over clouds, she leaned back into her seat. White noise. Bliss. Nirvana. She closed her eyes. Not to sleep, but to concentrate. She could still feel the thrum of the Rolls-Royce engines, and a bracing whiff of coffee floated by Jill's nostrils.

Jill's job was to reduce the risk of a terrorist attack on US soil through profiling. She needed to get the profiles finalized for the meeting today. Connecting the dots would bring some order to the move next week. The special ops team was to escort the nuclear missiles from Minot Air Force Base in North Dakota to Barksdale Air Force Base in Louisiana.

Yemen, said a voice in her head. She opened her eyes and pulled out the file marked YEMEN CONNECTION. She thumbed through the files on the three terrorists on the FBI wanted list.

The pictures of three men stared up from her lap, trying to communicate something from the dark pages. She felt her blood temperature rise slightly, knowing how easy these vile people were to inflict suffering on innocent others. A terrorist for Al-Qaeda—or any group, for that matter—didn't need much motivation to become an integral part of any scheme or attack.

Jill remembered reviewing a brief on Al Qaeda recruitment prerequisites. In the world of radical Islam, dominated by the Islamic Jihad, the requirements to join included good listening skills, manners, obedience, being vetted by someone in the group, and of course, the recitation of the pledge. Easy!

She sifted through the pile of papers on the leather seat beside her. Where is that pledge? A quick search unearthed it.

"The pledge of God and His covenant is upon me to listen and obey the superiors that are doing this work in energy, early-rising, difficulty, and easiness and for His superiority upon us so that the word of God will be the highest and His religion victorious."

Considering the recent testimony of Ahmed Bin Abdullah—one of Matta's flunky expendable front men brought in front of the US court system this past year—exposing the Al Qaeda recruitment centers network in over eighteen American states made Jill and the team's jobs critical. These centers were disguised as run-down social clubs or dingy bookstores and were often unnoticeable in Islamic communities. Because of the First Amendment, which gave anyone the freedom to exercise any religion, and the bureaucracy of the government, these groups could easily move fast and were hard to track.

Jill internally recited a mission statement she had memorized from an interview she had watched with Bin Laden before he was executed. It had become part of a ritual etched in her brain; she never forgot to turn over every stone to ensure she reported every detail. People relied on her relentlessness to achieve results.

"We have the right to kill four million Americans, half children. Punish, and you will be punished." Bin Laden justified this as an eye for an eye based on the number of Muslims killed worldwide in conflicts.

In many ways, Jill was sympathetic to the Islamic religion. Her first roommate in the dorm at college had been Muslim. Salma was a sweet girl, and they had become great friends. Jill respected her and her choice of religion.

But Jill couldn't stomach anyone who condoned terrorism; that was going too far.

She was in a foul mood now. She picked up the rap sheets and reviewed them again. But it wasn't long before she again lost concentration and found herself gazing out the window.

David.

Why hadn't she heard from him in five days? A picture flashed into Jill's head. It was an image of a pointed steel needle surrounded by fluff, and as her vision became more apparent, she recognized what was in the picture in her mind's eye. It was a picture of a building that pierced through cloud cover. It looked like the Empire State Building spire but different. A building that pierced through clouds had to be tall. Understanding her visions was vital; in most cases, it gave her profile the edge over others. This vision wasn't about the case; it was about David. She had never had visions about David before.

"We are about one and a half hours out, are you finished? We need the info ASAP," Tom barked, walking toward her from the galley. She gave him 'the hand.' He knew her well enough not to speak to her when he saw the hand. Jill's colleagues called it the F-off hand, and she liked the name. It fit.

She needed to stop drifting back to David's mood before he left for his assignment five days earlier. And true to pattern, her mind pushed past her heart. Her eyes struggled back to her lap, back to the faces of evil.

Her visions gave her an edge in her job, but solid science was also essential to profiling. Behavioral evidence analysis (BEA) was often overlooked, but it was where Jill shone. She was a BEA expert.

BEA was the first step to understanding and developing a sense of a criminal's profile. Equivocal forensic analysis (EFA) was the next step. After reviewing mountains of photos, Intel research, and investigative reports, she would form a clearer perception of who she was dealing with in the profile. Jill tied together different incidents to uncover some commonality that would reveal more about the perpetrator.

An INFOSEC—information security—briefing was her first review:

ALI SAED BIN MOHAMMED—WANTED FOR MURDERS OF US NATIONALS OUTSIDE THE UNITED STATES; CONSPIRACY TO MURDER US NATIONALS OUTSIDE THE UNITED STATES; ATTACK ON A FEDERAL FACILITY RESULTING IN DEATH.

ASHRAF REFEST NABIH—WANTED IN CONNECTION WITH THE AUGUST 7, 1998, BOMBINGS OF THE UNITED STATES EMBASSIES IN DAR ES SALAAM, TANZANIA, AND NAIROBI, KENYA. THESE ATTACKS KILLED OVER 200 PEOPLE. IN ADDITION, NABIH IS A SUSPECT IN OTHER TERRORIST ATTACKS THROUGHOUT THE WORLD.

NADAR KEAH LALANI—WANTED FOR INTERROGA-
TION. ESCAPED WHILE BEING QUESTIONED ON THE
ABOVE ASSAILANTS.

First, reports on the 2008 bombing spoke of activity similar to this
latest underground scheme. Before that attack, movements of crucial
Al Qaeda henchmen had also taken place. But the significance of the
shifts was realized only in hindsight. Similarly, next week's relocation
could be a potential target for a terrorist attack. The operation was
extremely hazardous, bringing the nuclear devices close to highly pop-
ulated areas in the US

If these men were apprehended, the potential for disrupting a
pending move of the nuclear missiles next week would be reduced.
Still, with the current state of affairs in the US, Al Qaeda recruitment
flourished, and they could not afford to take any chances.

Jill slowly closed the file on her lap and dipped into the well of her
intuition. Gazing over the horizon of clouds, she whispered, "What
am I missing?"

Jill went into her tunnels. Doing so was like riding a speeding
bobsled through all the notes and reports of the three men—too fast
for recognition as she tried to discover what she was missing. If she
noticed something that clicked, the racing bobsled in her intuitive
tunnels would stop short, and a clear image would appear in her mind.
But so far, no luck today.

Jill realized her leg was tapping; the hollow sound of her boot
hitting the metal footrest brought her back to the task at hand.

Then, without notice, Jill saw a picture in her mind's eye of a brief
she had read. The name Rashid jumped out at her. Then a sharp
insight hit her hard and fast. She snatched the folder from the seat
and snapped it open to a brief on Lalani. The speed of her movement
caught Tom's attention, and he approached her.

"It's Ali Bin Amr Rashid," Jill said, handing him the thick folder. "I think we have our man. He is the one piece that connects these three men to Yemen, but he is not Nadar Keah Lalani. Take a look at page three."

Tom reviewed the document. "See the picture of Rashid? Now go back to the first page. See the picture of Lalani? It's the same person, Tom. Lalani is not who he says he is."

CHAPTER THREE

The sky was a bright blue. Puffy cumulus clouds swirled around the morning sun as she disembarked from the plane. The captain had PA'd the time at 9:02 a.m. Once on the ground, Jill had the same uneasy feeling she had when she boarded the plane in Tucson. She glanced around and scanned the area.

Three o'clock. A man in a blue jumpsuit bent over, outlining the front and back wheels of the jet with black chalk blocks. His head was turned, and he wore orange sound mufflers clamped tightly on his ears.

Nine o'clock. A black 4x4, standard FBI edition, with someone behind the wheel. From his angle, the driver could not see her.

What is it that felt so... wrong? Jill wondered. Menacing.

"Is everything alright, Jill?" Concern emanated from Eric Wallace as he walked toward her from the black SUV. Eric had been her boss before she left the FBI over three years ago. His department was now part of the arm that worked with NSU and the CIA on homeland security matters. Jill still enjoyed working with Eric; after all, their mission was the same.

The rising sun behind him made Jill squint, but not enough to stop her from taking in his appearance. The fact that he wore a suit signaled the importance of the forthcoming meeting. The furrow etched in his forehead had aged him since they last met, and he had more gray hair than brown now, but he was still handsome in a distinguished sort of way. His amber eyes were kind as he reached over to touch her shoulder, squeezing it ever so slightly. Jill recognized the look in his eyes. She had seen it before—a mix of concern and pity. It was the same look he'd had when he and the team had finally rescued her from McGregor.

He knew her well. They had developed a bond during his wife's illness and eventual death. Eric had loved his wife intensely—the kind of love for which Jill had always yearned but had not had until she met David.

Jill smiled slightly. "I'm good, Eric, but I'll be even better when we close this friggin' case. It's dragging on way too long." Jill's right eye began to twitch, a sure signal that things would get more stressful. It was her body's red flag, and it rarely failed her.

Tom was already approaching the SUV, but Eric asked, "Jill, come on now. I know when something is bothering you. What is it?"

She stood silent for a mere second. That was all the time she needed to be reminded of their friendship and Eric's trustworthiness. She told him about the phone call from David's editor. When she finished, she pulled her windbreaker past her waist, straightening herself out before asking Eric hesitantly, "What do you think?"

They began to walk in Tom's direction, and before Eric answered, Jill added, "David's got a mind of his own. I don't think anything serious has happened to him. Do you?"

"You know, Jill, I've only met David once at your wedding, but from what I know about your life, he seems pretty together. He's an extensive traveler and has been 'round the bend a few times." Eric paused. "Has he been out of touch with you for extended periods?" He looked at her solemnly.

Jill shivered. She frowned, trying to recall. "Never this long."

They met up with Tom, who was standing by the open door of the SUV.

"How far along are we at determining that these guys you've profiled are the ones we are looking for?" Eric questioned.

Before Jill could answer, Tom piped in, "We think one of the men you have in custody is, in fact, Ali Bin Amr Rashid. If his true identity is exposed today, we can proceed with the move." There was that serpentine whistle again as he spoke and thrust the file into Eric's hand. "It's all outlined in here. Rashid has always been part of the group that goes after the broken arrows, sir."

Glaring at Tom, Jill wrestled back control. "Eric, Rashid is known as Dr. E. He's of Pakistani descent and is the brain behind Al Qaeda's uranium enrichment and weapons maintenance. There's one other thing—I think there is a Brazilian connection."

Eric knew, as did Jill, that Bin Laden's brother had resided there with his Brazilian wife when 9/11 happened. He was allowed to return to Saudi Arabia as part of the President's attempt to show concern about all religions. But he was safe and sound back in Saudi Arabia when they discovered he had helped set up and develop a significant Al Qaeda cell deep in the Brazilian jungle.

Eric leafed through the file.

"Lalani had in his possession a fake passport with a Brazilian visa in it. He's been there twice in the last month," Jill continued. "But in the intel—" Jill leaned in, "see here—" the pages flapped in the slight breeze as she pulled them apart, "see in this brief from the Brazilian Intelligence Agency, this is a picture of Rashid in Foz do Iguacu, Brazil. This picture is the same; it's Lalani."

Eric muffled a grumble too unclear to make out except for the words "redneck" and "third world," then said, "Looks like we have all we need here for now. Great work. Let's head to HQ; we have about an hour to prepare."

Sitting inside the SUV, Jill thought she saw a figure standing in the doorway of the hangar as they turned a tight circle. They had turned the corner before she could get a second look, and the silhouette was gone.

Jill juggled her thoughts as they drove along the Potomac River to FBI headquarters. The midnight black tint on the SUV windows dulled the sunshine, trying to work its way through the glass.

Was there someone watching me? If there was, why? Maybe I'm just tired.

Denying her intuition was a feeble attempt.

As they drove along the winding road, Eric continued explaining the details of the Al Qaeda capture, talking about how the departments worked together and complaining about how the CIA was always treading on their toes. She'd heard it all before.

Keep it together, Jill; keep it together. The mantra kept her sane on the short ride to headquarters, even as her thoughts drifted back again to David. Unprompted, she thought about what had happened five days ago...

That morning she had awoken to no sign of David. They had been married for over a year—still in the honeymoon stage, where David would often wake Jill up slowly by caressing her body. This day was different. She awoke alone except for the sunshine reflecting off the mirror beside her king-sized bed. Lying in the warmth, she pulled herself out of bed, lifted her red silk robe from its hook on the door, wrapped it around her olive-skinned tight body, and headed towards the kitchen. The smell of coffee told her David was home, but he wasn't in the kitchen. She checked the solarium—empty. Habit guided her to his office.

He must have been putting the finishing touches on an article with a deadline looming. As a correspondent for Time, his deadlines were always at midnight. To see David working this early on his assignment was an anomaly.

Perhaps he had a special evening planned, Jill thought hopefully, and with a slight spring in her step, she approached the office door. Walking softly, hoping to avoid disturbing him, she could hear him talking to someone in a low tone. She could sense the agitation in his voice, and she felt he was speaking to a female. Jill could often place tonality since she had studied this in her second year at the US Marshal Service.

When the conversation had ended, she peered in and offered a sweet, "Who was that, handsome?"

David abruptly pivoted around and tucked his mobile phone into his jacket pocket. Even in the early morning, David was striking. His rugged, strong Robert Redford-type face made her wonder why he became a journalist instead of an actor. She was happy with his choice; an actor would be far too vain for a life-mate. But she couldn't help but gush over his beauty. He was dressed for his regular squash game with his buddy Steve—a common event when David was home. His long, tight black running shorts accentuated his tanned quads. Jill loved a man with beautiful legs and a delicious tight ass. The top half of his body was covered with a Nike black jacket, shielding him from Jill's desire to walk over and straddle him into submission.

"It's just my editor on my case to get this article to him," he responded in a monotone.

As Jill looked at him quizzically, he added: "I have some bad news." David hesitated, averting his eyes from Jill to a spot on the floor. "I have to go back into the field."

"When?" She folded her arms slowly. Her jet-black hair slid off her shoulder as she cocked her head to one side.

"Tonight," he murmured, got up, and walked toward her. He hadn't shaved, and a dusting of hair darkened his chin, just as she liked it. Her heart sank fast, hitting a newly formed lump in her stomach.

"I have to head back to Doha to follow up on the interviews on those US soldiers back from Iraq. My editor feels there is enough information to get another story off the ground, and I guess I'm the only one available to do it. Sorry, my love," he said, arching one of his blond eyebrows. For a second, Jill thought she could see a twinkle in his blue eyes. He usually made her melt when he looked at her this way, but today she only felt unsettled.

"It's fine," she pouted. "I'm still knee-deep in my current assignment anyway. Coffee made?"

David pulled her into a tight hug. "You're not mad, are you, babe?"

Jill didn't answer; she just hugged him back. He knew, and Jill knew. Nothing more needed to be said.

The day turned into evening, and David was attentive for most of the day—yet somehow distracted. She asked him what was on his mind, but he didn't respond convincingly. He kept insisting nothing was wrong, but Jill knew better. Walking into their bedroom, Jill saw his suitcase, lying on the smooth wood floor, was already packed. Shirts were folded as if a professional launderer had done them. David routinely lined up his clothes on the bed, determining the best fit for each trip.

The sun was dipping behind Catalina's outside the bathroom window. The sound of splattering water with steam puffing up drew her to the shower, but she could not see him when she looked through the clear glass door. Then behind her, a feather-light touch on her shoulder signaled her to relax. His lips caressed the back of her neck, and the warmth in her belly melted her nervous lump. His fingers lifted her shirt ever so slightly, adding more heat to the steamy room. Jill began to feel the warmth of the tingle move lower. He gracefully slid his hands up her rib cage, taunting her, then cupped her firm breasts. His fingers pinched her hardened nipples, and he whispered into her ear, "Wanna clean up with me?"

The place between her legs began to ache and pulse. David slowly turned her around, then kissed her hard, his tongue lashing at hers inside her warm mouth. The shower mist fogged the bathroom as David lifted the cropped T-shirt over her head with practiced ease and admired her flesh. Then he cocked his head, turned, and walked into the hot rain. Jill pushed her shorts to her ankles, kicked them into a heap on the floor, and stepped into the shower. Sliding wet skin on wet skin, they played in the shower until the water ran cold. Then, wrapped together in a towel, David lifted her between the two sinks and plunged into her hard on the cool surface. The hot pleasure rushed through their bodies, and her head went light when she felt David's release.

A horn blaring from an impatient driver brought Jill back to the present. Her heart won that debate over her mind as she tried to understand what he must be going through to be out of touch for five days. She crossed her legs as they drove through the gate.

"Let's finish this," Eric said as they walked into a gray building.

Inside, suited men and women rushed past as if all were in a hurry. The pungent smell of Detrol dried her nose, and she winced. "Oh God," Jill whispered under her breath. Once again, Jill reminded herself she was right to leave the FBI when the posturing energy, thick as smoke, filled the halls. After being introduced to a series of faceless agents, Jill, Tom, Eric, and the suits were led to a large boardroom with a giant TV screen. Water and coffee jugs sat on a large table in the low-lit room.

Someone turned on the TV, and everyone focused on a small room where Lalani sat—or Rashid, as Jill believed. He sat there blindfolded with his hands tied behind his back. The camera did not show the interrogators, and the only indication of there being two of them was the tops of the papers from the angle of the filming. The speaker in the center of the table crackled as it began to record the event. The white coiled microphone that spoke directly in the interrogators' ears was also hidden.

It was Jill's job as a terrorist profiler to help flesh out the truth. The truth. There was never any real truth, she had concluded. Devising profiles of terrorists could be extremely tricky, as they often appeared to be ordinary people. Although serial killers and the like are sometimes said to be the "average guy next door," there was always something amiss that would help a crime profiler. Mommy issues, childhood abuse, those kinds of things—and there was always narcissism. But studies of terrorists showed that other than extreme religious beliefs, most are sane folks. Males between the ages of twenty and twenty-five were typical for field ops who acted like martyrs. Their goal was to blend in and appear normal. And this was where Jill thought Lalani was going overkill.

As they began the interrogation, Jill looked at Eric and gave him a clear signal—he leaned forward and pressed the mute button.

"Untie his hands and remove the blindfold," she said firmly. There are three primary goals when profiling an individual: a psychological assessment of the individual's social behavior, an evaluation of the possessions found on him, and the development of a series of questions for the interview. In this profile, Jill used investigative psychology, a technique different from that which an FBI profiler might use. The FBI used tools such as "thinking like a criminal." Instead, Jill compared links between background characteristics, the offender's behavior assessment, and previous threats and events, such as the hindsight of 9/11.

Eric repeated the request into a black box in the middle of the conference table.

Jill needed to identify a level of stress with offender profiling. Offender profiling is considered the third wave of investigative science—the first is the study of clues, and the second is the study of the crime itself. It's often used with psychological profiling, which includes identifying a person's mental, emotional, and personality characteristics. Jill had already determined (per the brief) that the man behind the screen fit Rashid's description and closely matched the photo. Jill wasn't there to interrogate in a "Guantanamo Bay" kind of way. She'd leave that to the others. She was there to confirm they had the right man in custody. That was the only reason she was there. And she was convinced this man who called himself Lalani was indeed Ali Bin Amr Rashid, or Dr. E., the brain behind Al Qaeda's uranium enrichment and weapons maintenance.

The room fell silent, and the lights dimmed even more. Penlights glowed on pads of paper as the suits took notes. Jill watched and listened intently. Then she noticed something. Rashid's lip twitched on the right—a sign of disbelief or contempt. She saw it only once, but it was there. The interrogator continued in Arabic, reading off Jill's list of questions.

They weren't leading questions, or at least Jill didn't think so. She was tired of this case, and her instincts told her she was right about who Lalani was—Rashid. He refused to answer any of the questions, but when the interrogator began to speak of Brazil, he shifted in his chair and looked agitated. He knew what the bully boys had in store for him—how could he not? The interrogator slid a paper in front of him. Jill knew the drill; he was being told to admit he was Rashid, to sign something to say so. If he didn't sign it, the man threatened in Arabic; he would be worse off once they got through with him here. It was Rashid, all right, Jill thought as he signed the paper.

"Do you need anything more, Jill?" Eric asked. The static on the speaker sounded like white noise from a blank TV screen. Looking around, Jill realized that the interrogation had paused, and all eyes were on her. It took a moment for her to collect her thoughts. She straightened and said crisply, "I have what I need."

The room emptied fast. Eric motioned to Tom to leave him and Jill alone. The bright fluorescent lights hummed above them. There it was again. That look, that look of pity. Eric walked to her, reached out, and grasped her arms.

"Jill, I know you're worried about David, but today... you're just not yourself. I don't need to tell you this, but I will. It would help if you stayed focused. National security is at stake here, maybe even world security."

For the first time in years, Jill felt her eyes begin to fill. Eric still had that kind, fatherly look as he said: "You need to figure out what is going on with David, Jill. Why not take some time off? I'm sure Sven will give you a break. Your job, in this case, is pretty much finished. Take some time, and come back in a couple of days. We can wrap up any loose ends."

He looked down his nose sternly, not waiting for her reaction before he ordered softly, "Take the jet back to Tucson, Jill. Tom can stay on and finish the brief. This part is just the bureaucratic crap anyway."

Gently he put his hand on her lower back, guiding her toward the exit. Slightly miffed, Jill allowed herself to be maneuvered out the door.

"But..." Jill started to protest.

"I'll put a call into Sven; he'll give you the time off."

"No," she retorted. "I don't need a babysitter, Eric." Then Jill thought carefully before saying, "I'm going to Doha?"

"I know you, Jill, and I know I can't stop your stubborn ass," Eric sighed. "But if you go to Doha, be careful. We don't have the authority or jurisdiction in Doha nor the budget to assist you when you get there. But I will put in a call to ops and ask them to give you any information they have, as well as the clearance you will need."

Eric stopped and looked Jill in the eyes. "David is okay, Jill, you know that. He is out there somewhere. He's just not able to reach you."

Jill could tell he was feigning confidence. But before she could object, he slipped out the door with these parting words: "Don't worry about the case. You've done a great job. I'll e-mail you when we complete the report."

CHAPTER FOUR

11:42 Zulu Time — Somewhere Over the Midwest

The same flight attendant was on the Lear returning to Tucson and approached Jill. Heather knew Jill was married, but Jill hardly ever spoke about her personal life. Today was different.

"You okay, Jill?" Heather asked inquisitively. "You don't look that great; it's almost three p.m. Have you eaten anything?"

"Have I ever told you about when I first met David, my husband?" Jill asked in an emotionless, almost robotic voice. Without waiting for an answer, Jill gazed through Heather rather than at her and continued...

"It was on a rafting trip down the Colorado River, starting from Lee's Ferry, Arizona, and going down to Phantom River." Jill's eyes moved from Heather to the small portal window where clouds dappled a blue expanse. "I went there to guide about four times a year on those large river rafting boats whenever I could get away for a few days. That trip, that particular day, felt different. I guess you could say I was in the zone. Then I saw David. There was an immediate spark, and when we began to talk, I discovered his calm confidence and independence. He was just the kind of man I was looking for..." Jill's voice trailed off.

David.

Jill looked over at Heather. "I need some time alone, Heather, okay?" Heather rose from her seat with a shrug. Jill didn't care if she was ticked off. She needed to think about what she was going to do next. She'd already put the call into Sven—she hadn't volunteered the reason behind her request, and he had approved her time off without question. She said nothing about David because she had no intention of having her boss think: "Poor broken-up Jill can't function because of a man." He was an ass. No. She was ambitious and had to be careful not to appear like a sniveling lovesick puppy, even though she felt like one! That would clearly be a career-limiting move in the man's national security world.

Once back on the ground, Jill felt that odd something-is-not-quite-right-but-can't-put-my-finger-on-exactly-what-is-wrong feeling. A shiver rolled through her when she got into her car, but all she could do was shrug it off as nerves. Besides, Jill was too busy to concern herself with possible paranoia. She had to figure out where to start and what to do. The rumble of her car was comforting as she drove toward their house on the hill.

Mountains surrounded Tucson in every direction. The Santa Catalina Mountains to the north were close to the city but not as close as the Tucson Mountains in the west. If they had bought a home to the east, it would have been in the Rincon Mountains. It wasn't as quaint as Page, Arizona, where she grew up, but Jill didn't mind as she shifted into low gear and began her ascent into the foothills of the Catalinas. Home is what she needed now. With a glimmer of hope, she pictured David there.

Jill glanced in the rear-view mirror. Tired eyes below a knitted brow looked back at her. Still on the main highway and aware of her fatigue, she noticed a black SUV traveling steadily in the far left lane. When she stole a second look, it was gone.

"Come on, Jill, keep it together," she mumbled, annoyed with herself. Ten minutes later, she pulled into her garage and sighed heavily before entering the house.

Somberness surrounded her heart as she sat in the comfort of the glass house in the hills. The trip back was a blur. How she got there, Jill couldn't quite remember. Sitting in her office, she stared at nothing, ignoring the papers strewn across the cluttered desk. The words Eric spoke to her still pricked at her pride. "What's happening to me?" Jill hushed.

"Grams, Grams," she whispered. At that moment, a bird, a chickadee, perched itself on the windowsill.

Jill eyed the small, vulnerable bird. It chirped, then swiftly flew away as Jill reached past a dirty coffee mug on her desk and picked up the phone.

Crap—voicemail. Thank God there was only one.

"Jill, this is Stan Brown. Can you please call me at this number on my satellite phone? It's important." The voicemail clicked off.

"What the hell do you want, you piece of shit? Anything you have to say is never important," Jill thought. Stan was David's father, but David had forbidden Jill to communicate with him, or any other members of his family for that matter, since their last falling out close to a year ago. It was a nasty fight, most of which Jill had the misfortune of witnessing, before exiting as gracefully as she could and thus missing the finale.

David had told Jill about the many disturbing and sometimes shocking experiences while being raised by Stan, his bullish, narcissistic father, and Carol, his trophy-wife mother. Whenever he spoke of them, sadness and anger filled his eyes. But David would never tell her what the final straw was on the fateful day of "the family feud." Jill suspected that his family didn't like the fact that he had married a

Native American. If that was the case, Jill didn't care. She had become immune to various forms of racism and snobbery, having experienced them her whole life.

Funny how things change, she thought as she reflected on David's family and how they had rejected her. People now brag when they have Native American blood in them. But David's family was stuck in backwoods Texas where the Ku Klux Klan still exists, even to-day. David hadn't told his family about their wedding until late last year—when it would be too late to voice their protests. And it was around that time that Jill first met them. But after the big bust-up, whatever was left of the frayed relationship was doomed.

A beep pulled her from her ruminations as the fax machine sput-tered to life. It was a note from Jeff, David's editor. The fax screeched as the details of David's assignment, itinerary, and other information came through.

Fly to Doha, Qatar Meet PRO Interview soldiers at the command post for the Iraq war Location in Doha Special clearances

His assignment seemed simple enough. Next to his itinerary was a list of phone numbers. Jill called the first number on the list, the Le Meridien Hotel in Doha, Qatar.

She mentally went through what she knew of the destination, Doha, which was the capital of Qatar, a small peninsula off Saudi Arabia in the Arabian Gulf. Doha meant "the big tree" in Arabic. Qatar generated most of its revenues from oil and natural gas, of which it had vast reserves, and some from tourism, banking, and commerce. Doha itself was a relatively modern city. Its tribal roots stretched back several hundred years, though it had been virtually unknown in the West until the discovery of oil in the neighboring Gulf countries.

The hotel receptionist spoke broken English with a Southeast Asian accent. It took Jill longer than she would have liked to identify the woman's lilt, but she guessed it was from the Philippines, and Jill was surprised by her willingness to give private information freely. Jill thought of no privacy laws in third-world countries and made a mental note to take a refresher course on identifying accents.

"Yes, ma'am," the Filipina said sweetly. She told her that David had checked in on schedule—but checked out the very next day, even though he had been expected to stay for four nights.

The phone almost missed the cradle as Jill scrolled the list of numbers before returning to the second number at the top—the US command post for the Iraq war. David was to have met a Major Evens, it seemed. As she dialed, she wondered how Time had acquired these numbers. "Special clearance" written after the number answered her thought.

After a series of transfers, she got to a staff sergeant who replied to her query: he sounded like a New Yorker, Jill thought, already exercising her ear on the accents again.

"No, ma'am, we were expecting him 'bout four days ago, but he didn't show up," he explained. "Reporters do this from time to time; we're not concerned, ma'am. I had lined up everyone he wanted to speak with, but they weren't bothered at the no-show—it gave them a little unexpected leave."

She thanked him and hung up. A ball of dread began forming in the pit of her stomach. Something was clearly wrong. David was very precise—almost anal—about keeping appointments.

She began to read the draft that David's office had faxed to her of the story he was working on, "Lives of Soldiers Fighting in Iraq;" he had started writing it on his first trip to Doha. The content was predictable: Don't like fighting, doing it for my country, miss my family. God bless America—yadda yadda yadda. Nothing unusual jumped out at her.

As Jill's anxiety grew, she became restless. She needed to move to think correctly. She sprang out of her chair, grabbed the draft of David's piece, and made her way through the house. The sunset glow danced on the painted walls, changing from a dark red to okra to a mellow green as she walked past the kitchen, into the living room, and headed towards the bar.

The bar was the room's centerpiece, with a six-foot green gecko mosaic outlined by red tiles.

Talisker, a single malt whiskey from Scotland, was her current favorite brand—and on this day, a good friend. Jill's hand shook slightly as she lifted a Scotch-filled carafe from one of the shelves below the bar and set it on the top. "This will take the edge off," she said out loud.

The ice machine churned as cubes rattled into a highball glass, to which she then added a healthy measure of Talisker. She reached for the glass now filled with ice that had rattled out of the ice machine. She downed it like a cowboy in an old Western film. Jill didn't like to spoil the taste by adding a mix. Tasting and drinking—Scotch is an art form, and Jill had treated her palate to many premium single malt whiskeys. There were over thirty primary smells of good single malt. Talisker was sweet yet smoky when its aroma met the nose. She recharged her glass, this time with about half a measure, raised it to her lips, and sipped the Scotch, fully allowing herself to enjoy its sweet and subtle salty taste.

Fortified, she traded the glass of the amber liquid for David's draft article, and almost immediately, her stance stiffened. In the comments section at the end of the article were the words "keep identity anonymous." Then the name "Hamrain."

It's a unique name, at least in North America, she thought.

Then Jill recalled seeing it somewhere before, which had been recent; she was sure of that. "But where?" she said to herself. Armed with what was left of her soothing Scotch, Jill walked briskly down the hall and stepped into David's office. She stopped abruptly once over the threshold.

Jill was always impressed at how immaculate David kept his office—unlike hers. Everything was in its place, no coffee cup stains from late-night edits, no slips of paper scattered willy-nilly on his desk. A photograph on the wall, taken when they first met, displayed the rich colors of the Colorado River banks. The water was gin clear. It was framed in black and matched the oversized southwestern-style desk David had built for his office.

The dustless desk offered no signs of Hamrain or any other helpful information, for that matter. To Jill, this was odd. She distinctly remembered David having several files on his desk; he always did when working on a story. He liked to keep things organized and easy to reference. Where were all his files? He must have taken the folders with him, but why? That would be unusual. She needed to know what the hell was going on.

She glanced down at David's desktop computer. He always kept everything on his laptop and was very possessive over his MacBook. But he had told Jill that he always backed it onto his desktop. "Just in case," he would say. She reached over and turned it on, thanking the powers that be that that—David rarely changed his password. She logged on without a hitch. David was equally organized on his desktop computer, although he loathed Windows. Needing structure was a little quirk of his. Well, more than a quirk—more like a compulsion. He enjoyed teasing Jill because her email inbox was full of opened, undiscarded emails.

However, when she tried to access his most recently viewed documents, she got one error message after another. It looked like they had all been deleted. Why would he delete his records, his history? That was unlike him.

Jill moved the mouse to the recycle bin. Empty. "Well, well." The chair squeaked as she leaned back and stared at the screen. A couple more sips, and she continued her search. She started with the following logical command: to show all his hidden files—something a person could easily do in the control panel. A few 'restores' in advanced settings led her to a backup of one folder. Strange. Inside, she discovered a file called Hamrain. As she read the more detailed electronic 'post-it' notes, which included David's comments to himself, she absently sipped the Scotch and felt its slightly nutty, spicy finish before it traveled down to her stomach.

Most notes directly referenced the story, but one was somewhat cryptic. "Al Binood... Doha. LSA.," it read. The last three letters, LSA, were bold and underlined.

What is Al Binood? Jill wondered. She knew the word Al meant "the" in Arabic, and Binood sounded like it might be part of a last name. LSA didn't hold any meaning for her, yet it seemed vaguely familiar. Additional searching and reading uncovered little else of interest other than the names of soldiers from his interviews and others to whom she might potentially speak. She hovered the mouse and clicked. Print.

Jill had to stand and lean over the large pine desk that filled David's office to reach the phone. She dialed Kali.

Jill had worked with Kali Lucas for more than three years. She was one of those rare people you meet that instantly know you will be lifelong friends no matter what "happened at the office." After all, being Jill's research assistant could be challenging at times. Kali was the one Jill turned to when she needed to substantiate a hunch or her intuition, a process that could take hours, even days, and often frustratingly lead to dead ends. If this bothered Kali, she never mentioned it. She always dressed quirky, kind of a 1970s bohemian type, with curly red hair that she tamed by tying back into a ponytail. Her breasts strained against her shirt most days, the cleavage often distracting admirers from the dried Navajo choker Jill had given her for her birthday, which she adored.

She came over to the house sometimes when David was away. Though neither gossiped with others, they enjoyed doing so between themselves. They could easily spend an evening making fun of their workmates over a bottle of wine—particularly Tom and his feeble advances toward Kali.

After a brief exchange of greetings, Kali quickly picked up on Jill's stress. "You're not worried, are you? You know David is fine, right? Doha is in the Middle East, right?"

"I don't know." She sighed heavily and then continued, "I'm a bit concerned, so I'm going to take some time off to see if I can figure out what's happening. I couldn't find much on David's computer except for a reference to Hamrain, a name called Al Binood, and a reference to LSA."

"Got it; I'll see what I can find out about these names and give you a callback."

After hanging up the phone, Jill breathed to clear her head. She stared out the window. The red rock hoodoos gazed majestically back at her. She had seen the rock take on many colors depending on the time of day. The mountains in the distance always inspired her. One giant rock had sheltered their wedding ceremony—David and Jill at sunset in the mountains on a hidden ledge, with a few friends, Kali, Eric, and a Justice of the Peace as their witnesses.

Her hand lifted to touch the cold mobile phone in her top shirt pocket. Had it rung or vibrated? Had she missed a call or message? She flipped it open. No missed calls, no SMS, nothing. There was no point wasting time as she waited to hear back from Kali. She turned around to face the computer and began typing. First on her list was to find a flight to Doha as soon as possible, for as little as possible. But the ordinarily low-cost web reservation systems were not kind to her today. The only flight she could find to Doha was through Washington, and the only seat available was in first class. Ouch! She paid the $11,000 fare by credit card, thankful she diligently kept the balance near zero, even though her limit was nearly double that. She wondered if she should have tried harder for something cheaper when the phone's sound startled her. She answered it before the second ring.

"Oliver."

Kali was subdued as she explained that she couldn't find any information on LSA or what it might mean. "I'll keep looking," she promised. "Al Binood is either a person's name or a restaurant in Doha," she added. "I'd go with the restaurant, as the system isn't coming up with any people by that name. I've sent you a map and satellite photos of the command post; they're in your VPN," she finished.

"I'm going to Doha, Kali, today. I feel like it's something—"

"You need to do. I figured as much. You'd better keep me posted, and, oh, Jill, be safe." She always seemed to finish Jill's sentences, though Jill hadn't yet decided if that was something she liked.

"I will," Jill said softly and hung up. She didn't bother to check the map and photos. She had to pack and leave for the airport to catch the flight. To access her VPN would require a secure computer, which David's was not.

Anticipation competed with dread as she looked around her dark bedroom. David had painted the high vaulted ceiling dark brown, and as she walked through the oversized Mexican double doors, she stopped in awe, as she always did, at the king-sized Mexican bed David had built her for her birthday. The thick solid legs overpowered the room, even with the tall vaulted ceiling. David had selected the hand-painted tile embedded into the headboard because it reminded him of her. He would often say, "Simply beautiful." The thought increased Jill's anguish as she walked through their large bright bathroom and into the walk-in closet.

David's clothes were neatly folded in the checker box cupboard next to which hung his shirts and his only suit. He didn't wear suits often—only for special occasions, a nice dinner out, or a work function. To the right was an array of Jill's clothes stuffed on different shelves; smaller items spilled over the edges. Clothes drooped haphazardly on hangers.

Jill turned back to David's side of the closet—though the closet was an understatement, for it was bigger than most bedrooms. She rifled through David's shirt pockets, momentarily pausing to inhale his smell from one that he had worn and not yet laundered.

She loved to smell the crook of his neck after they lay in bed, content and at pleasure. The pang in her heart brought her back; determination overpowered despair, and she hung the shirt on the peg from which she had taken it. Pulling herself back to the present, Jill rummaged through the rest of his shirts and suit, the breast pocket of which yielded a business card. DR. GLEN BELL, FORENSIC DNA SPECIALIST, MD.

Jill looked closer at the floor lamp next to the enormous east-facing picture window. But before she flicked on the light, her eyes were drawn to the winding road leading to her driveway. A vehicle, almost too dark to make out in the dusk, was parked on the edge of the jagged rock. She would have missed its headlights being flicked off a split second later.

David, Jill thought. Her heart leaped a little; then she came to her senses. David wouldn't stop mysteriously on the road like that and certainly wouldn't turn his lights off if there were a problem.

Jill reached into her uniform shirt pocket for her mobile, and while staring toward the vehicle, she hit speed dial one for David's mobile.

"I'm sorry, the mobile customer you are trying to reach is switched off or out of the service area." Jill snapped the phone shut and slipped it back into her pocket.

The car was about a mile away as the crow flies, longer by the winding road that hugged the mountainside. "Now, who are you?" she said snidely. There was no movement around the vehicle. A minute passed before Jill became impatient and marched over to the bedside table, opened the drawer, and pulled out her snub-nosed revolver. "Screw you, Matthew McGregor!" Jill barked as she rolled the chamber and stuffed it into the back of her fatigues. Whoever was out there was no McGregor, but she had sworn to herself the day he almost killed her; this maniac would never terrorize her again.

"Riding the rail" is what her doctor had labeled McGregor's form of torture. That's what they called it, he said. Or at least they did back in the Civil War era. It was mainly about humiliation, pain, and then more humiliation. Jill could endure the pain; the humiliation brought her to her next thought.

As she had done ever since finishing her therapy sessions for post-traumatic stress disorder, she took her doctor's advice and used the tragic part of her past to overcome adversity. And this was one of those times. "Screw you, McGregor," she whispered, almost hissed, again to herself. Then she moved. Fast. She snatched her car keys off the table and ran out the door, full speed, toward the garage. She skidded in the gravel when she saw the garage door was open. Did I leave the door open? Jill could not recall.

She looked around. The only thing she heard was the tree frogs croaking. She stared in the direction of the stopped vehicle, then back at her car. "Screw it," she barked as she jumped into the car, turned the key, and heard the engine growl.

She crawled the car out of the driveway, lights off and guided by moonlight reflecting off the cliffs to her left. She edged slowly along their dark and jagged facade, aware of the treacherous mountain drop on her right. She'd gone maybe a quarter of a mile when an animal skittered across the road.

"Shit!" she swore, simultaneously stepping hard on the brake. They'll see my brake lights light up the cliffs, dammit! Sure enough, the black SUV headlights came on in a flash while it reversed and spun around, splattering gravel and dust as it started to race back down the winding road.

Jill turned on her lights without hesitation and jammed her foot on the accelerator. Her back tires spat gravel, and it took all her upper body strength to control the steering wheel and the horsepower beneath it.

Jill knew this road like the back of her hand, and there was no way in hell she would let a random car get the best of her. "You bastard!" she shouted. "Watch this!" She shifted gears, revving the engine even higher. She was soon within about five car lengths of the fleeing vehicle, whose brake lights flashed on and off as it rounded the sharp corners.

Jill needed to think fast. What would she do if she caught up with them? Run the random SUV off the road? Maybe it was just someone who had lost their way in the mountains? What the heck is wrong with me? Jill second-guessed herself. But she knew what she had felt all day. "One plus one equals two, girl!" She was being followed alright, and now she was determined to find out who and why. She could almost hear Kali as she egged her on: "You go, girl!" And that's precisely what she did.

Jill did some mental calculations. She knew the PIT maneuver—pursuit intervention technique—well. She had opted for more training after Matthew McGregor and was confident she knew what to do and how to do it. The PIT maneuver was a series of vehicular moves to stop a pursued vehicle. The pursuing vehicle would push the car's back end in a forceful and particular direction, causing the pursued vehicle's back wheels to lose traction, thus spinning them in the opposite direction. The technique was used by most, if not all, law enforcement in the field; it was very successful if executed properly. But Jill knew her car didn't have the required bumper guards.

"What the—"

Jill braked fast, and the car started to swerve to the left. An animal, maybe a wolf, stood between her and the black SUV. Blinded by Jill's headlights, the creature stood stunned in the middle of the road.

Jill pulled hard on the emergency brake, barely hanging on to the wheel as the car spun out of control.

"Shit," Jill cursed, just before the vehicle's ass end scraped around the cliff's edge and came to a complete stop.

"Shit, shit, shit," she yelled, hitting the steering wheel. All she could do was watch the SUV's fading taillights blink around and down the winding road. She could never catch them now. There was no use even trying.

CHAPTER FIVE

19:20 Zulu Time — Washington, D.C.

The plane was full of movement and chatter, which annoyed Jill as she snaked her way to her first-class seat on the Qatar Airways flight to Doha from Washington. She stowed her carry-on, sank onto her seat, and took a moment to regroup. She was one of the last passengers to board. The clock on the screen in front of her blinked 11:20 p.m., only twenty minutes before the scheduled departure.

Finally, she was on the last leg of her journey to find David and was exhausted. After Jill lost the black SUV in Tucson, she returned to the house and called to update Kali. She'd had to pack fast to make the Tucson/Washington connection. The drive to Tucson airport and the flight to Washington were uneventful. No sign of the SUV or anything else that looked in the least bit suspicious. She got a quick call from Eric, concerned after Kali briefed him about the SUV and the aborted chase. Jill knew she was being followed but couldn't find a plausible reason why anyone would want to tail her—it didn't make sense. She felt better knowing that Eric would dig into this potential personal threat. She loved the fact that he still watched out for her.

Jill took a moment to register the details of what the $11,000 charge to her credit card had bought. The cabin layout was well de- signed: it was open, airy, and ergonomic, and none of the seats were crammed together. Her plush Indian-red recliner was large, roomy, and equipped with a personal 17-inch screen.

She looked around at the other first-class cabin occupants who would share her bathroom for the 14-hour flight and wondered what type of people could afford such extravagance. There was only one other woman dressed in an abaya. The floor-length black robe, which boasted a beautiful gold beadwork trim, flowed over the woman's seat. Jill knew that many Muslims believe that Islam's principles require that women cover their hair, but just as with other religions, there are also many interpretations of the practice. This woman sported a simple black headscarf that outlined but did not cover her face. She was not wearing the black mask burqa that Jill knew some Gulf Arab women wear. A rather large diamond ring adorned the middle finger of her hand.

The rest of the cabin was filled with men. Some were preoccupied with the in-flight entertainment and associated controls; some read newspapers in various languages; others were focused on their laptops. A man across the aisle from her bulged out of his too-tight suit and shouted in Arabic to the young flight attendant, his hand gesturing his displeasure. The flight attendant attempted to calm him with gorgeous olive skin, jet-black hair, big, black-lined, cat-like eyes, and bright red lipstick.

Jill was thankful when a second attendant arrived with a juice, water, and champagne tray. Jill quickly reached for a glass of champagne, but the attendant pulled the tray back slightly, whisked a small napkin onto a flat area on the arm of Jill's chair, and gently placed the bubbly down. She was well-trained in the art of service, her demeanor lacked professionalism, and her condescending smile made Jill think she was none too pleased about serving passengers. This thought was reinforced when she pirouetted and paraded back to the galley with a sashay.

An endless flow of red wine followed the champagne, and while the meal that accompanied it was tasty, Jill barely touched her food. Jill wobbled when she stood up to let another flight attendant flatten her seat and make her bed with sheets, a pillow, and a duvet.

The flight attendant whispered, "Here, ma'am," as she gently spread the sheets out, neatly tucked in the corners, covered the bed with cushions, then handed her a set of neatly wrapped branded pajamas. The plastic crinkled as Jill grasped the nightwear groggily and then set off to the bathroom. The corridor was dark now; the hum of sleep surrounded her. "Would it be so hard to make a bigger first-class bathroom?" Jill grumbled to herself while she struggled to don the pajamas in the tiny space.

On her way back to her seat, she scanned each individual, looking for a glance or any sign that any one of them might be watching her. Nothing. With resolve, she laid down and, before long, faded into a fitful slumber.

Large lights above her slowly changed from blue to pink, and a disoriented Jill bolted upright. The PA crackled with the Captain's voice: "Ladies and gentlemen, we are beginning our descent into Doha." Jill begrudgingly recalled her reality as she sipped her coffee, fortified by the fact that she'd had several hours of alcohol-induced sleep.

Doha airport was confusing. There were signs in Arabic and English, but they seemed to direct people nowhere. Jill decided to follow the general flow of passengers, hoping they also might be headed to the baggage claim. At passport control, a row of glass booths housed blank-faced men wearing crisp white robes. From conversations with David, Jill knew that the traditional men's robes were called dishdashas or kandouras. Red-checkered head scarves or gutras that hung over their shoulders and down their backs were held in place by twisted black coils called agal that sat like fallen halos on their heads. Jill watched her passport get stamped with a quick thump. She reached for it and thanked the official, who waved her through without acknowledgement.

Jill gasped for breath outside the terminal as she hit a wall of heat and humidity. It was like walking into a sauna. "What the hell! Is this for real?" she asked herself. Beads of sweat swiftly formed on her forehead and upper lip as she looked around for a taxi. The sun was setting over the massive highway in front of the airport. To her left, typical airport chaos—the rattle of carts bumping across the concrete, people looking down the line of cars for their own, people busy stuffing luggage into trunks. Several men in dishdashas were smoking and talking loudly all at once. Jill could not tell by their body language if they were happy. Another mental note to add to her list of additional skills to hone: research the body language of Middle Eastern cultures more thoroughly.

A man dressed in pants, a bright yellow dress shirt, and a tight navy blue tie approached her with a clipboard. He said something in Arabic, then quickly switched to broken English when he saw the confused look on her face.

"Taxi, ma'am?"

Jill nodded.

He directed her to an all-white sedan. A small man jumped out, smiled, and in a thick East Indian accent, said, "Taxi, ma'am?" His head bobbled, and Jill nodded again. He hurried around the car, took her bag, put it in the trunk, held open the back door, and gestured for her to get inside. He rushed around to the front of the car, like a character out of The Amazing Race, and jumped in. Before Jill could tell him where to go, he put the surprisingly clean vehicle in gear and accelerated. The sudden momentum pushed Jill back into her seat and jolted her feet to the floor. She couldn't help but chuckle to herself, despite her fatigue.

She explained to the driver that she needed to go to a restaurant called Al Binood, to which he responded, "Yes, yes, ma'am, no problem, no problem," his head bobbling again. He seemed to know where she wanted to go.

So far, Doha looked as she imagined it would from the images she had seen online. The four lanes that comprised the road they were traveling suggested that it was likely the main thoroughfare. The sun yawned behind them as they drove. On her right, the waters of the Arabian Gulf sparkled a beautiful turquoise blue, highlighted by a pale pink and cream-colored sky. Stunning human-made enhancements, including an expanse of a stone-paved walkway between the road and the open sea, complemented the natural beauty. It was lined with lush greenery and waving date palm trees. Jill imagined how lovely it would be to stroll there with David once they were reunited—if it wasn't so Goddamn hot, that is!

As they drove towards the cluster of tall, congested Doha proper buildings, the city began to engulf the taxi. The hustle and bustle, and concrete-jungle-like environment, immediately changed her mood. The sound of honking horns clogged the air over the thick lines of vehicles driven with reckless abandon. Throngs of people hustled through the streets, and Jill noticed various races and cultures. Women covered head to toe in black abayas and shaylas that revealed only their eyes scurried children along by the hand, some with maids trailing behind, babes in arms. She thought that men in dishdashas sauntered in twos and threes, many of them looking rather arrogant. They moved much slower than the smattering of men of Indian and Asian descent.

Others, dressed in Western clothes and what appeared to be pajamas, contributed a threadbare component to the overall tapestry of
the sidewalks. Some men in pajamas held hands and walked in large
groups. A cornucopia of small shops jammed with a colorful assortment of goods on the ground floor of just about every skyscraper. The
city was full of life. Amidst the chaos of city sounds and blaring horns,
which could be easily heard through the taxi's closed windows and
above the air conditioning on high, Jill detected what sounded like
chanting.

It must be the evening call to prayer, she reminded herself. "Ashhadu an la ilaha illallah, wa ashhadu anna Mohammad rasulu Allah."
There is no God but Allah, and Mohammad is his prophet.

Jill remembered David telling her how he felt. It was a soothing
sound.

It had been a chilly November night as the two of them sat in the
hot tub sipping a delicious Cab Sav. David spoke while Jill listened.
He enjoyed telling her tall tales about his adventures and the countries
and cultures that fascinated him. He captivated her with his vivid
descriptions, and she learned much about the world from his fabulous
stories. Although Jill was a specialized terrorist profiler for the US,
there seemed never to be any budget to fly her into areas where most
terrorists were based. But David often traveled to many of those exotic,
if sometimes dangerous, places, and he became her personal conduit
to parts of the world she had not, at least until now.

Jill returned to the present with a sudden jolt as the taxi screeched to
an abrupt standstill at a red light. The rapid halt propelled her into the
back of the front seat. "What the hell?" Jill gasped. The driver glanced
back at her in the rear-view mirror but didn't seem bothered by his
passenger's discomfort, as if this was a regular occurrence. Jill looked
around the now dark streets and realized the surrounding buildings

looked familiar—but how could that be? She had never been here before. Or had she? They had made lots of U-turns and skimmed around traffic circles. It didn't take her long to figure out that they had been going around in circles for quite some time.

"Al Binood, you know Al Binood?" Jill asked.

"No problem, ma'am, no problem," he bobbled.

Jill had no idea what time it was, but she knew it must be getting late, and it was becoming clear the driver hadn't a clue how to get to Al Binood.

"Hello, can you take me to Le Méridien?" she said, somewhat exasperated.

"No problem." Again with that predictable reply.

The lobby of the Le Méridien was bright gold and gaudy. The only noticeable difference from an American hotel was the number of men blatantly staring as she walked into the smoke-filled lobby. Over the years, she had received many compliments on her tight body, and she was used to being gawked at by now. Some people thought she was a fitness model, and she would inevitably get the question, "Are you from Italy?" She sometimes admired herself in the mirror, appreciating how her dark hair, green-gray eyes, and olive skin were ever-present gifts from her Navajo genetics.

As she waited for her room key, she observed the bright gold and marble decor, leaving her almost as cold as the frigid air conditioning that made the place feel like a meat locker. She began to scan the room, out of habit but also on the against-all-odds hope that somehow David might be there. She returned her glance to one man in particular—he seemed to be staring at her—then she continued scanning the rest of the lobby. She was brought back to the task when the young Filipina woman behind the counter held up a pen and asked her to sign the check-in form. When the woman gave Jill the key, Jill asked if there was someone who could help her locate a restaurant. The woman pointed, and Jill followed her finger across the room to a short man in a gold uniform, complete with a long-tailed jacket, in the corner.

She went over to the corner desk where he stood, but after a fruitless back and forth, she realized the small man would not shed any light on how to get to Al Binood. As she walked toward the elevator, Jill thought she felt someone staring at her from behind, but when she turned and glanced back, no one was there.

Once in her room, Jill could not escape the growing dread in her stomach. She kicked off her shoes, threw her black pants suit into a pile on the floor, and headed into the spacious bathroom for a hot shower. When the water turned cold, she barely had the shampoo rinsed out of her hair.

"Shit!" she grumbled aloud. She toweled off, took one of the two fuzzy robes out of the closet, wrapped it around her lithe body, and plopped down on the bed.

"What now?" she asked herself aloud.

Even onboard in expensive first class, there was no natural deep sleep on the aircraft or any aircraft. Jill pondered the value of the trip. She was not a tightwad like David, but it was still a lot of money to spend for a fourteen-hour journey. Jill lay down on the comfy bed. As her mind began to calm down, she had a strange feeling that someone was watching her. But her brain was too tired to register what her gut was trying to tell her. Soon darkness enveloped her.

CHAPTER SIX

05:37 Zulu Time—DOHA, QATAR

A crow lands on the old gray split rail fence. I watch it as I lay on the warm blanket, grass prickling through. The scent of white lilies fills me when a soft hand touches mine. My mother speaks in her native tongue while tickling my tiny toes. I don't understand what she is saying. She holds out a small leather pouch and points at the crow gazing down at us.

Jill awoke disoriented. She rolled over to see the bedside clock: 8:37 a.m. Today the hunt for David was about to begin. But she didn't leap out of bed as someone else might have. Instead, she remained curled between the crisp sheets, desperately trying to recall her vision.

The pouch—the pouch.

Grams always carried a pouch of earth from the sacred mountains of their homeland. Why, in the vision, was her mother giving her the pouch? She told Jill many stories about the pouch's power. "All things are equal, and everything has a spirit," she would say to her. She was a singer, a healer, and she taught Jill that she, too, might have inherited her clairvoyance.

"Hmmmm..." Jill hummed out loud. She would only have these visions when she thought deeply before sleeping. She hadn't had one since the day after David left; she couldn't remember. It had been a very long time.

Jill had her pouch. Her RV pouch. As a retired Remote Viewer, she had taken an oath not to use what her intense Viewer training had taught her outside of the FBI. Besides, she felt she could no longer Remote View since McGregor because all she could sketch was that location—the place where he held her captive. And continually reliving the experience was the main reason she started a career in the USMS—US Marshal Service. She couldn't continue viewing that location again. In truth, Jill had lost her RV mojo. She couldn't seem to connect to the energy path she needed anymore. Frankly, she was glad to have a desk job, and for the most part, she felt safe.

Jill contemplated what the vision had meant as she stepped into her navy Capri pants and slipped on a smart, slightly wrinkled green shirt. She walked into the washroom, finished her morning flush, brushed her teeth, and put on her face, which consisted of her favorite dark burgundy lipstick and black mascara.

Sunlight burst into the room when she opened the curtains. She felt the sun's heat, even through the thick glass. Below the dust-ridden window was a sea of dingy, worn-out rooftops stacked with dilapidated air conditioners.

Jill was excited that she was close to seeing David, even though she had no idea how to locate him. Jill's carry-on sat on the desk where she had left it. She opened it and pulled out her notebook. As she mind-mapped, things would often randomly pop off the page, which rarely happened when she worked on her laptop. She quickly recorded last night's vision, then flipped to the previous page, where she found her final vision—the one she'd had the morning after David left for Doha.

David and I are lying on a blanket in the warm sun. He is smiling at me as I giggle while he tickles my toes. A shadow passes over us as we look up. A crow flies fast over our heads and lands on the fence beside us.

Jill sat and stared blankly at the page, flipping back and forth between what she had just written and what she had written the week before. The similarity prickled her. As she leafed through the pages, a business card slipped out of the notebook and fluttered to the floor. She picked it up: DR. GLEN BELL, FORENSIC DNA SPECIALIST, MD. It was the card she had found in David's suit pocket just before she had pursued the mysterious SUV. She had forgotten that she'd stuffed it in her notebook when she packed for the trip. She wondered for a second time why David would require a DNA specialist. Perhaps the Internet would yield some clues.

She pulled her laptop out of the bag and placed it on the desk. She accidentally snagged a small leather case with her ring. It tumbled to the floor. She looked down at the weathered pouch. It somehow looked different on the plush carpet. She bent over and picked up the worn taupe case. It was the size of a small makeup bag.

"Hello, you," she cooed, as if greeting an old friend. Comforted, she put the pouch beside the business card on the desk and switched on the laptop.

The Le Meridien login screen informed her that she needed a password, but no one answered at the front desk.

She needed coffee anyway and, more importantly, food in her stomach, so she headed to the lobby.

In the smooth elevator ride down, Jill remembered that it might be the Muslim holy month of Ramadan, during which you cannot get coffee, food, or even water, for that matter, until after sunset. She was pleased when she entered the lobby café and saw guests loitering around, sipping from cups.

Jill ordered a cappuccino and was happy to receive it in record time. She opened her notebook to the page she had made notes on while trying to fall asleep on the plane. It was full of seemingly random words with arrows drawn between them—a way of provoking thought. It looked like a naughty child's scribbler who had doodled and daydreamed when she should have been paying attention to the teacher.

Al Binood was circled in the middle of the page. Her eyes scanned the words around it. Her conclusion: she needed more information on the restaurant—if it was one. She decided to call Kali to see if she had found out anything more. Circled in the top right corner were the words "mobile phone." She would ask the hotel where she could rent one when she went to get the login password for the Internet.

Across the bottom left-hand side of the untidy page, she had scrawled "Major Evans" and "clearance." Jill had contacted his staff sergeant to arrange to go to the command post. She had hoped he had managed to organize the list of soldiers David wanted to interview. The word "PRO" and a question mark were in the bottom right corner.

As she continued to review her notes, something didn't feel right. Her intuition made her slowly raise her head. She scanned the dining area. Lady-with-the-Martha-Stewart-haircut was busily showing diagrams to hotel staff. Training, Jill thought. A little boy, who looked about three years old and seemed to have no parent, ran around servers and tables like they were part of his private playground before darting over to the windows and licking them.

"What the—?"

A handsome Arab man sat alone in one corner, back to the wall, sipping coffee. He stared at her. She stared back. Their eyes locked for a long second until she felt an uncomfortable twinge, then she looked away first. She shrugged off her mild discomfort—just as she had yesterday when she first entered the hotel—and returned to her notes. Before long, she felt his gaze boring into her again, and she looked back. Jill wondered if this game of peek-a-boo was part of Middle Eastern culture. Then, without further thought, she plucked herself out of her chair, maneuvered around the table, and strode purposefully toward him. As she got closer, she felt slightly intimidated by his striking good looks. His strong features and intense brown eyes might have come straight off the cover of GQ. His stubble—neatly shaped like a manicured lawn on his broad chin—accentuated his dark features. Long, wavy hair covered his ears—something you would see on a rock star—and it made his cream linen suit look out of place for a man of this culture.

He nodded slightly, mysteriously, acknowledging her approach, even as his eyes moved cautiously around as if he were concerned that someone might see them speak.

"Do I know you?" Jill asked boldly.

"My name is Zayed Saleem," his voice barely audible. "You must be Jill. I have been expecting you."

She took a slight step back. "Me? Have you been waiting for me? Why?"

"David asked me to look out for you," he replied softly. "And no, you don't know me."

A heady mix of hope and astonishment overcame her, and she rushed out, "How do you know David? Do you know where he is?"

He rose briefly as a matter of courtesy. The wrinkles in his linen pants indicated he might have been there for a while. His hand, palm up, signaled in the direction of the other chair at the table. "Please, Jill, please sit down. I am David's PRO."

Slightly hesitant yet anxious to find out as much as she could about David's whereabouts, Jill pushed the chair back and sat. She leaned into Zayed. "You have my attention; go on."

"The last time I saw David was about three days ago." Only a hint of his tongue curled as he spoke—he smelled strongly of musk.

"I'm the public relations officer for Time in Doha. David's contact here. They hired me to help him. You can call me a contractor of sorts." He lisped slightly and leaned back, looking a bit smug.

"Where is David now?" Jill eyed Zayed intensely. She didn't flinch, nor did he.

"That's the problem," Zayed said, maintaining eye contact, his voice still low. "He told me he was going to go undercover on an assignment and would be out of touch for two days."

"If you're his PRO, why didn't he tell you where he was going? Why the secrecy?"

"He said he didn't need my help this time and had it covered. He did say that it was a risky story and that the help I could give him was to take care of some things he may need me to do in Doha and that he would be in touch. I haven't heard from him since. Before he left, he said that you would surely show up if something went wrong and he couldn't reach you."

Jill almost missed it. Barely noticeably, Zayed's glance lowered. Liar! Jill had studied many faces as a profiler. Jill didn't hate much, but she did hate liars. She learned during her training that the US would never use a lie detector test on a suspected Arab terrorist because lie detectors work by registering heightened anxiety if and when a person lies. A lie detector test wastes time if a person feels no compunction about lying. Most Arab criminals do not have the same connection with lying as

Western criminals would. In fact, some suspected Arab criminals have been known to achieve 100% "accurate" scores on lie detector tests, which no individual could obtain by honest means. In any event, Jill saw Zayed's eyes dart downwards. Intriguing, she thought, for this was something positive. He may have been lying, but he cared about it. Jill needed more information.

"He gave me a detailed description of you," Zayed explained. "He thought you might come to this hotel to locate him if he was not back in a reasonable amount of time."

Looking into Zayed's dark eyes, Jill recalled that when she called looking for David at this hotel, there was no message left for her.

"How would David know that I would come? And what things did he ask you to take care of?"

"It's clear by your presence that he must know you well," Zayed said, Yoda-like. "When I did not hear back from him, I paid the hotel clerk to notify me of any reservations under your name or David's name."

"What did David want you to do for me?"

"He just wanted me to ensure your safety until he came back," he replied, then did some fishing of his own: "I take it by your presence here that you haven't heard from him."

Jill felt uncomfortable confiding in Zayed. Her jaw perched squarely on her hands now, elbows on the table. Jill inched closer to Zayed.

"No, I haven't heard from him in almost a week. That's why I'm here—to try to find him." She thought carefully before she asked her next question. She didn't trust Zayed, but she had no choice but to work with him; he was all she had at this point, and PRO had been written on the fax from David's office... So she blurted it out.

"Do you know of a restaurant called Al Binood?"

He lit a cigarette. A whiff of Marlboro crept up Jill's nose; she pulled back. She hadn't noticed the small black round ashtrays that littered this side of the café.

"You like one?" His index finger tapped the Marlboro-branded case on the table. He turned his head and blew out smoke, then butted the cigarette when Jill shook her head no.

"Jill," he paused, looking into her eyes. "Yes, I know of this place. Why do you ask about it?" He showed no emotion, no movement for Jill to decipher.

Curiously, and before Jill could answer, he said, "I will help you take you there, as I am an Arab man, and this is not a place for a lady to go alone. David said you were stubborn but didn't tell me how much. They will not speak to an English-American woman. We must go unnoticed. You will need to change your clothes. I will return with a local dress for you to wear."

Jill leaned back in her chair, arms crossed, her leg flipping nonchalantly up and down. "Why should I trust you?"

He stood and looked down at her. "I really don't think you have too many options." He placed several colorful bills on the table. "Meet me back in the lobby in twenty minutes." And he walked out of the café.

Jill rented a mobile phone from the hotel gift shop, where she obtained the Internet password before heading back to her room. Bright sunlight streamed in through the window, causing a glare on the computer screen. Out of curiosity, Jill strode to the window and touched the glass; it felt like it was on fire. No wonder the air conditioning was on high. She sat down at the desk and Googled Al Binood. Nothing. Zayed was right. She needed his help. Her chair creaked as she sat back, staring at the Google page.

"Zayed, you say," Jill spoke to the screen. "Your grammar and syntax are off a bit, Zayed, my new friend. What are you hiding?" She knew it could be a language barrier. But slower speech, almost mumbling, was a clear sign of deception. There was no way in hell she was going to trust him. "No way in hell," she repeated out loud. He was right, though; she didn't have much choice, and he could earn her trust. Maybe. But what was David's and Zayed's relationship? And why hadn't David told Zayed where he was going?

Jill grabbed the phone and dialed Kali, who sounded groggy when she answered. In her haste, Jill had forgotten about the time difference. She immediately apologized to Kali for waking her.

"I won't keep you, Rine," Jill said quickly, hoping her friend wasn't too pissed off or too tired to talk. "Have you found out anything more about Al Binood?"

"I've uncovered an off-chance connection that it may be an Al Qaeda meeting place," she said, her voice a little thick. "But the information was so obscure; it may be a long shot. Oh, and Jill, have you seen any reporters? 'Cause CNN's dogs are on it. It's been all over the news that an American is missing, but it's only a tagline. You know those vultures—they get a whiff of a story and move on it. So far, no messages on your voicemail, so I don't think they know it's David yet."

"You can bet they will uncover his name soon. Kali, can you send me an e-mail if anything changes with the media? I need to keep on top of whatever comes out." Before Kali answered, Jill added, "I'll call again soon. Oh, and Kali, I met an Arab guy in the lobby; Jeff mentioned there was a public relations officer. Arabic, he says his name is Zayed Saleem. Can you see what you can find on him?"

"How do you know him? Do you think he's dangerous?" She sounded slightly concerned.

"Well, he was here waiting for me. He said he hadn't heard from David. But you know me, Rine," Jill said wryly.

"Yeah, just be careful, Jill." But Kali's words fell on deaf ears.

Jill had no intention of visiting Al Binood unarmed. She needed some sort of weapon. She could not bring her gun onto the aircraft as she was not on official US Marshal business, and guns were illegal in Qatar. Jill had read of American security contractors being thrown into Qatari jails for merely having a couple of live bullets in their luggage. Not something she needed right now.

She smirked as she pulled out her keychain lighter and marveled at the cleverness used to disguise her switchblade. The knife's sleek, cold metal had never been discovered by even the most observant of airport security. She changed into her dark fatigues, slipped the knife into a side pocket within easy reach on her right leg, and left her room.

Zayed looked different sitting in the plump lobby chair. His head nodded, motioning her toward him. His spotless white dishdasha appeared freshly laundered and starched, and he sported traditional Arabic headgear—a black agal held in place by the flowing gutra that he had lifted back on both sides and then neatly crossed over at the back. Jill studied him up close. He resembled a figure from an old Arabian movie, a modern-day Lawrence of Arabia.

Sitting across from him was a woman dressed in a black abaya, complete with the hijab and burka, holding a large blue shopping bag. Jill could see only her dark brown eyes. She was surprised when the woman looked back at her without a hint of shyness. Her eyes were expressionless at first, then Jill saw slight crinkles at their edges, and she knew the woman must have been smiling.

"She will help you dress to blend in," Zayed said. The woman stood, then waved her hand, directing Jill to follow her. They walked across the gold lobby to a room next to the hotel concierge desk and opened the door. The room was empty, with faded pear-green walls and a small cot in the corner. The silent woman removed the contents of the blue bag and placed them on the unmade cot—an abaya, a black scarf, and a small cotton cloth cap. Without a word, the cloaked woman, who now stood before her, began to stroke Jill's hair off her face gently, as if preparing her for a wedding. Jill stiffened slightly. She wasn't accustomed to strangers being in her personal space, let alone touching her in such a familiar way. But something was comforting about this woman's presence.

Maneuvering around as deftly as a Park Avenue stylist, the woman pulled Jill's hair back into a ponytail, then up into a bun. Jill felt the tautness as the tight cap covered her hairline; it was like she was preparing to race in a swim meet. She brushed her fingers along the edge of the cloth cap; not a single hair strayed where it might be seen.

The silent woman stood before her, holding the black robe to Jill's shoulders. She scrunched it like pantyhose into a ring and gently slid it over her head. The cloaked woman's face was close to Jill's, and she glimpsed into her misty brown eyes rimmed with crevassed lines. After several adjustments, the woman in black clapped her hands. "Yalla, yalla," she said and motioned Jill to turn around.

The glossy polyester robe hung heavy. Jill looked down and saw the tips of her toes poking out from under the hem. She wondered how much she would sweat today. Now the woman began to wrap the scarf tightly around her face, meticulously pinning and tying it. Jill did not expect that she would breathe easy with her mouth and nose covered. Jill suddenly felt a sense of relief. There was no mirror in the room. No one could see her; no one knew who she was. Turning Jill around one final time, a look of satisfaction lit up the silent woman's eyes.

"Alhamdulillah. Praise be to God," she said thickly as she pulled Jill back into the lobby.

Zayed was still in the same spot pouring from an Arabic-style coffee pot. Steam rose as coffee hit the toy cup. He looked at Jill approvingly as she approached.

"Khalas, khalas. Finish." His upright fingers touched quickly, then he opened them again. The dismissed woman turned and crossed the bright lobby, her abaya billowing as she walked out the door.

"What now?" Jill asked.

Zayed stood, said Khalas once again, and headed toward the door, Jill trailing a step behind him.

Unexpectedly, the heat didn't seem as invasive as the day before. Could it be the abaya? Jill wondered. A passing taxi tooted twice when he noticed Zayed's hail. The robin's egg blue Corolla pulled up, and Zayed opened the door for Jill to get in first. She hesitated. Jill thought of the taxi she had taken from the airport last night and kicked herself for not appreciating it more.

The driver was dressed in loose-fitting pants and a long over-shirt with slits up the side, which Jill remembered was called 'shalwat kameez,' the pajama-like clothing that is the national dress of Pakistan. He also sported a bright orange, well-trimmed goatee, contrasting with his baby blue-colored attire. A little white crocheted beanie adorned his head. The plastic on the seat crackled and crunched when Jill slid across it. The gaudy seat material shouted through the plastic, reminding Jill of heavy curtains in an old movie theater. Zayed said something to the driver in Arabic, and the car jerked forward. The door smudged with fingerprints and dirt rattled ominously, and Jill noticed the absence of a door handle on her left side immediately.

The driver's beady eyes peered at her through the rear-view mirror, tilted at such an angle that he could see her body. Jill wondered why he stared at her cloaked presence erratically while driving. It made her think of last night's taxi driver professional in comparison. Jill closed her eyes several times as the car jerked forward and sideways. Honking cars cut them off. The streets were busy, and the driver turned on the Arabic music when Jill talked to Zayed in English.

"The streets seem abnormally clean," Jill said, trying to take her mind off the drive.

"We have very cheap labor here, so we have a lot of people to do the work in a short time; they usually clean the streets at night."

The loud music filled the car and left no room for more chitchat.

Suddenly, they made a sharp right and popped over a speed bump into a giant parking lot. It took Jill several seconds to realize it was not a parking lot but a back street with cars parked in disarray; too many cars for the number of buildings on the block. Cars were parked down the center of the lot, making progress virtually impossible. In some instances, the vehicles were double-parked, making passing unattainable. Nevertheless, the small taxi snaked its way through the vehicles until they came to a bright yellow sign set back from the street. Jill thought it strange to see an English sign for Nestlé Tea in this part of the world, but there it was in its bright yellow glory. Below it was Arabic writing, and Jill spied the words in English: Al Binood.

In front of Al Binood lay several dozen sand-stained, tattered, square cushions about eight inches high. A TV perched on a makeshift stand was in front of the low seating area. The TV looked vintage 1980s and in bad condition, but a power cord ran from it to a socket in the wall. Dust coated everything. Dingy white plastic chairs on the cobblestone suggested this must also be an outdoor meeting place. Zayed said something in Arabic or Urdu; Jill wasn't sure, to the driver, handed him some money, then reached his hand over to help Jill out of the car. It was easy to slide across the plastic fabric, and Jill was thankful for his help when the bottom of the abaya touched the ground and got in the way of her feet.

"So this is it?" He nodded and, with annoyance, moved his finger to his lips, signaling her not to speak. This gesture pissed her off, but this was his turf, so she kept her mouth shut and fell behind him. She wasn't used to being told what to do. They walked past the chairs and cushions and through a rickety front door.

Jill stopped abruptly and took in the scene before her. She stood in wonder at what she saw. The one-room area was in desperate need of repair. One of its four walls consisted of a bank of dirty windows that surely had not let the sun through in at least a decade. One particularly filthy pane had a long taped-up crack in it. An abundance of plastic tables and plastic chairs checkered the room. On the tables were ashtrays and a smattering of faded plastic yellow flowers. There was a door at the back of the room, which Jill thought might lead to a restroom, but she saw no sign. A large picture of an obviously crucial Arabian man was on the far wall beside the cashier's desk. A prince or president, she assumed, based on his decorated gold-trimmed clothing.

Zayed motioned her over to a corner table. Jill's abaya swept the dirt, leaving a hint of a trail across the floor to where she sat at a wobbly table. Only two other patrons were in the place, and they looked to be Arabs. A gaggle of slight servers staff members, all male, stood around anxiously, waiting to serve them.

One broke from the group, brought coffee in an Arabic-style decanter, and poured the brown liquid into miniature cups. Looking down at the steaming coffee, Jill tried to work out how to drink it with a burqa. Not wanting to raise suspicion, she let it sit there untouched. She looked around the room for anything that appeared irregular. Everything did.

Meanwhile, Zayed engaged the waiter in conversation as the tiny man grinned widely and poured him another cup of coffee. Zayed pulled a photo of David from the slit side pocket of his dishdasha and showed it to the waiter. It took all Jill had to stop from grabbing the picture and questioning the man herself and not knowing the language. However, she forced herself to stay quiet and evaluate the discussion as best she could. Although she could not speak Arabic or any of the many languages commonly spoken in the Gulf region, she understood body language; judging by the server, he did not seem to know the man in the photo. Too relaxed, Jill thought. The server then called over another of his colleagues. Looking closer at the picture, Jill reached over and gently pulled it from Zayed's hairy hand. Her chest swelled as she looked at David, so close to her heart and now in her hand. He was sitting in the hotel lobby, Le Meridien, the same place where she was staying. The picture was taken from afar as if done under surveillance; David wasn't looking at the camera, but to Jill, it felt like he was saying hello.

As she returned it to Zayed, another waiter nervously approached their table, slightly built. Jill guessed he was from Bangladesh. She based this on her research profiling terrorists from Dhaka. She recalled that they were more frail-looking people with smaller, rounder, and flatter faces than their Indian neighbors.

"You know this man?" Zayed asked in Arabic. The small man looked at Zayed, then at the photo, and back to Zayed. A bead of sweat rolled off his forehead. He looked around the room. Then, without further warning, he bolted towards the back of the café and fled through the unsigned door. It clapped shut behind him.

Jill was surprised that her first reaction was one of pause, as usually her instinct would be to run after him. Then she heard Zayed's chair fall over backward. The flash of Zayed's crisp dishdasha told her he was well ahead of her thought. Jill dashed past the curious staff the next instant and raced after Zayed.

The sunlight was blinding after being in the dim café, and Jill winced at the brightness—only to find Zayed holding the escapee up against a wall and shouting at him in Arabic. They were standing in a small gated courtyard. Jill had read that in Arab culture, people were taught not to raise their voices, let alone hit another, but Zayed's stance was forceful. He was shouting, holding the man with one hand and threatening him with the other. The trembling man began to speak to him in broken Arabic when Zayed pressed his body into the wall harder—more shouting from Zayed.

Finally, he loosened his grip, and the man slumped down the wall onto the ground. He was whimpering and looked like he might break into tears. Jill knew it was fear. Raw fear. She'd seen it before; she'd felt it before.

Zayed stomped over to Jill and grabbed her arm. "We must go now!" He whisked her out of the courtyard and down a back street, where he hailed the first taxi he saw. Zayed motioned her not to speak. "Shuay, shuay. Patience," he hissed, opening and closing his upright fingers. Anger once again bubbled inside Jill at being ordered around, but the look on Zayed's face told Jill to stay quiet on the trip back to the hotel.

Back at Le Meridien, Jill and Zayed jumped out of the taxi as they started towards the large hotel's glass doors when Jill noticed that Zayed was doing sector scans. Surveillance scans were something she would normally do if she felt threatened. Situational awareness was instilled in trained forces and all agencies, including the police and military. Typically, a sector scan consisted of assessing potential danger, knowing your exit routes, and understanding who and what was surrounding you. Zayed was doing a sector scan clock style; she knew it well. First, you look ahead: twelve o'clock. From twelve to three is sector one. Sector two is from three to six. Sector three is from six to nine. The last is from nine o'clock back to twelve. Military, she thought at once. Telling.

"What did he tell you, Zayed?" She opted not to say to him that she recognized his trained skills. Not just yet, anyway.

"We'll talk in your room, Jill."

Jill followed Zayed's accelerated pace through the lobby into the elevator and up to her room. It seemed the most logical and safest place to go, but apprehension stopped her when they reached the door. She had not been in a hotel room with another man since she met David. She fumbled with her key and paused again before entering the room. Once the door closed, she removed the thick black abaya. Zayed watched her, but his eyes dodged hers when she looked back at him.

She pulled the snug headdress off and threw it onto the bed; she flicked her head and released her hair. Then she pivoted to face Zayed. "What the hell was that?" Jill hissed.

"Yani, calm down. David said you had a bit of a temper."

"Don't yani me, screw you." Jill pulled off her abaya with such force that it lifted her shirt up past her black bra. Zayed did not seem to care as he watched her adjust herself.

"Listen, Jill, khalas, listen." Jill simmered and listened, adjusting her shirt and fixing her hair. Zayed's eyes did not leave her body, and she recognized his silent attraction. "The server told me that he shouldn't talk to anyone as it would endanger his life and disgrace his family. He said that David was at the café four days ago and met with two men."

"He saw David?"

Zayed nodded. "These men apparently spoke English and were well-dressed Arabs. He recognized one of the men as a friend of his uncle. The server didn't think much of the trio—until he overheard them discussing a man's name that would catch the attention of any-one within hearing distance." Zayed hesitated. "His name is Matta."

"Matta?"

"Yes, Matta. And they were also looking at a map of Afghanistan."

"I guess one of the men caught the guy watching them. It seemed he recognized him too and went over and took him aside. The man who knew his uncle threatened the server by suggesting that he has three little nieces and that he will take them from his uncle's home if he repeated anything he had heard or seen."

Jill didn't know what to say. Questions flooded her mind. "Why Matta? Why David?" And does this relate to the case I was working on before leaving to come here? "Why were they looking at a map of Afghanistan? What was the name of the uncle?"

Zayed shrugged. He didn't know. "The server's name is Punjabi, so I guess his uncle's name would be the same. I thought David must have been planning a trip to Afghanistan. He may be on his way there now. I think David is somewhere along the Turkmenistan border, as the server spouted something about the top of the map. Turkmenistan is above Afghanistan on the map. I did some business in Afghanistan about five years ago. Kabul, mainly."

Jill looked puzzled. "What were you doing there?"

"A family business trip," he replied evasively. "Airline parts."

"Do you think David's disappearance has something to do with Matta?"

"I have no idea," he responded, his accent growing thicker with concern.

Thoughts entered her puzzled mind and then fled. David must have stumbled upon a great story, something worth risking everything for that Pulitzer. David was a risk-taker; it was undoubtedly shown in his choice of assignments and stories.

Jill picked up the hotel phone and started to dial. Zayed's hand grabbed hers and forced her to drop the receiver. She angrily pulled her hand out of his.

"Don't touch me. Do that again, and I'll break your arm." She knew she was bluffing because even with her HTH hand-to-hand training, she could gauge by his size that he would not be an easy mark. Besides, she didn't know who she was dealing with and what his fighting skills might be. "I am contacting my office—they can help find David."

Zayed looked at her squarely.

"My contact has access to Interpol," she said firmly. "They can sometimes pinpoint things such as mobile phones if we know the region or other intel that might be available." Their eyes were fixed on each other, and neither budged. Then his body language relaxed, conceding to her determination to do things her way. He retreated towards the door.

Just before he walked out, he turned back and said, "It's in your best interest to have me help you, Jill. David asked me to watch over you. I made him that promise." He closed the door behind him, leaving Jill wondering who he was.

CHAPTER SEVEN

"Screw you." Jill flipped the bird in the direction of the closed door. She was more than a little miffed by Zayed's smugness. She did not know this man, nor did she feel like being bullied, but at this point, she didn't have time to waste thinking about Zayed.

She glanced over at the time and realized that Kali would now be just on her way to work, and she would need to wait another forty-five minutes to call her. Jill knew Kali was the most efficient one to call and that she had security clearance to speak to Interpol on her behalf.

She looked around the room and saw things she hadn't noticed before. Gaudy burgundy wallpaper with twists of gold lined the space. Jill hurried across the room to the desk and turned on her computer, praying for high speed. The speed from her earlier search was mediocre. She was pleasantly surprised when the speed test proved even higher than at her Catalina home this time.

No e-mail from David or Kali. "Damn." The rest of the e-mails were insignificant. Then she spotted a name she hadn't wanted to see. Stan Brown, David's father. When she clicked on the name, she wondered how he got her e-mail address. It was not public knowledge, and for her life, she could not remember giving it to him. Perhaps he had called her work, and they had given it to him, she half-heartedly thought.

The message was brief:

Jill,Please get in touch with me regarding David.Stan

"Whatever," she said as she closed his e-mail.

Jill surfed for any information on Afghanistan, Turkmenistan, and LSA. She Google-earthed the region in Afghanistan and got a feel for the terrain. It looked somewhat mountainous. The time passed fast, perusing different maps and photos, and then she grabbed the phone.

Jill explained to Kali the encounter with the server and what he had said and gave Kali her mobile number. "Pay-as-you-go is all they have here, so call the hotel when possible."

"I'll call Issy—you remember my Interpol sleuth—and give you a buzz back," Kali spouted.

"Oh, and check out a man named Zayed Saleem; he says his family is in the airplane parts business. This Zayed is definitely trained, Kali. Check any military ops you can get. He's Arab, just not sure from which country—also any information on who frequents Al Binood or anything that might link him there? Scan relatives of Al Qaeda. If Matta is involved, I think David has stumbled onto his Pulitzer." Jill did not notice that she had gently placed her hand on the small leather bag on her laptop's right side.

"Gotcha." Kali hung up.

Jill leaned back, propped her feet up on the desk, and pondered. Staring blankly at the TV screen beside the desk, she thought, What am I missing?

The TV was blaring, and Jill felt comforted as it drowned out her thoughts. Her thoughts of gloom. No new reports on CNN about the missing journalist as the taglines zoomed by fast. She was on the fence about whether to be happy or not about that fact. With missing people, the quicker you get the story onto the news with the details, the more likely it would be to find them.

David's not officially missing. He's working on a story. She kept pushing that thought to try to convince herself.

Jill recalled a document in one of her files that disclosed the Pakistan Secret Police had executed a CNN reporter for obtaining a connection between Matta, Dr. E, and a laboratory located in Pakistan. Trying to remember the journalist's name, Jill jumped when the phone rang.

It was Kali with some welcome information. Kali told Jill that her investigation and conversations had revealed two clues regarding what David might have found of interest to make him go into a dangerous country such as Afghanistan.

"LSA means Lost Soviet Arsenal," Kali said excitedly. "There was a report about camps along the border of Turkmenistan and, in particular, a town called Kushka. Documentation shows that there is evidence of voice recordings to substantiate the possibility that enriched uranium existed in this area in 2008."

At this point, Jill felt like kicking her ass to the door and back to Tucson.

"What kind of profiler am I if I can't even figure out what LSA means?" In her defense, Jill told herself, We don't use that term. We use loose nukes, suitcase nukes, or even broken arrows. "Shit!"

"Well, we know it now, so don't sweat the small stuff," Kali chimed.

Jill was still pissed at herself for missing the acronym. Kali told her that she would load the documents to the VPN for her to download. "I'll send you an e-mail when I'm done. It shouldn't be more than a few minutes."

Jill looked over at the mini-bar, contemplating what she should do in the meantime. David had commented on the increase in her drinking when she was under pressure. But to Jill, the comfort settled her when her body and mind couldn't do so on their own. She couldn't blame that one on McGregor; she'd always been that way. This was her vice.

But today was different. This new information affected her life, her family, and David. Jill often brought her cases home with her, and although she was not directly out in the field, profiling took her into the dark abyss of evil. Sometimes the darkness overwhelmed her heart, knowing what she knew.

Being a terrorist these days does not cost much, and finding black market weapons seemed easier than buying ice cream. Unlike some major TV news reporting in the US, even as far away as Australia, there were reports of suitcase nukes. They even had serial numbers in some of the articles. Reports of US forces uncovering anthrax camps, reports that Matta had these nukes as close as Mexico—her mind boggled when she didn't see public warnings on any of the US news stations. Jill often wondered if the President had censored the news so the public wouldn't understand the threat behind it all.

What if the nukes were in Mexico? Three thousand illegal aliens crossed the border into the US daily. It's only a matter of money and time before some of these illegals would be from Al Qaeda. Only a small two percent of those caught were non-Mexicans, or SIAs, Special Interest Aliens from Arab countries. Not long ago, Jill had been asked to assist the CIA in an interrogation of a woman who was a terrorist courier. She had traveled back and forth illegally across the border to and from an Al Qaeda cell just outside Los Angeles. It's too easy, she thought, too easy.

Jill needed to have a clear mind. She would not miss another stupid thing, as she reprimanded herself again about the LSAs. She looked down at her hand after it brushed the leather pouch, almost as if it were calling her. She untied the string and opened the pouch. Inside were eight clay tablets, each branded with its own number. Jill's mind began to numb until she heard a familiar sound.

"You've got mail!"

Pushing back to the present, Jill read Kali's e-mail that reported that the files were ready for downloading, and then at the bottom of the e-mail Kali had written:

Eric has a potential lead who might have been tailing you. He said there were reports of a black Cadillac Escalade stolen from the airport in Tucson. He thought it might be related to the move, so he contacted homeland security. They're running the flight lists now. It'll take a while with the volume of flights. Will keep you posted, chickee! O.

Jill logged into the VPN and began downloading the documents. Kali had also included satellite images of the Turkmenistan border and a map from Kabul, the Afghanistan capital, to the small town of Kushka. A rather extensive report on Russian rebels attached was too large to review right now. Jill read the last words in a piece of news from the Washington Times, saying that diagrams of US nuclear power plants had been found in an abandoned Al Qaeda camp just outside of Kushka.

Saving the documents, Jill sat back. She sighed. It was several silent minutes later. Numb minutes when it happened. The epiphany was Leila. Leila Sorel.

"Leila, why didn't I think of you before?" Jill spoke to herself, excited. "Maybe she has heard from David?"

Leila was a colleague of David's and was one of the first colleagues David had introduced to Jill. Leila was tall, had a dark complexion, large green Asian eyes, and verged on stunning. She was a freelance photojournalist for Time. Leila also looked physically strong. Jill noted the striations in her arms when she reached out and shook her hand in greeting. Her bone-straight hair accentuated her tight short bangs; she often joked about how she ended up so tall with her Asian descent.

Although they had not been on many assignments together, David and Leila would often converse on the phone or at Jill's home about article concepts and tricks of the trade. Work stuff. The Pulitzer. Like David, Leila seemed fearless, taking on assignments in war-torn countries with only her camera to guide her. She was a feisty, strong, opinionated woman, and she and David often ended conversations in a debate. Some might call her a bit of a hothead. To Jill, she was David's friend. Leila's passion was Afghanistan. Some of her best shots were from that country. Leila had won many awards for her photos.

Looking at the time and hoping she would find Leila reachable on her satellite mobile, Jill snatched the phone and pushed hard on the numbers.

"Sorel," the firm voice answered.

"Leila, it's Jill. How are you? Where are you? I'm in Doha."

"Well, girlfriend, you get 'round now," she said with interest.

"Where are you, Leila? Have you heard from David?"

"What do you mean, Jill? What are you talking about? Why are you in Doha?"

Jill explained the recent events to Leila, who immediately became concerned when Jill mentioned she needed to go to Afghanistan.

"I don't think you should go, Jill. I know you are trained in ops and know your stuff, but this is for experienced field agents. Have you spoken to Jeff? Can the company help you?"

Jill realized she had not heard from anyone at David's work for two days. "I haven't been in touch with Jeff since he called me. Frankly, I haven't been in contact with anyone. I suppose I—"

"Jill, what is your mobile?"

Jill gave Leila the details.

"I'll get back in touch with you after I call the office. I'm in London at the airport, but morning is about to break in the States. Jill, please stay put until you hear back from me."

Without waiting for a response, Leila abruptly hung up.

"What was that about," Jill hushed to herself. Leila seemed worried. No, it was more than that. Jill couldn't put her finger on the niggling feeling she had.

Torn between sleep and a desire to keep researching, Jill took a break. She looked over at the open pouch and thought about attempting to RV in search of David. The thought of seeing that sketch of McGregor's location again made her cringe. If she knew in her heart that David was in trouble, she'd do it; she'd have to push through the fear, push past herself, and take the plunge. She hesitated again, contemplating, then went over to the bed, laid down, and closed her eyes. David.

She felt relieved after understanding what motivated David to go to Afghanistan. He was driven by the story, adventure, and justice, which was enough for him to be out of communication with her. However, she was unsure whether to search for him or go to Afghanistan. She decided to wait until she heard from Kali regarding Zayed and would call her after a few hours of sleep.

Yup, that one's a no-brainer. Perhaps I will just stay in Doha. Her intuition grumbled. Jill's brain went from dancing a jig to a slow waltz. Fog blanketed her thoughts as she drifted into a much-needed deep sleep. Bliss.

CHAPTER EIGHT

22:12 Zulu Time—DOHA, QATAR

She couldn't breathe, her body told her mind, as she was startled awake. Jill tried to fight the strong hand that gripped her mouth.

"Quiet!" he whispered. It was Zayed. "Someone is coming down the hall. You're in danger."

Jill's arms pushed hard against his chest, and he lifted his weight, releasing her.

"What are you doing? Get the hell off of me," she hissed.

"We don't have time," he said, and without hesitation, he handed Jill a gun. In the dark, Jill released the magazine from the Glock, squinted to see the rounds, then jammed it back in. She pulled, then released the slide, chambering a round. Zayed was dressed in dark black army fatigues similar to the ones Jill had on when she had fallen asleep. Darkness surrounded them in the small room. Instinctively, they both moved to the door, their bodies tense, backed against the wall.

With the tinkle of the lock being picked, the door handle quivered ever so slightly. A man emerged from the light in the hallway. Before Jill could move her brain from thought to recognition, Zayed smacked him over the back of the head with the butt of his gun. The man fell hard.

"Grab your things," Zayed commanded as he looked at the fallen man. "More will be coming; we must get out of here now."

Jill looked at the time: 1:22 a.m. She grabbed her computer, the small leather pouch, and anything else her eyes revealed in the pitch black. She threw them into her carry-on, and they fled silently down the dark fire exit stairs and out of the hotel.

Outside, the cool air was a break from the daytime desert heat, but Jill still wore her clothes from the night before and was thankful for that. Their boots smacked the side street as they ran into the dark. Jill followed Zayed to a large white Land Cruiser.

"Quick, get in!"

Before Jill could slam the door shut, Zayed accelerated. He drove frantically through the stream of parked cars. Their bodies lifted as they hit the large speed bumps at high speed. Out onto the dark street, cars blurred as they passed them. Several turns later, when Zayed slowed, Jill could unclench the handle above the door.

With no apology, Zayed began to speak. "I know this man. I recognized him when he walked across the parking lot at the hotel."

"But how did you get into—"

Before Jill could finish asking how he managed to break into her room undetected, Zayed pulled out a key to her room. Feeling somewhat violated, she wondered who the man was.

"You were watching the hotel? Why?"

"You cannot go back to that hotel. You must stay underground. You are in danger."

"Who the hell was that guy, Zayed? Tell me! And why do you think I am in danger?"

"He is a rebel from the Chechen Mafia. They are running the Al Qaeda cell here in Doha. Guess I am not the only one paying for information about you. The question is: What is their interest in you?"

"What were you doing at my hotel? Who are you, Zayed, and where the hell are we going?"

"I have told you already; I am here to help David. Quiet now, just for a few minutes, I'm thinking."

"Screw you."

Jill felt the gun inside her pants pocket. She looked at Zayed, and when he didn't return her glare, she stared out the window. They were on a highway now, water on her left and desert on her right—it appeared they were leaving the city.

Jill scrolled her mind, searching her memory for the briefs she had read about the Chechens. Then, the sting of what she recalled made her mouth drop open slightly. Jill remembered David telling her about one of his colleagues at Time who wrote that Matta had refurbished "broken arrows." When she went to Sven with this information, he dismissed it as Matta's grandstanding. Jill's research proved him wrong; Matta had purchased twenty live nukes from the Chechen Mafia. It was confirmed in a US State Department brief and was leaked to the international media. The US media failed to cover the story. Even after pressing Sven further on it, he tried to appease Jill. He told her the CIA was saying that the brief was false. She knew it wasn't, and frankly, she didn't know why Sven would attempt to make such a stupid statement. And if it was true, the Chechen Mafia potentially had more nukes for sale.

Jill's brain began to tick the boxes—one hell of a story, David, one hell of a story. Jill decided to tell Zayed what she knew about the Mafia and its connection with Matta. With the adrenaline dissipating as they drove along the gloomy streets, Jill wondered if she could trust Zayed with the new information she had received and her decision not to go to Afghanistan. "Fake 'til you make it, and never let them see you sweat" was her motto. I will take as much from this guy as I can, for now, anyway.

"What do you know about the Chechen Mafia?" Jill asked Zayed.

"They are now a growing movement contributing to Islamic radicalism. They are a powerful organized crime group—drugs, gun running, and sex slavery. Depending on what David was working on, I guess that they wanted you as a hostage or something like that. David must have stumbled upon something good—real good."

Jill thought she heard a hint of a German accent in his words again, for it was the longest he had spoken to her at one time.

"Have you ever heard of the term LSA?"

Zayed noticeably grimaced. "What is it you think you know, Jill?"

Answering a question with a question pissed her off. His response made her wonder what he knew about the broken arrows and what he knew about her. Hadn't David told him what she did for a living? ... guess not!

"Well, the Chechens and Matta have one thing in common, you know, that whole terrorism war," Jill said smugly. "It can't be a coincidence, Zayed."

She wasn't going to tell him everything she knew. He didn't say anything, which gnawed at her intuition.

"With the Chechen Mafia's involvement, I need to find David now more than ever. I am going to go to Afghanistan." She didn't have a choice; she had finally decided. Then she said, "And I need your help."

She would be better off with someone who spoke Arabic. She only hoped that Kali's search on Zayed turned out positive.

Without so much pause, Zayed said, "You need to get out of Doha unnoticed—and now. They're a big group, Jill; you cannot go to the airport, and Qatar is a peninsula. You cannot drive off of it as it goes into Saudi Arabia. They have their connections there, and the border will be watched."

Then, in what seemed to be a bizarre suggestion, he added, "We need to go via boat to a place in the United Arab Emirates. I know of a city that we can get through to unnoticed. Port security is next to nothing... Abu Dhabi. Insha'Allah!" He looked over at Jill and said intently, "God willing."

"Insha'allah yourself. I am not going anywhere by boat."

Jill had heard of Abu Dhabi. The number of reports she had scoured over the years would be enough to fill her office and more. She had seen pictures of Dubai and its grandstanding architecture but not many photos of Abu Dhabi.

They sat in silence while Jill's intuition began to recede.

"Do you know someone with a boat? How long would it take us to get there?" Jill asked. Her left hand held the seatbelt strap for support when they made a fast U-turn.

"It is about an eight-hour trip by sea to Abu Dhabi."

Thinking of the amount of sleep she would miss made her sigh heavily.

"Grab your abaya and put it on."

Jill reached over the seat, rummaged through her carry-on, and found the black robe. She unclasped her belt and balanced her body on the console, straining to put on all the pieces. Jill looked over her right shoulder, and in her peripherals, she noticed Zayed had a full view of her ass, bent over the seat. His face was angled ever so slightly in the direction of her butt. She snatched the black cloth and turned back onto the chair.

There were no mirrors like in the cramped room the woman had helped her get dressed in. Jill, unsure what to do next, fumbled with getting the cotton beanie tied correctly.

"You need to tie it at the back under your hair," Zayed attempted to assist.

Her body moved forward slightly as the Land Cruiser slowed down. Jill flipped the robe over herself and told him she needed his help with the black veil. They veered around a narrow street, bounced hard over two more speed bumps, rounded a corner, and stopped directly amid a village on the water. Only the moonlight reflecting off the rippling water brought light to the docks.

He pushed the truck out of gear fast. As Jill jumped down from the SUV, her black robe fell over her fatigues, dusting the ground. Zayed went around the front and stood directly in front of her. Jill could feel the heat of his breath on her forehead as he wrapped the scarf around her head. Without moving, he said, "I will need to hide the guns; we cannot travel with them."

Jill agreed, but it made her uneasy. Her hand tangled under the long gown, and she pulled the gun out and gave it to Zayed. The weapon looked tiny in his oversized hands.

"Stay close to me, and don't speak," he said, walking toward the boats.

He was taller than her, bigger than David. Jill noticed that he was muscular in a Rambo sort of way, admiring him from head to toe in his tight attire. Eye candy. She always appreciated a person, male or female, who cared for themselves physically. Reaching into the backseat, she grabbed her carry-on and followed Zayed.

CHAPTER NINE

Narrow wooden boats were lined up end to end along the docks. Butted against each other, they did not look like a vessel you would see in North America. The long wooden structures looked like miniature pirate ships, and their decks were decorated with outdated electronic equipment, black engine parts, and clothing hung to dry. Water slapped their sides, making them rock gently.

Jill was looking at a fishing village. All along the concrete street and adjoining wooden docks were hundreds of fishing nets that resembled wired igloos piled on top of one another.

People scurried around the boats, getting ready for nighttime fishing. Not far away, she could hear a loud engine trying to start. It went out with a loud backfire, followed by the sounds of the effort being repeated.

All the boats looked the same. Each had a long pointy nose and a double-wide, two-pronged fork at the back end. A cabin, presumably housing the cockpit, was the only structure on the deck. They were stained in a dark brown, except for the three whitewashed tips, and were all about 100 feet long; they looked substantial enough for an eight-hour journey, stable on the water.

This ship can't be the boat Zayed had mentioned to me.

Noticing Jill had stopped keeping pace, Zayed glanced back at her. She could tell by his look that these boats were what he intended to travel on. She gawked at the run-down condition of the vessels, and his firm face answered her question.

"How are we going to get anywhere in this type of boat?" she said pointedly.

Zayed waved his hand and then closed his fingers upwards. Begrudgingly, Jill kept quiet.

Walking along the breakwater, they moved towards the second-to-last dock. The little Indians working on the ships did not glance their way for fear of retribution. It wasn't polite to stare at a woman in an abaya and even less polite if you were a laborer imported to work.

The moonlight lit a feeble passageway, and they sidestepped the shadows down the unsteady plank onto the dock. Passing one boat after another, Jill was thankful that the boat she'd just passed wasn't the one taking them to Abu Dhabi.

Zayed didn't notice or care as he stopped directly in front of the last boat on the end of the rickety, cracked dock. An unsettling feeling flittered in Jill's stomach when he motioned her to stop. Pussyfooting down the long scanty plank alongside the wooden ship, he yelled something in Arabic to the cockpit. An Indian man dressed in navy blue slacks and a pressed white shirt appeared from a small door. The window on the door reflected a moonbeam as Zayed began to speak slowly to him. After several minutes of discussion, the Indian pulled out a phone from his breast pocket, dialed, and started talking in a different language. Hindi or Urdu, Jill didn't know for sure as he glanced over at her. Flipping the phone shut, he waggled his head from side to side and said, "No problem, boss."

Zayed turned and looked at Jill, then lightly commanded, "Yalla yalla."

The dock rocked from side to side as she wobbled over to Zayed. The ship squeaked as it hit the rubber on the pier. Zayed lunged onto the boat first, then turned and held out his strong hand to help her up over the side. The hull wasn't that high, but it would be almost impossible to leap onto it while adorned in her black dress. Jill was thankful the Indian looked away when she lifted her legs over the edge, knowing he would be surprised to see her army boots.

Jill prayed for air conditioning, but it was the least of her problems once on board. She immediately felt uneasy—not from believing she was in danger but in a seasick way. Jill didn't have sea legs, and the fear of motion sickness began to penetrate her brain and stomach. From a young age, she had not fared well, even in the back of a car that wasn't being driven straight. No one knew this about her. On the Colorado River, where she volunteered as a pilot on the large rafts, she seemed to have no problems. But she had never been on any large body of saltwater. All she could do now was try not to look stupid in front of Zayed.

Zayed followed the Indian to a pint-sized door at the front of the vessel. Looking through the tinted glass as she walked past, Jill could see steps leading up to the cockpit and a staircase descending into the craft's belly. The small Indian tour guide did not have to crouch when he descended the wooden staircase. Zayed and Jill ducked their heads and went down into a living area.

The floors were wooden planks that continued up the walls. A large clock hung on the far wall, shaped like an oyster, and the hands were attached to a pearl. It read 2:16 a.m. The galley, sink, and mini fridge were to her left. The saloon was full of pirate character, like a backdrop from a Johnny Depp movie, and was clean, to Jill's surprise. To her right were built-in benches with white vinyl seats, giving a feeling of newness. Pinned to the floor with large protruding bolts was a fitted wooden table lined with teak grout. Two closed doors were directly in front of them like perfectly spaced little rectangles. The symbol on the left with a picture of a toilet hinted at what was behind door number one.

The Indian signaled them to door number two, and it scraped slightly across the floor as it opened. Inside the room were four cots, two on each side, one above each other in bunk bed fashion. They were about three feet wide enough to fit a fully grown man comfortably. Although it wasn't the Shangri-La, the bunks looked relatively clean—almost like what you'd find in an old army hospital.

Zayed motioned the Indian to leave with the familiar hand gesture he gave Jill and a "khalas." The Indian smiled, waggled his head from side to side, turned, and left the room.

They were alone. "I know it's not much, but it will take us out of here safely, insha'Allah."

"What does any of this have to do with God?" Jill spat. "I will take this bed," she added, plunking her carry-on onto the bottom bunk on the right.

"This boat is owned by one of my colleagues, for whom I have done some work. Although equipped for fishing, it's moored only in the harbor for what one might call suspicious activity, as far as Islam is concerned." Jill thought she saw a glimmer of amusement in his eyes. "He would loan the boat out to friends so they'd have a place to drink forbidden alcohol. And sometimes, these men would enjoy the hired company."

Jill knew what he meant and averted her gaze down at her bed. She didn't know how she should feel about the history of her new cot.

Pointing towards the stairs, Zayed said, "He won't come back in unless he asks me first, as I told him you would be taking off your abaya." Jill knew the connotations of this. No man is allowed to see another man's wife's hair or skin. Tonight, the Muslim religion would be of benefit.

"I will leave you to change and get some rest." He watched her pull off her cultured attire and added, "I will, however, be resting here." He tossed his compact pack onto the bed across the narrow aisle from Jill's. He turned quickly and closed the door. The light at the head of the beds cast a yellow glow on the dark wood walls, giving a sense of a cabin at summer camp. It was just enough light for Jill to pull the sheets back to look for any critter that might have found comfort there. Thankfully, the crisp sheets boasted a newly laundered scent of fresh jasmine.

Jill sat on the bed and decided not to take her boots off until she got in. Her eyes moved to Zayed's backpack, quickly glanced at the door, then back to the pack. It would take only a minute for her to go through it. She reached over and cautiously lifted it, rolled it over, and saw the clasp. Glancing again at the door and back to her treasure hunt, she was determined to figure out who Zayed was.

"What is this?" She hadn't seen a clasp like this. Open it fast. Her eyes darted from the door to the clasp. The clasp appeared to be a black plastic type of square box. On closer examination, the backpack was made from flak jacket material. "Bulletproof," she whispered. Her fingers brushed the little black box, looking for a clasp. Then as simple as a child's bike lock, the lid of the box slid horizontally in a circle, revealing a fingerprint receptacle. "Damn it."

Jill hurriedly tried to place the pack in its original spot when she thought she heard a noise coming from the other room.

She opened the door slowly and found Zayed sitting and staring at nothing in deep thought. His black hair draped his shoulders with a bit of a wave; his muscular chest pushed against his tight black T-shirt. For a nanosecond, Jill thought she felt something stir deep within herself.

She looked away as he began to meet her gaze, then she turned and reached for the bathroom door handle. Jill had always had a bathroom fetish. David would wait at the restaurant door until she slipped into the bathroom to determine whether they would stay and enjoy a nice meal—or bolt out of the restaurant, thanks to the bathroom's lack of cleanliness.

This bathroom was much different than the rest of the ship. White fiberglass surrounded it; the floor in front of the toilet was also a makeshift shower with a wood-stained grated rack built above the drain. It was made from a prefabricated mold with a built-in sink and a toilet. Jill lifted the lid of the toilet—it was clean. Relief enveloped her, and at that moment, she knew she could make the eight-hour journey. Glancing up, she saw a tiny fog-framed mirror on the wall but could not see her whole face. Probably a good thing, Jill thought to herself, feeling the beads of sweat pucker on her skin in the sweltering room.

Zayed was no longer there when she stepped back into the main room. The door to the bedroom was open; the space was empty. The backpack was still in the same spot. She grabbed her pack, carried it back into the saloon, and sat on the white leather sofa. She reached in and grabbed her phone, but there was no reception. At least no missed calls meant no news.

Sitting in silence, Jill examined the room. In front of her was a stovetop built into the black countertop. Below it was the fridge, and Jill quickly plucked herself up and opened the door; it was stocked with water, juices—and beer. Beer! She chugged a quarter of a can to quench her thirst while she sat wondering what the night would bring for her, for David—for us.

She sipped the rest of the cold beer and began to relax. She thought about what had happened earlier tonight. What does someone from the Chechen Mafia want with me? And what does this have to do with David?

Her thoughts were interrupted when she heard the cabin door open. Zayed clunked his way down the stairs.

Jill held up the beer and asked, "Is this okay?" He nodded, but she knew he was displeased by his dismayed look. He's just tolerating me. Jill offered to get him one, but he said he didn't drink; it was against his religion. Although Jill knew Zayed was an Arab, she hadn't thought he was a devoted Muslim. It was a hard thing to picture, a feeling she had.

He looked at Jill intently. "We are leaving port, and you need to get some rest. We have a long trip ahead of us to Abu Dhabi." As he left the room to prepare for sleep, Jill asked him about their plan for arriving in Abu Dhabi, but he curtly replied, "We can discuss it after we get some rest. Give me five minutes, and then you can come in when you want." He abruptly closed the door.

The bench seat puffed as Jill sat back down. The wave of exhaustion was pushing her past her desire for another beer. Just one, she said to herself, to help her sleep. That always sounded good to her. The roar of the starting engines brought her pleasure when she felt the room temperature drop. Jill looked around the small room and noticed a tiny vent tucked high on the wall. She stood up and crossed the saloon, waved her hand before it, and touched it. Heaven, air conditioning!

Jill opened the fridge, grabbed a water bottle, cracked it open, and drank half. The rolling boat made her stumble as she muddled her way to the bedroom. Tiptoeing in, she could hear a slight purr from Zayed.

Was he sleeping already? His back was towards her. Jill sat down on the side of her cot. For a second, she held back from taking off her boots and listened; she wondered if she should leave on her boots. After the night's events, she didn't know what to do. Then she pulled her feet out of the boots and lifted her tired legs into the bed. She looked across at Zayed, still motionless. His rhythmic breathing was consistent. The beer, the dim light, and the rolling boat combined to lull her senses. Longing for David, she faded.

Jill sat up fast, only to be thrown onto the floor.

"Get up," Zayed ordered. Another jolt, and she was flung in the other direction, slamming her shoulder so hard against the side of the bunk that she winced with pain. Jill realized she was tossed around the room like a crumpled piece of paper.

"We must be in rough sea!" Zayed yelled. "Stay put; hold onto something! I'll see what is happening."

Her stomach swayed. Unsteadily, Jill went from the bedroom to the bench seat and grabbed hold of the table. The light from the galley still on from last night shined brighter than she thought it should. She heard her empty can of beer on the floor, rolling from side to side, dancing to the ship's chaotic rhythm.

The boat creaked as it rocked. Jill couldn't see outside and had no idea what time it was. Her stomach started to tap on her esophagus. The bridge door opened, whacking the wall with it.

"Jill, come up now," Zayed said, just in time.

"Ouch, shit!" Jill's hip hit the solid sink hard as she tried to grope her way up the stairs.

She tasted salt as a spray of water hit her tongue. Balancing herself with one hand on the back of Zayed's thick calf and the other on the side of the cockpit, she lifted her head to get her bearings. The horror of what Jill saw tore a screeching sound out of her lips. She didn't know she could make such a sound.

The curdling fray of massive white bubbles churned to her right. Surrounded by giant swells in the darkness, the Indian captain was sweating, trying to maneuver the creaking boat. They hit a wave, and then there was a hard thump and a downward plunge as the ship crested, knocking Jill off her feet. Zayed pulled her up into the cockpit, protected from the wet spray. She sat down to the pilot's left on a bench, and Zayed sat between them. Jill could not see the Indian now, but she wished she could see his facial expression. It would give her an idea of his competence in piloting this old fishing boat to safety.

"We are going to go closer to shore!" Zayed yelled above the crash of waves. "We need to get out of the rough sea!"

"Why are we so far out?" Jill questioned frantically. The next wave attacked, and Jill grabbed his thigh hard.

"Pirates, this area is full of them!" Zayed told her they had to sail out of view of the shores as modern-day pirates combed the shorelines for unsuspecting boats. "Then there is the Saudi Arabia Coast Guard. They will not let us into their waters," he finished, yelling over the sea.

Whack! Another thud from the rough sea. This time Zayed hooked his arm solidly around her shoulder, pulling her close. She looked for anything solid to grasp, as even Zayed was thrown around. She could not see land; the large swells blocked her view of the open sea.

Time passed slowly. Finally, the swells began to shed their boiling whitecaps and became dancing giants. Rolling in the distance was something solid—land on the horizon. The salt crusted on her lips. Being careful not to lick them, she felt the rest of her face. As she passed her fingers over her skin, the dry salt made her feel like a blind person reading Braille. Jill looked down and realized she had no boots on her damp feet.

Still holding her tight, Zayed said more calmly, "The worst is over. Why don't you return to the cabin, get warm, and rest?" He slowly pulled his arm up and off her shoulder.

"How long until we get to Abu Dhabi?"

Zayed asked the Indian in Arabic. The Indian replied. Zayed looked back at Jill. "Two hours."

Below deck, the room seemed to have changed somehow, and Jill couldn't figure out how. She reached down, picked up the beer can, and placed it into the sink. In the bathroom, Jill was torn between trusting the water on the ship and not washing her face. Turning on the tap, Jill cupped the water, smelled it, and splashed her face.

Standing still for a second, she wondered how to let another man other than David hold her so close. She dismissed the exchange as pure chivalry.

Jill stepped back into the galley, walked over to the fridge, and retrieved a water bottle. She drank it down fast, diluting the salt on her tongue. A pang of hunger twinged as she laid back down on the cot. The rolling boat rocked her into a deep sleep.

CHAPTER TEN

I fly high above the desert when I swoop down and land on a hoodoo. Below me, I see something familiar, but I don't know what it is. The day's heat ruffles my feathers as I try to understand what I see.

A knock on the bedroom door startled Jill awake, and her body snapped upward. "Yeah?"

"We are pulling into the Abu Dhabi port," Zayed shouted through the door. "Get dressed and come up on deck now."

Aye, aye, Captain Crunch. Jill reached into her bag, pulled out her notebook, held it up to the faint light, and turned to the page where she had last read her visions.

Click, click, click. Jill kept pushing the pen button while she reviewed her notes. What, now I have a view from a bird's perspective? "Enough of the mystery, Grams!" Jill's brow furrowed. She wrote the word "family" and circled it without a hint of intent.

She stepped into her boots, pulled on the black robe, and spotted Zayed's pack on the rumpled bed with her last glance. She plucked up the bag and looked at the locked black clasp. She glanced around the room, flung his backpack onto her shoulder, turned, and walked up onto the deck. She was momentarily blind in the bright sun. After her vision had cleared, looking to her right, she saw water that was a beautiful turquoise, calm water; the slight breeze felt refreshing against the newly risen sun's heat.

"What time is it?" Jill queried as she handed Zayed his pack.

"Close to nine," he replied. "Thanks."

The ship was parallel to a grand building checkered with hundreds of windows on the shoreline to her right. She realized it must be a hotel when she saw all the beach chairs and umbrellas dotted across a breathtaking beach. The center of the building had a giant square with a large dome on top of it. The peak of the dome had a mosaic painting laced with gold inlay. Surrounding the square were low-to-the-ground buildings that stretched for hundreds of yards.

Jill looked over at the pilot, and Zayed then mumbled something barely audible. How dumb that I have to wear this. Does he think that the guy didn't see me in the storm? Moron. As she gazed up toward the water's edge, she was surprised to see a large island connected by a busy road, with a sizable shopping mall and a tall sign on a post that read IKEA. Stretched high into the sky above the mall was a tower with a round spaceship-looking structure. She was impressed by how modern the buildings looked. Further along, the brimming horizon was another island with open-faced square tents that dotted the sand as far as she could see. When their boat passed the last tent, she noticed white people—two adults and a small child—enjoying the day before it got too hot.

Jill turned around fast when she heard a sound. Jet skis zoomed past their boat, several chasing and almost hitting each other as they popped over the vessel's wake. Arab teenagers, that much was clear to her. Jill didn't understand what they were doing, and her thoughts turned to the Chechens.

She wanted to speak to Zayed but knew he would silence her with that damn hand, and frankly, she wasn't in the mood to be muted again.

When they cruised past the island, Abu Dhabi sprawled out before them in all its contemporary splendor. Everything sparkled as rays of sunlight bounced off the city's glass towers. The view from the sea was stunning until the boat turned left, and the scene quickly changed. They were approaching a ruddy fishing village, similar to the one in Doha but smaller. Just before they reached the dock, Jill spied something. Ahead on two rusted steel posts stood an extravagant portrait of an Arabian man—the size of a giant billboard—towering over the boats.

As they coasted up to the main dock, several Indians scattered about and began assisting the pilot with tying the boat. The ship's buoys squeaked as they rubbed against the old wharf. Just as they were about to disembark, Jill noticed Zayed reach into his pack, pull out an envelope, and hand it to the captain. He smiled at Zayed without a word, just nodded, and with the boat secure, descended below deck.

"Let's move," Zayed ordered.

The docks were busy with boats coming in from the previous night's fishing. The loud voices of men filled the air as they offloaded their catch directly onto the dock. Bartering in Arabic and Hindi, deals were being made as Zayed and Jill zigzagged past the fish for sale. In front of the docks was an open fish market, and as they walked by, Jill eyed neat trays of ice complete with fish of all sizes and colors.

Most of the crowd was gathered at the end of the building. Zayed was again doing his clock surveillance. He stopped so fast that Jill bumped into him. Swiftly he pushed Jill to the right, launching her behind a dumpster.

"What the hell are you—"

Zayed hissed, "Quiet! Two men look like our friends in Doha. I don't think they saw us." Zayed leaned forward and then cocked his head around the dumpster. He quickly looked back at Jill. A man who was squatting above his fish looked curiously up at them. "It looks like the same guy from the hotel, and he is not alone."

"But how would they know we were coming here by boat?"

Zayed was silent for a moment and then said, "Everything has a price, Jill. He probably asked around, offering a cash incentive for any information."

For the first time, Jill noticed that there weren't many women on the docks. "I need to get to a phone. I need to find out what the hell is going on." For a moment, Jill thought of marching up to the two men and asking them, "What the hell do you two want from me?" None of this made any sense. And then it hit her out of the blue. "Zayed, I was being followed the day I left the US."

This information seemed to take Zayed by surprise. "It could be connected." His voice sounded perplexed. "Did anyone know you were coming to Doha?"

Dumbfounded, Jill thought about it. Her office knew, and so did David's. She hadn't mentioned it to anyone else.

"Let's just focus on losing these guys," Zayed said. But Jill could tell by the worried line in his brow that he didn't know what to do.

Shoot, move, communicate, survive. Then Jill piped up. "We need to split up. If they paid someone in Doha, they would know that there are two of us, and they would also know that I was wearing this." Jill pinched her black robe.

"I'll distract them."

"You don't have a weapon."

"You need to get into a taxi and get to the airport. The airport has security and police; they can't do anything to you there." The taxi stand was approximately one hundred meters from where the two men stood. "I'll run past them, and they will have to react fast," Zayed suggested. "They won't have a weapon, either. I'll get a taxi. It'll be too fast for them to think, and they will follow me. Once they follow me, Jill, get a taxi and get to the airport. I'll meet you there. Okay?" Zayed looked at Jill for confirmation. Jill thought when he repeated, "Okay, Jill?"

Jill nodded. She knew she could fend for herself if she had to, but she had on this robe, and she couldn't do much wearing it. She contemplated taking it off, but Zayed whipped around the corner of the dumpster before she could decide.

Jill followed fast and peeked her head out. She spotted the two men who shifted and then braced as Zayed ran toward them. They looked like deer caught in headlights as he flashed past them. Zayed jumped into a taxi. Gravel spat as he sped away. As Zayed suspected, the two men raced after him, jumping into the next taxi.

Looking through the bodies of people, Jill saw piles of fish remnants that filled the gutters. Men sat on stools at cutting blocks, filleting fish with ease.

Alongside the building, a line of gold-and-white taxis awaited their next fares. Zayed's scene had caused a commotion on the sidewalk at the front of the taxi line. Jill monitored her surroundings as she briskly walked to the last taxi in the line, jumped in the backseat, and hissed to the driver, "Airport," then "khalas!" The driver seemed pleased to be jumping the line and slowly drove away.

The driver, wearing pajama attire, was from Pakistan and drove quietly. Jill was getting increasingly peeved that she couldn't speak to anyone and getting more pissed off with all this cloak-and-dagger bullshit. She plopped her backpack onto the grungy seat beside her. Jill wondered what would happen to Zayed if the men caught up to him. Her thoughts strayed to the day she left Doha. Could it possibly be the Chechens following her when she was in Tucson? Did it have something to do with her current case? She had no answers.

As they drove through Abu Dhabi, Jill noticed it was strikingly similar to Doha—but larger and more spread out. The car was old and rickety. Jill looked at the clear plastic envelope attached to the back of the driver's headrest. His ID photo looked like any of the many terrorist mug shots she was used to seeing in her files. The driver's name was Abdu Bin Amin. Jill did her surveillance, which was much more subtle than Zayed's. Everything around her depicted any other average city—just newer.

The traffic flow changed drastically as they left the congestion of the city. The car began to rattle more as the driver sped along, too fast for Jill's liking. They darted around slower-moving vehicles, and her left shoulder hit the door as he jerked the car over a lane. A large white patrol SUV screamed past the dodgy taxi, going more than 120 mph, followed by a large white Land Cruiser. Bumpers almost kissed as they flashed past. The patrol jerked fast in front of them, and suddenly the taxi driver walloped the brakes. Jill grabbed the driver's seat in front of her to support herself. Then her body was thrown back in the seat when the driver accelerated.

"Hey, slow down." Jill scowled.

Grudgingly quiet, she couldn't help but see something in his stern stare back at her through the rearview mirror. What was it?

As the taxi sped down the freeway, the grassed median strip flicked past in a green blur. Sprinkler systems lined the lush area for miles, it seemed. The road was bustling, crazy drivers abounding, and Jill figured her driver was one of them. They appeared to be holding a steady pace when suddenly the driver slammed on the brakes, accelerating a millisecond after they passed the speed camera. Holding onto the handle above her door window, Jill concentrated on hoping she would get to the airport in one piece.

Jill stared out the window and watched as a grand structure dominated her view. The massive white mosque was unlike anything she had seen before. She was astonished at what she experienced at the fishing village and how it fit with such beautiful architecture.

It took about thirty minutes to get to the airport, but to Jill, it felt like being on an endless roller coaster. She was surprised to see Zayed when she pulled up to the airport. He was speaking to what appeared to be a police officer. She looked at Zayed, and he gestured for her not to stop and to go instead into the airport. Once inside, she looked out the glass walls and did her scan. Nothing. Two minutes later, Zayed was inside. "What was that about? What happened to those two men?"

"Did you not see the car crash on the way to the airport?" Zayed asked with surprise. "It was their taxi. Guess I had a more experienced driver."

"But why were you talking to that policeman?" Jill asked.

"Informed him of the accident; it's what any good citizen would do. I told him I thought they were drunk. That should hold them up." Zayed smirked. "We need to get moving, Jill. It won't be long until they catch up to us. We must be past security so they can't follow us or find out where we are going."

Speechless at his nonchalance, Jill followed Zayed to security.

The airport was filled with passengers and security guards. The terminal looked like a giant octopus-shaped spaceship and was remarkably small, with gaudy lime-green ceilings. Zayed spoke to one of the security guards, who pointed him to the only stall where they could buy tickets. A large gold sign hung behind the desk: ETIHAD, THE NATIONAL AIRLINE OF THE UAE. "Great, this should be interesting," Jill grumbled to herself.

The Filipina lady behind the counter wore a gray hat with a poly-ester cream veil cleanly tucked under her chin. After several minutes and a few "yes, sirs" and "yes, ma'ams," they determined they could get to Kabul via Tehran. The first leg of the flight would be on Etihad, with the second on Afghan Airlines. Both of these airlines did not sound very inviting to Jill, any way she looked at it, but the good news was they would not have to wait long. There were several flights a day to Tehran, and with only a two-hour layover, they would be landing in Kabul at around 8 p.m. local time.

The blank-faced security man at the X-ray machine didn't consider what was in Jill's bag. He was busy chatting with other Emirati men dressed in security clothes. She smirked, thinking about her flashlight pen concealed under her abaya.

After security, Zayed piped up. "You can take off your abaya now if it makes you feel more comfortable." He approached her, pushing the boarding passes into his breast pocket.

Jill was relieved. She looked for the usual female triangle silhouette. Zayed pointed as if reading her mind. "There, over there."

Jill saw only an obscure picture of an abaya. She marched over to the washroom door, hesitated while looking at the symbol, then walked in.

The room was immaculate for an airport, she thought. Large toilet stalls with doors to the floor were a nice improvement from North American standards. The first stall she attempted to open displayed a large square porcelain box inset into the ground. There was no toilet, only a hole in the white glass with two steps on each side and a foot pedal for flushing. Not! On her next attempt, she found a regular toilet. There was no toilet paper—just a leaky water sprayer attached to the side of the stall.

Jill took off the black robe and stuffed it into her carry-on. She hoped she wouldn't have to wear the dark garment in the heat again. Exiting the stall, she wondered how the black-robed women used the washroom—with no toilet paper, they must spray themselves clean while gowned. She shuddered at the thought.

Jill stood in front of the mirror, staring. Somehow she looked different. Perhaps it was dehydration from the heat, but she noticed small lines ever so slightly crinkling around her dark-circled eyes. Reaching into her carry-on, she brought out a small red bag. Her image transformed as she glided on the dark maroon lipstick. A bit of eyeliner and mascara, and she was ready to greet Abu Dhabi airport.

Pulling out her mobile, she turned it on. Jill waited, glancing at herself in the mirror. On the screen came two words: NO SERVICE. "Shit," she blurted when she looked around to see if she was alone. She suspected that this pay-as-you-go phone would not get international service. She needed to contact Leila and Kali, and with fading hope... David. She needed to get intel on the Chechens that were following her. She was, however, feeling a bit more comfortable with Zayed assisting her in Afghanistan, and for that, she was thankful. There was hope in finding David, she thought to herself as she looked at the phone. There was. And she was going to figure out how. She did not know if the phone was unlocked, so she could use a different country's SIM and turned it off to save battery power. She adjusted her hair one more time and exited the washroom.

Zayed leaned against the wall to her right. At first, he didn't see her, and Jill could tell by his facial expression that something was not sitting well with him. As Jill walked through the crowds of people, something felt off-kilter.

Suddenly, Jill stopped fast, just as the airport began shaking like an earthquake. Jill looked around; no cups on the tables were moving, and none of the crystal glass in the gift shop ahead shifted nor rattled. Jill was stuck as if someone had hit pause on a DVD.

Zayed calmly walked over to her and said, "Sea legs. It's you, not the building."

What a strange sensation. Jill felt as if she was rocking uncontrollably.

"Come, Jill," Zayed said softly, soothingly.

"I need to find a phone to call my office. See if anyone has heard anything," she claimed.

"Zein, fine, I'll be here."

Jill found it hard to hold his glance and turned away. The giant, tiled circular roof in bright lime green made her think the architect was smoking some heavy shit when he designed the building. Small shops were all around, and she could only count twelve gates. Airport-style chairs were scattered everywhere. Jill saw a security guard and approached him about a public phone. He didn't seem to know what she was asking, to her dismay.

"What airport doesn't have public phones?" Jill snarled to herself. Then she saw a bunch of men standing around an array of computers.

Jill didn't see a connection for her laptop, so a public terminal would have to do. She couldn't log into VPN but could check her email using the US Marshal's secure webmail system. She hoped for some news. Jill silently crossed her fingers that the servers were not blocked, given the state of affairs in the Middle East. As she began to log in, a strange thought crept into her mind.

Slowly, Jill looked up and around, then over at Zayed, who was puffing on a fag and getting ready to light another. A quick, soft surveillance scan. The airport was busy, and nothing caught her eye. Paranoid. If she had more time, she would spend it profiling. First Zayed, then the Chechens. When she profiled, her instinct would push her into the tunnels. Push her to find the answers that she wanted to uncover. She needed her notebook to do this, and Google was always a bonus, but she also needed privacy. Perhaps on the plane, she would find some reprieve.

Logged in, Jill saw several messages regarding work updates. One was from Eric, stating that the missiles had been transferred successfully. She was in luck when she found one from Kali. The email contained more information confirming that her destination should be Kushka.

In 2005, US operatives discovered a biological weapons laboratory under construction in the Kushka foothills, with evidence that Russian scientists were helping Al Qaeda develop anthrax.

Kali reminded Jill that it was 300 miles through mountainous terrain and attached two articles on recent bomb attacks by the Taliban. Jill quickly read them and noted several of the town names. *I must look at the map once I get settled on the plane.*

No word from David or Leila. As for Zayed, Kali said that she could not find any information and had called Jeff, David's editor, to see what information he knew about him. She asked if he was possibly using an alias. The email ended with Please be careful, Jill.

Jill sent a quick email with Zayed's full name that she heard him tell the boat's captain. She noted that bin meant "son of," hoping it helped her search.

Zayed Mohammed Bin Saleem

Jill gave Kali her flight itinerary in case David got in touch. Just as she was about to close her webmail, a pop-up told her... New Mail.

It was from Stan Brown again. But this time, his email was a little more pointed.

Jill,

I know you are reading my emails. Why are you not calling me? Please, it's important.

Stan

What could he possibly want? Jill knew that it could not be about David's whereabouts. If anything happened to David, she or her office would be the first to know. Maybe the newscasts were now disclosing David's name?

She emailed Leila.

Leila, please email me. I will explain later why I had to leave the hotel. Hostile.

Jill

Jill looked around for a television and wondered why Stan had contacted her. Two large screens to her right zapped the logo of CNN. Jill clicked send. Having Kali call Stan Brown was her best bet, as now and again, they would hear from David's family about some new dramatic crisis hoping to get David's attention. Jill couldn't deal with anything like that right now.

Jill closed the browser, erased her history, and walked closer to the TV entertaining a large gathering of brown men in casual shirts and trousers. Standing there, she looked over to where Zayed sat. He was intently watching her. After about ten minutes of tag lines on CNN, Jill resigned herself to the fact that no new information was released about David yet.

Zayed continued to stare at Jill as she walked in his direction. His scrutiny affirmed for Jill her thoughts of uneasiness about him. Or was she just being paranoid again? Paranoia was a symptom of post-traumatic stress disorder, and Jill had to work hard at deciphering between paranoia and instinct. Most days, it was easy, but it was hard when stress raised its ugly head. She chalked her thoughts up to paranoia.

Well, for now, anyway. Shifting in his seat, he softly scratched his ear and asked, "Any new information?"

Jill hesitated, then plopped beside him, still feeling slight unease about what Kali had just told her or hadn't told her about him. Jill was still puzzled by his presence. Then without giving it another thought, she said, "My contact confirmed that the LSA briefs came from a town called Kushka. She also sent me directions and how to get there."

"Kushka?" He was surprised.

"Do you know of this place?"

"No," he said, sounding a bit elusive. "Where is it?"

"On the Turkmenistan border. Right on the border, actually." They sat in silence.

"How long do you think that will take us?" Jill asked Zayed, shattering the lull.

He wasn't sure and said it would depend on the condition of the roads.

"The last time I was in Afghanistan, most roads were well paved on the main routes anyway," he said. "The question is... is Kushka on a main road?"

To her, he sounded like he already knew.

"Kali sent me a map, and I have it on my laptop. When we get on the plane, we can look at it. But I do need to find a phone. I should call Stan, David's father."

There was an immediate shift in Zayed's body language. Jill looked him straight in the eye and said pointedly, "You know Stan Brown?"

He hesitated; his eyes darted left up, then left down. He was searching. Jill knew it. He was about to tell her a lie. "David's spoken of him," he said matter-of-factly.

"David spoke to you about his father. Why in the hell would he do that? What did he say about him? Was this recent?" The questions came fast.

His eyes darted again. "I don't recall. Something about contacting his father. He never said why."

"That's it?" Jill sat back and considered this unexpected reaction as Zayed nodded. Why would Zayed lie? And who gives a shit about Stan Brown? Was Zayed just being polite about it all? There were just too many questions now, and Jill needed some time to herself and in the tunnels.

It wasn't long before their flight was called. Zayed and Jill would not sit together for this as they had bought last-minute tickets. She was grateful for this as she pulled out her notebook. The Captain announced over the scratchy PA that the flight would be 34 minutes. Not enough time. Not enough time.

CHAPTER ELEVEN

08:20 Zulu Time—Tehran, Iran

Tehran's airport terminal was very different from Abu Dhabi's. It was a massive building, similar to any major US city. Inside, the terminal was sparkling clean, with high ceilings and walls brushed with a dark rust color that complemented the beige marble floor tiles.

Jill and Zayed didn't speak as they went to the next gate. Once there, Jill sat on a hard orange vinyl chair, opened her laptop, and looked at the map. The clock at the gate said 13:12. She knew Afghanistan had mountainous terrain, but the satellite images did not do it justice. Jill would have to be connected to the Internet to see the terrain from different angles, and she kicked herself now for not doing this earlier when she had the chance.

"There appears to be only one road to get to Kushka," she told Zayed, showing him the map.

As he studied it, she noticed how long his eyelashes were as they blinked against his olive skin. The veins in his muscular forearms bulged as he held her computer. After several minutes, he turned the laptop back to her without a word. Jill looked up and down the map and ran her finger along the route to Kushka. Along the way, she noticed one of the cities Kali told her had been attacked by the Taliban.

It appeared to be about fifty miles from the route they were taking. A hint of relief hit Jill, knowing she would not be close to those areas.

Jill lifted her gaze from the computer to the large windows show-casing the aircraft, and her mind drifted to thoughts of David. Jill pictured him in Kushka at a local hotel, working madly on his story. She remembered watching him many times at the eleventh hour in his office, intensely punching the computer keys. David was always too enthralled in his writing to notice her standing there. She never disturbed him. Jill hoped that was what he was doing, and she could picture there not being a phone in northern Afghanistan. Well, she prayed for that ideal scenario anyway.

"Zayed, you said you've been to Afghanistan. What are the hotels like there?"

"Jill, why do you think of such things right now?"

"Never mind."

Darkness began to cover her thoughts when Stan Brown invaded them. Why was he trying to reach her? She did not know. She felt a twinge of anger and regret when she thought of David's parents. They seemed normal enough when she first met them. But the too-perfect impression was truly a façade. When David was younger, he later told Jill, he often hid in his room to avoid being whipped by his father's belt. However, his father never hit David's sister, Margarita; she was always the loved one. Jill teared up at the memory of their conversa-tion. David was a proud individual, and it took him a while to let Jill into this part of his past.

"He used to lock me in my room like a dog and wouldn't feed me for the rest of the day. Sometimes he would turn off the power in my room, and it was almost unbearable on hot summer Texas nights," David had recalled. "That was his way of punishing me for not completing my homework on time or putting out the garbage.

He would taunt me, especially if I had friends around, and especially when he was drinking."

Jill often wondered if some of David's quirks were caused by such a strict upbringing, like being an obsessive neat freak. When they spoke about his family, it reminded her of how her father had abandoned her mother when she was pregnant and how much Jill felt blessed that she had cool grandparents. With Jill, the craving for self-discovery and closure would briefly flare up, but it left just as fast as the notion came.

From the outside, no one would have guessed at the underlying dysfunction. David's father was a successful businessman in Texas. Margarita was two years older than David, and as the family favorite, she got the first car and pretty much the first anything. "She had all the new clothes and annoying rich friends, compliments of Mother," David had told Jill. "Mother is a doormat for my father, and she has never stood up for me. I always found a way to separate myself from her. She was emotionally vacant and sometimes extreme in the way she thought. I could never do anything right in her eyes, and she let me know it with her scathing, hurtful remarks. Margarita is the same—a younger version of my mother."

When Jill met his sister, she had no choice but to agree. Jill profiled her and concluded that she had a borderline personality disorder. Recently, they had been notified by other family members that she was being treated for a psychopathic disorder. Probably a good thing since she had more plastic surgery than Joan Rivers and had been married more times than Elizabeth Taylor. Jill couldn't help but think of them right now. She sometimes wondered why she hadn't known more details about them before she married David. She wanted a family as great as they first appeared; now, she couldn't help but feel ripped off somehow. She would call Stan. She would put her disgust aside because she needed to stay focused. She needed to find David.

Jill came out of her daydream at the barking words from a loud gate agent. While Jill was standing in front of the gate, in the absence of a PA system, the man yelled in vague English something that sounded like, "Boarding now!" Zayed and Jill boarded together.

The flight was just under one hour this time, and they sat together. The plane was much smaller than the Airbus 330. Jill reached into the seat pocket in front of her, filed through the glossy cards, past the little white barf bag, and pulled out the airplane description card. It was a ritual of hers; she always looked at the card describing the exits and then confirmed how many rows she was from the exit.

This Boeing 727 was an older and inferior plane compared to the ones she had flown on recently. She began to feel a little nervous. The name alone, Afghan Air, made her wonder how safe they were. She assumed that airlines in Afghanistan were more worried about the Taliban than ensuring the maintenance was done correctly. With this thought, she looked at Zayed; her body lurched back as the roaring engines drowned everything out.

They both gripped the armrests as the plane vibrated. The plane angled up, and Jill felt a tickle from the hair on his arm touching hers. He didn't move, nor did she. Jill laid her head back, and just as she began to close her eyes, the engine's hum lulling her to sleep, Zayed spoke up.

"How long have you known David?" he asked. It was the first time on the trip that his voice held a hint of kindness. She'd come to accept the intensity and gruffness of his personality. "You seem very devoted to him to go to an unsafe place like Afghanistan."

Jill sensed an air of sadness. "I'd do anything for David. Besides, I'm a US Marshal and can handle a little heat in Afghanistan. My colleagues would have insisted I not go if the trip were too dangerous."

Without reserve, Zayed rested his warm, callused hand on her forearm. His dark, probing eyes peered into hers. "Maybe your friends knew that already and didn't bother to try." Their eyes locked for too long, and then they both looked away.

As the plane was positioned for the descent, the captain came on and said something in Arabic. Zayed looked at Jill with concern and warned, "Tighten your seat belt."

Jill was about to ask why when the plane banked hard to the left and the nose angled downward. They descended fast, turning sharp lefts. It felt like they were on a corkscrew. One man shrieked. The plane suddenly leveled, and you could cut the relief in the air with a knife when the tires bounced the aircraft onto the tarmac. Jill's eyes bugged out when Zayed said, "Surface-to-air missiles. They have to be careful to avoid another incident."

When the plane came to a complete stop, she looked at Zayed and said softly, "Do you think we'll find him, Zayed?"

He offered no response.

CHAPTER TWELVE

11:17 Zulu Time—Kabul, Afghanistan

Dusk settled upon them as they disembarked the airplane. They clunked down an old set of metal stairs onto the tarmac and followed the line of shaken travelers across the patched pavement. It was significantly cooler in Kabul, Jill noted.

The terminal was worse than she had imagined. The green-gray paint-chipped walls betrayed its age. The letter L was missing from the sign saying "KABUL," implying no budget for maintenance. Jill's nostrils wanted to shut down when they inhaled a smell unlike any other she had experienced. It seemed to be a combination of concentrated house cleaner, sweat, and wet sand. Her instant reaction was to clamp her nose shut with her hand, but she resisted.

Only a few people were standing at arrivals, and the clock behind them read 16:04. It struck Jill as odd for an airport. Typically, airports were full of people waiting for their visitors to arrive. It must be a security issue, she thought. There was no shortage of guards with automatic weapons dressed in gray jumpsuits with AK-47s resting over their shoulders. They didn't look in their direction while talking and smoking and seemed oblivious to their arrival. The customs agent was dressed the same as security and only grunted as they passed through the security machine. Exiting the building, a sea of colorfully dressed people had gathered: the arrival crowd. Jill always enjoyed waiting at the arrivals gate. It gave her a sense of joy to see the delight of others as they welcomed loved ones home from their destinations. She often thought about what good therapy it would be for anyone depressed to spend some time at the arrivals gate.

Zayed did his scan again. Jill did hers. At eleven o'clock on the scan, a woman approached Jill carrying a small child. She held out her hand and begged. She was dressed in a bright blue abaya; the headdress was much different than Jill's. There was a mesh mask over the eye area; it was even more restrictive than the burqa she had been wearing from Doha. Zayed said something slightly forceful in what Jill thought might be the local language, Pashto, and the woman shyly ambled away.

Most of the people in the crowd were men. They were dressed similarly to the taxi drivers in Abu Dhabi, yet not as clean-looking in their faded clothing. They wore turbans wrapped loosely in balls on their heads.

Jill and Zayed pushed through the crowd and approached several taxis lined up with drivers smiling, waiting for a paying customer. The black-and-white cars were run-down and riddled with dents and chipped paint. Zayed chose one, and Jill wondered how the trip to Kushka would be in that car. Would it even be able to make the journey? Zayed leaned his head in the window and spoke to the driver. Another whiff smacked her in the nose. Jill could not distinguish the smell. It was part sewage, body odor, and maybe burnt jet fuel. They entered the decrepit car after some discussion between Zayed and the driver. The driver honked his way through the wave of people.

During the ride, Jill saw yet another large portrait of someone famous. Next to the grandiose headshot was a military fighter jet painted in camouflage green. As they drove under the wing toward the security gate, Jill noticed the number eighty-two painted on it.

At the security checkpoint, the guard in military fatigues flicked his automatic rifle, signaling them through. Jill thought there was no point in checking the taxi or for any security leaving an airport, and she curiously looked back to the inbound guardhouse. They were stopping vehicles going into the airport. A guard held a long stick with a mirror to scan underneath cars. Jill felt thankful she lived in the US as they left the airport grounds.

Kabul was as she imagined. Even at night, she could see the devastation of war and poverty. The sides of the roads were lined with homeless, hopeless-looking people huddling together to stay warm. The sounds of honking horns added to the cacophony. Cars hit one another like taps on the shoulder and then continued driving. Chaos surrounded them this night, and Jill looked at Zayed, convinced they could not make the trip in the rat-trap taxi.

As Jill had read, Kabul was over 3,500 years old, and before the civil wars in the '90s, it was deemed a relatively cosmopolitan city. Now it just looked worn out. The gloomy gray buildings showed the strain from the plague of unrest. Kabul linked other significant centers in Afghanistan via a ring road connecting Kandahar and Herat. This route would be the first part of their trip to Kushka.

Before Jill spoke her concerns, Zayed whispered, "We are going to go to a hotel, find a driver, and then leave in the morning. We have a better chance of getting through the checkpoints then."

Jill was relieved that they did not have to embark on the long journey tonight, but the relief lasted only a moment when she began to wonder about the condition of the hotel. It must be better than the boat ride they took—anything would be better than that.

The taxi driver made a hard U-turn and stopped at a big gate. Two guards came out while a third watched knowingly. One guard had the leash of a scrawny German shepherd and held the dog tightly as it sniffed around their taxi. The guard with the mirrored stick gave no expression. Only the beret tilted ever so slightly on his head showed a hint of personality.

The driver exited the taxi, walked back, and opened the trunk for inspection. They passed inspection and continued up a long driveway to the hotel. Jill was taken aback when a sharply dressed porter came out and opened the door. He had a white earpiece that curled down the back of his neck, and Jill was comforted by her first impression—until she saw the doorway was equipped with a metal detector. She resigned to the fact that they were in a former war zone and walked through.

Stepping into the hotel was like stepping into a different country. The lavishly decorated lounge area had a distinct Moroccan flavor, with clean marble floors contrasting the spittoons placed every twenty feet along the walls. The walls themselves were painted a dark Indian red. Behind the lobby desk stood two men, and Zayed approached, speaking to them in Pashto, confirming to Jill that Zayed must have been here before to have been able to speak this language. She could not know how well he spoke it, but they seemed to understand him. The taller of the well-dressed clerks pointed to a man sitting behind a desk in the corner. While they conversed, Jill looked around and was surprised to see an ATM in the lobby. Does it even work? she wondered. She had no need to use it as one of the things her training had taught her was always to bring as much cash as possible; she was more curious to understand how a hotel like this could survive in the middle of war-torn Kabul.

Tired, she walked over and relaxed on one of the colorful couches and waited for Zayed. Within minutes he was back, and he handed Jill her room key.

"I managed to get a car and driver for tomorrow. They have room service, so go ahead and order some food and get some rest. I have to go out and arrange for the trip to Kushka. My room is next to yours. I will get a wake-up call at six a.m. Is that good for you?"

"Where are you going, and what do you need to arrange now?" Jill queried pointedly.

"I am meeting with the driver tonight to ensure we can trust him. It's not a big deal, so please just go and get some rest. We have a long trip tomorrow."

"Whatever," she responded in a rebellious tone. She was tired of Zayed's arrogant behavior. Jill turned fast, marched toward the elevator, and sharply punched the button. She refused to look back at Zayed.

Upon opening the door, she arrived at her room and was instantly elated. The king-sized bed was covered in a bright red Moroccan-styled bedspread. A flat-screen television sat at the end of the bed, and across the room, she could see patio doors with a balcony. Jill put her carry-on down, walked to the window, and looked out. The view was of scattered lights in disarray from buildings along the horizon.

She turned around and spied the door to the bathroom. She was happy that it was spotless. Hand towels were rolled beside both sinks while a bright orange orchid bloomed in a small vase. Before she could think of having a shower, she picked up the phone to call Stan Brown. Voicemail. She didn't leave a message. After all, what would she say? I know you are a disgusting pig, but what do you want?

Jill undressed, turned on the shower, and entered the sizable tiled tub. She let the hot water massage her until she almost tipped over from exhaustion. She pulled down the thick white robe that hung neatly on a hanger behind the door, wrapped herself snugly in it, and headed back into the main room. Pulling the crisp bedspread down, she sat and contemplated what to do—the room's beauty and a hunger pang made the decision easy. She hadn't eaten much in the last twenty-four hours. Fast snacks on the plane were all she could bear. But now she suddenly felt famished. She knew that she needed to eat to keep her strength. After all, she really didn't know what she was getting herself into or what she would encounter tomorrow. She needed her strength right now. But even with thoughts of reason calming her mind, her heart somehow ached even more. After ordering room service, she plugged in her laptop and connected to the Internet. The speed was good when she checked her email.

Nothing from David. She sighed and clicked on the email from Kali. It was a short email:

No luck with the Zayed name. It's as if he doesn't exist. Jeff left me a voicemail saying that he would ask his PA to get the information on Zayed that you requested. But still nothing yet.

She couldn't reach Stan Brown, and Leila's phone was switched off—no new reports on the news.

Jill stood up, walked to her carry-on, and pulled out the leather pouch and notebook. "Hello," Jill muttered with a smile. She snapped the laptop shut, pushed it to the side of the desk, placed the notebook down, and began pulling out the eight pieces of clay. Jill put them randomly on the desk, fished for a pen, and opened her notebook. She dated the top and scribbled a question.

"Where is David?"

Jill abruptly stopped, dropped the pen, and shivered. She looked down at the blank page and closed her eyes. You can do this, Jill. Stay focused. And then, as she had practiced with her shrink, she blurted, "Screw you, Matthew McGregor. Screw you!"

Without hesitation, she moved the pen square in the middle of the blank page and stared at it. Looking over at the numbers, Jill whispered, "Optimum trajectory. Optimum trajectory." Jill attempted to stay focused on the academics of Remote Viewing to keep her mind off that goddamn haunting sketch. She picked up a number with trance-like movements and clicked it down on the desk—one by one by one by one. She thought that pure intuition only comes from a thoughtless mind but shouldn't. Remote Viewing was only successful when the mind was quiet... open. Jill began to hum. Looking through the numbers, she moved around on the desk; Jill said the question over and over again: "Where is David?... Where are you, David?" The clay numbers scraped slightly. She moved the numbers around on the desk in a random fashion and hummed. "David." She tried to open it, tried to see the target number. But her hand kept moving them. Focus, goddamn it. Focus.

She was working hard, trying to peel off the layers and get to the core of peace—that place where the Remote Viewers went.

She saw it first before she heard it. The sketch was rammed in front of her view. It was drawn in black charcoal with finger smudges on the edges. It was a drawing of a square hole, like an entrance to a cave. Around the cave was a sign carved into the side of the rock. Luray.

"You bitch, you whiny little bitch," spat Matthew McGregor as he forced the sketch upon Jill.

Jill screamed and almost knocked the chair backward as she pulled herself back to the room, waking her from her trance.

"No, no, no!" cried Jill as she angrily swiped the clay numbers across the desk and they scattered onto the floor. She grabbed a wad of hair as if she would pull it out. Sitting forward, curled over the desk, Jill cried for the first time in a long time.

Time passed, and her wails turned into sobs, and she attempted to regain her breath. She looked over at the numbers scattered on the floor and sighed. Defeated. She had never felt so frustrated; she was so upset with herself. What the hell was she thinking coming here? David needs me, and I can't escape this hell.

She didn't know how much time had passed when she was interrupted by a knocking on the door.

"Room service."

She pushed her food around the plate while sipping on her glass of cheap vintage. Jill could not stop staring over at the numbers she had placed back on the desk. She hadn't pulled them out for some time now, and she wondered if she would have been able to see something, anything.

She excused herself as being tired. But there were no excuses, not anymore. She got up, put the tray outside the door, shut off the lights, and lay in bed. Her cried-out eyes were still swollen as she watched the building lights filter through the curtain. Jill thought of David. The thought passed as the exhaustion of a hard sob pushed her body into the sheets.

CHAPTER THIRTEEN

03:30 Zulu Time—Kabul, Afghanistan

The long wooden tree branch cuts into the hard, rocky sand. A large circle is drawn, encompassing a cryptic symbol. The symbol is something I recognize. The hum of chants surrounds the sand painting. The symbol has two large outlined figures and two small ones. Stick figures. They looked like upside-down Us with round heads. The bodies are cut in half, with only the top of the silhouette showing—the Navajo symbol of family.

Answer the phone, she thought, as she was pulled out of a deep sleep. And indeed, it was blaring intrusively.

"Hello?"

"This is your wake-up call!" the recorded voice spoke in monotone.

Jill jumped out of bed, groggy from a deep sleep. She stepped over to the desk, pulled out her notebook, and quickly wrote a summary of her vision. She didn't have time to analyze it now. Fumbling through the balance of her clean clothes, she went into the bathroom, showered, packed, and was about to open the door when she heard a knock. Zayed's sharp features and freshly manicured whiskers boasted an excellent night's rest.

"You get everything done, okay?" Jill said bluntly.

A nod from Zayed was his only response.

They headed downstairs and checked out of the hotel. Jill squinted in the bright sun. She did her normal scan for anything that seemed suspect. Nothing. A man in a light blue uniform greeted them. AL GAZAL was stitched across his top pocket. He spoke broken English and looked Afghan with his long orange-dyed goatee. When he smiled widely, you could see he was missing some teeth. Zayed nodded in recognition. The hotel grounds appeared different in the daylight. They were filled with beautiful bright orange flowers, trimmed grass, and a large water fountain on the other side of the valet drive, gurgling spray. To her right was a black 4x4 sedan similar to the ones they used in the US Marshal Service.

"Come," the man motioned to Jill. She put her pack in the back and noticed plastic bags stuffed with junk food and a liquor box. The waft of cigarette smoke threatened her nose when she climbed into the backseat. Frankly, the smell of stale cigarettes before coffee pissed her off. But she said nothing.

The man held up a map and pointed to Kushka. Zayed and Jill agreed on the route. First, they would head along the Kabul River on the main highway. It would take them to Peshawar in Pakistan, Highway A76 if they continued. They would then go south on what looked like a gravel road into the mountains until they reached the small town of Kushka. Jill noticed the map was slightly different from the one she had. Although it was faded, she saw Xs jotted with a black marker.

"What are those black marks?" she pointed to the page.

"Checkpoints," he responded in his thick accent.

Zayed handed the driver four envelopes filled with cash for the checkpoints, and their journey began.

Jill watched Zayed give the man money, which provoked a question she had had before but never asked. Where did Zayed get this much cash? The driver seemed friendly enough, but Jill was puzzled by how easy it seemed for Zayed to have found him. A driver that spoke English in Kabul could not be an easy find. She tried to place the name Al Gazal and decided it must be a taxi service of some sort. Jill was reluctant to ask him because the driver was within earshot, so she turned to gaze out the back window instead.

The more she thought about it, the more Jill realized she didn't know much about Zayed at all. She went back into the tunnels now. As she sped through her memories in fast forward, the images were too fast to recognize as they flashed past. She hadn't had time to get into the tunnels in the past few days, not while awake. It was a gift of hers. Usually, when something didn't sit quite right when she was profiling, she would go into her quiet office, put her feet up on her desk, and stare at an object. While her instinct searched her memory, like nature's computer scan, something always pulled up an image. Something that her intuition made her see. Something only her intuition could feel. Today it stopped on two images. One is the Chechens. Two, Stan Brown. She looked at Zayed and wished she could pull out her notebook, but she didn't want him to see her notes. They were private.

Jill thought back to what Kali had said about Zayed. The Arab that waited for her arrival in Doha seemed like too much of a coincidence, and now traveling the highway in the SUV also seemed too convenient. But she was here now. Shoot, move, communicate, survive. And with that resolve, she sighed and moved on.

Anticipation at finding David consumed Jill and briefly took her mind off Zayed. There was no dread, no fear in her psyche. Well, not yet, anyway. But she needed to understand what the Chechens and Stan Brown had to do with her. She should have tried to reach Stan again—now more than ever. She kicked herself.

The city was awake now, and a mix of people was on the busy streets. Men in business suits walked alongside others in robes. Some were holding hands with each other. Jill knew in this part of the world that men holding each other's hands were not sexual but more of a sign of friendship. She'd seen it in Doha and Abu Dhabi alongside men Eskimo kissing—nose to nose. Most vehicles were civilian cars, SUVs, and then the occasional motorcycle. Several wagons were pulled by horses, and seemingly endless numbers of people on foot.

As the scenes flicked past, Jill decided they must be on one of the famous Silk Routes described in the report from Kali. These Silk Routes were used mainly to transport silk made in China and shipped to Rome. In return, the Roman traders returned gold and ivory on the same road. Now, these routes carry drug traffickers, Taliban, and opium smugglers.

The driver in the front seat began to speak. He explained that the opium trade was rampant in his country.

"The government... does nothing," he said. As they left the city, he pointed to several landmarks of war. Blown-up trucks, twisted metal, and building rubble lined the valley toward the gray mountains ahead. Signs warning of landmines were posted about every kilometer. While he continued his grim story, Jill noticed the beautiful colors of the city they were leaving behind. The terracotta, yellow, navy blue, and hints of purple impressed her. But as the city colors faded behind them, the bleak frontier of Afghanistan began to emerge. The blue of the sky highlighted the barren foothills. The further they snaked away from the city, the lighter the traffic became. They passed a few aid and military vehicles but little other traffic. In the distance, Jill could see what looked like tiny villages sprinkled on the face of the dreary mountains.

This road, at least, was smoothly paved as they traveled quickly up toward the mountains. The driver grew quiet. Several times during the ten-hour journey, she wondered about her visions—the Chechens and why they were after her. Why am I dreaming of family? It must be about David. The thought did not sit well with her, but she couldn't figure out why.

They stopped at the checkpoints, and the bribes moved them through. It turned out their driver was experienced at this because he would open the back of the truck at every checkpoint, and the non-smiling guards, dressed in green army fatigues and carrying automatic rifles, would politely take a bottle of vodka. The driver commented that sometimes these guards were so poorly paid that food was more valuable than vodka. With the fall of the Soviet Union in the early 1990s and its breakup into a dozen countries, Jill could understand why. But she had thought things were better now for the displaced Russians. Not in Afghanistan, it seemed. The driver's vodka donation plus US cash was something the guards cherished, cherished more than the country that had caused their situation.

These checkpoints were set up for the opium smugglers, and it was mainly women who worked as mules to transport the lethal heroin mix. The guards needed to indulge in corruption to maintain a satisfactory lifestyle, so they stopped every vehicle, whether it contained a woman or not. The guards appeared intimidating when they came out of the run-down bolo-type steel trailer. They spoke a dialect of some sort of Russian. They seemed confident, waving their black truck through one checkpoint after another.

They got fuel and food—if you could call it food. Hard-crusted wraps, some stale potato chips, and a melted chocolate bar, in a town called Chaghcharan, about two-thirds of the way to Kushka. The sun had begun to set as they crested the last mountain. In the distance, Jill thought she could see Turkmenistan. They must be getting close; her heart ached to see David.

During the journey, Zayed sat limply, relaxed. He made no sound, and the movement of his eyelids indicated he was in REM. His sideburns trailed into the hair on his cheeks. His large nose arched in the middle before it rounded over and hooked, meeting his full lips. Who are you, Zayed? Jill thought.

The GPS voice was an English female, oddly in a British accent. The driver piped up: "Kushka, five minutes," and with that, Zayed awoke.

Kushka looked very different from Kabul. Even in the dusk, Jill could see that Kushka was far greener and more colorful. The poorly lit streets were filled with the shapes of people walking. A motorcycle honked as it zipped past them—one and then another.

"It looks like the primary mode of transport is motorbikes," Jill said. Her voice sounded louder than she had intended.

"Or horse carts," the driver joked.

Zayed asked the driver to take them to a hotel, and the driver explained there was only one main hotel in town.

They saw very few women wearing abayas. Royal blues and bright yellow outlined with red—colorful dresses appeared to be the local favorite.

They pulled up to a run-down government building. The driver pointed to the building and said, "This is the hotel." The sign on it was not in English. A cross between Arabic and Russian, Jill wasn't sure. Zayed asked the driver to wait while they went into the makeshift hotel to see what was available. Jill blinked hard when she walked in. It was as if they'd come off a deserted US highway to a motel that hadn't been refurbished in decades. Spittoons lined the hallway, and her first impression was one of conflict. The gray marble floor and front desk were clean and almost sparkled in the light. But the windows were dirty, and most were cracked. Jill stretched her back by pulling her arms forward while Zayed spoke to the attendant at the front desk.

A moment later, Jill's attention was drawn to Zayed as he walked toward her. He looked uneasy, and when he turned to speak, she felt as if she could read his mind.

"We have to share a room," he told her matter-of-factly. Jill felt her skin flush, but the strength of his words told her they had no choice. "No record of David being here."

She wasn't going to have any of this crap. She marched over to the desk and asked about getting her room. The clerk just shrugged and said, "No English!" Jill had a thing about hotel rooms. It was different than sharing a room on a ship. To Jill, being in a hotel room meant hotel sex. It was an agreement between David and Jill. No women in his room while he was on assignment—not for any reason. David adhered to the agreement, and now Jill was faced with a breach of trust.

Jill's shoulders slightly slumped when Zayed said, "Wait here, and I will get our bags." He left, not waiting for her reaction.

"David would understand," she told herself. But dread hit her stomach as they walked down the long hallway toward their room. She didn't want to be put in this position. It wasn't as if Zayed had a beer belly and stank of too much cologne. He was strikingly handsome. She liked his strong stature, rock-hard muscles, and even more powerful demeanor as a man. But she was in love with David, and really that's all that mattered, didn't it?

Twisting the key, Zayed opened the door, and Jill stepped in. But she stopped so fast that Zayed bumped into her and knocked her slightly forward. The room was filthy, seedy, and dark, lit only by a harsh light bulb dangling from a wire. Dark stains dotted the cracking paint on the walls. There were two small beds and no other furniture.

Apprehensively, Jill walked toward the only other door in the room. "What a shithole!" she blurted out loud. Water dripped from the toilet before spattering along the grungy floor, trickling toward the lopsided rusty bathtub.

"Don't worry," Zayed soothed, coming so close that she could feel him. "There is no hot water anyway. They only turn it on from 8 a.m. to 8:30. We will find David tomorrow and leave here. We are lucky to get a room with a bathroom; they said only two rooms have toilets."

"If David hasn't checked into the hotel, what the hell are we still doing here?" Miffed at where she had to stay, she pushed past him, reached over to the closest bed, and went through her ritual of pulling down the stained bed cover. The other occupants were apparent. Cockroaches scurried off the bed and disappeared into a hole at the base of the floor. Jill looked down at the sheets and decided she would sleep standing up.

Zayed sternly said from behind her, "I have to go out and find someone to help us locate David. If he had been here, someone would know. He's blond and American, so he'd stand out."

She stared down at the hole-ridden floorboards in thought. "I'm going with you," she said just as sternly.

"It's too dangerous," he protested. "Women do not go out after dark."

Jill thought for a moment. "What do you need to go and do?"

"I need to find a contact or someone with any information. I will start with the hotel clerks and see what I can find out. Money helps!" he finished.

"What? What are you going to ask them; have you seen this guy? Seriously," she mocked.

"I'll be back shortly. Do not open the door for anyone. I have a key so I won't be knocking." And with that, Zayed closed the door behind

him, turned the key in the deadbolt, and his footsteps faded down the
hall.

CHAPTER FOURTEEN

14:56 Zulu Time—Kushka, Afghanistan

"Whatever," Jill mumbled, still wondering if she had made the right decision not to push to go with him. The room did not hold any welcoming décor. An old clock with no glass face cover and missing its second hand read 20:26. Lowering herself gingerly onto the bed, Jill thought about this trip. She was a US Marshal who had rarely been in the field since her FBI days, let alone somewhere like Afghanistan. She started to feel some regret. What am I doing here? she asked herself. You're so tough, Jill; now what? Ever since her episode with her attempted Remote Viewing, she had been feeling insecure. She felt like giving in to her woe-is-me pity party. After all, she liked her nice cozy office filled with plants and a plump couch for late-night caseloads. It felt safe to her, or perhaps it was just a cop-out when she left the FBI after McGregor. She didn't get back on that horse and somehow liked being at the top of the safe game.

She knew there was probably no Internet but had nothing else to do. Pulling her laptop from her bag, she waited for a wireless connection. She got out her notebook and began to review her visions. In the absence of "You've got mail," "You've got no Internet," chimed back to Jill. Apprehensively, she leaned on her carry-on perched behind her against the wall and closed her eyes, trying to think. David, where are you? There was no answer back.

The sound of a key unlocking the door woke Jill so fast that she slipped off the edge of the bed and onto the dingy floor. Quickly jumping up, she brushed her hands down the back of her pants as Zayed walked in.

When he turned to lock the door, Jill saw a large black duffel bag draped over his left shoulder. He walked past her and tossed it onto the other cot. Tiny particles of sand fell off it and onto the bed cover. Before she could ask, Zayed unzipped the dirt-ridden zipper and began to sort through the bag, revealing several guns, grenades, some paper, and maps.

Perplexed, Jill asked, "Where did you get this stuff?"

Without looking in Jill's direction, Zayed responded, "I hired an intelligence broker in Doha to help us here in Kushka."

Jill stared at him, mouth agape. "How did you hire an intelligence broker when we had to leave the hotel so fast?" She tried to remember when they first talked about Kushka. Was it on the way to the fishing village in Doha?

"Before we left Doha, while we were on the boat, I called a friend who knew an IB, one that dealt with this kind of information over here," he said. "He arranged to have the GPS coordinates left for me at the hotel."

"But," she paused, trying to think fast. Her head tilted slightly. "How did they know where we were going to be staying? And how can you trust anyone here, Zayed? You're telling me that you potentially compromised our safety, my safety? Did you even think of David?"

"I have people I trust, Jill." He smiled crookedly. This statement pissed Jill off even more. "Besides, the coordinates were in encrypted code. No one would know what they meant, and the instructions were left for me under an alias." Then, with a condescending glare, he said, "It doesn't take a rocket scientist to know this is the only hotel in Kushka, Jill."

"How did you get a GPS?" she demanded suspiciously.

"Calm down, Jill. I asked the driver to wait so I could use his GPS. The geocache was buried close to the hotel, and the marker was easy to spot."

Geocache. Jill knew what a geocache was, but how did Zayed? Geocaching, now a modern high-tech treasure hunter's sport, began in World War I, but it wasn't called geocaching back then. Markers were left for men on the frontlines to hide what they needed to protect. Nowadays, in military operations, GPS coordinates give almost the precise location with predetermined markers to mark the exact spot where something of value was buried.

Over one million caches worldwide were listed on websites where would-be Indiana Joneses would hunt via GPS. Contained in the geocaches was a nominal treasure. They didn't typically include anything of monetary value but something a treasure hunter would value—perhaps a coin or trinket. Included in these caches were a logbook and pen; for the finder to log their discovery, they had to replace the treasure with something of a higher value. More than a hundred countries had geocaches, and over five million 'geocachers' played the game the last time Jill read about it.

Airplane parts, my ass. There was no way Zayed worked in the airplane parts industry as he had told her. This man had too many connections, too much knowledge, and too many secrets. Jill's brow furrowed as she thought of what to do next. She knew he wasn't a mere salesman or PRO and tried to benefit him from her paranoia. She tried. But alarm bells kept ringing in her head. "Where did you get the money to hire a broker?"

He began to speak, but before he got a sound out, Jill could see him mouth the word David as if in slow motion. Then she felt the back of her neck tingle. Jill tried to keep her poker face as she stared at Zayed, silent. No flicker in her eye. Her only thought, and she had thought it before, bullshit!

Jill knew David's spending habits, and there was no way in hell he would leave money in someone's hands—let alone someone in the Middle East whom Jill had never heard of before. To put it mildly, David was a tightwad. Not to mention Jill would have noticed a significant amount of money missing from their joint account. She didn't monitor David's spending habits very often, but she would have noticed something out of sync that didn't mesh. And he didn't use their joint credit card; otherwise, she wouldn't have been able to afford the first-class trip to Doha. David made good money as a freelance journalist, but Jill would have noticed anything unusual.

Her gaze turned to the bed on which sat the Glocks. She just confirmed Zayed's bullshit. It wasn't her paranoia. It was blatant, and now she knew for sure. Somehow, now more than ever, she needed to trust herself. She needed to get off that goddamn shrink's couch. Screw the pity party. She needed to take control, and she needed to do it now.

With this newfound information, Jill needed to figure out what to do about Zayed. She was in the middle of the world's end with a man she did not trust.

Why did Zayed come all this way for a man he barely knew? Think, Jill, think.

Zayed entered the bathroom, leaving her alone with the armory on the bed. Her hand reached for a gun. Caressing the cold metal and tapping her foot, Jill recalled her time with Zayed. Whatever was nagging her brain grated hard like a child's whine. First, his stance, the way he held himself. Second was his scanning. He knew a military surveillance tactic and used it well. And now, with the geocache, all of this confirmed her suspicions. She wanted so much to believe Zayed was helping because he was David's PRO. But that was just foolish, and she knew this was untrue. What kind of training would he have? Before she could factor in a conclusion, Zayed returned from the bathroom.

"I reviewed the information in this document," Zayed said. "There is a man in the old souk about two blocks from the hotel."

"Hotel, my ass," Jill blurted gruffly. Zayed frowned and reopened the document.

She needed to figure out who he was, what he knew, and his motive for dragging her along with him. I need to get closer to him to learn more about him. She considered her options. She could just outright ask him—Jill style. But then she didn't want him to know that this new information confirmed her suspicions. Not until she knew who he really was.

The hundred-watt light glowed down on them as Zayed, still reading, sank onto the cot across from Jill. He looked up to find Jill staring through him. He leaned his back against the wall, not caring.

"How much money did David give you, Zayed?" Jill said matter-of-factly.

Zayed began to blink slightly faster. "He gave me $25,000 US dollars."

"Twenty-five grand? Why would he need to give you that much money?"

"Contacts cost money, Jill—a lot of money. Don't worry; I am sure he got the money from Time. If not, I am certain they'll reimburse him. They pay well for information."

Jill caught the blinks and continued pressing. "You said you knew David for a couple of years and helped him with introductions to the key people so he could get the story. When was this? When did you meet him?"

The right side of Zayed's mouth wrinkled up, but he said nothing. She looked back. The pregnant pause made Zayed growl, "You don't trust me." His accent was thick with anger.

Then Jill did something that didn't make sense to herself. She pulled herself up fast, walked over to the cot beside Zayed, and sat cross-legged with her boots tucked under her legs.

"I know I asked you this before, Zayed, but why are you going to such lengths to help me, to help David?"

With his head cocked, he looked at her inquisitively and then said, "Miss Jill, you must not think I am the enemy. Why would I stop the Chechens from taking you?" His lusty eyes brightened as he leaned forward.

A knock on the door caused Zayed to jump up, grab a gun, and rush to the door. Just before he grabbed the grungy knob, he glanced back at Jill and gestured for her to move behind him. Jill did as he asked and watched Zayed fling open the door.

Before he was about to square a bullet between the man behind the door, Zayed whipped the gun behind his back.

"Si-si-si-sir," the young man stuttered. "Here is the map you asked for." His shaky hand presented a bright baby-blue map.

Jill sat back on the cot next to the geocache, listening to the faint talk at the door. She knew he had lied about where he got the money; that was an easy read—blinking speeds up when a person is lying. She enjoyed confirming this by studying politicians giving their campaign promises or their version of the truth. Especially the infamous line from the one who said, "I did not have sexual relations." He boasted seventy-nine blinks.

She had to keep Zayed at bay for now, and for now, she needed his help. Jill felt, in the core of her being, that even in his presence, she was alone.

With the timid delivery boy gone, Zayed locked the door and pulled out the key. He somewhat impatiently said, "I will go find the café." Jill didn't say anything. "We found the café on the map," he said. "I'll see if the informant will speak to me." His overbearing attitude was back. "And I will go alone."

"I will not have it, Zayed," Jill said in a way that made him know she meant it.

"He will not speak to a woman," he rebutted.

Jill turned her back to him and crossed her arms. Less than a minute later, she had come up with a plan. "I can dress like a man, and I will." Without waiting to hear his thoughts, Jill pulled her switchblade from her pants and marched to the bathroom. "Give me one of your larger shirts. No one will know I am a female if I don't speak." She didn't look back for acceptance.

Inside the dirty bathroom, Jill stood in front of the mirror and, for a brief moment, reconsidered. No, I have to do this. The tap was dripping into a bowl, at the bottom of which was wet sludge. There were no windows in the bathroom, and she didn't want to consider what was inside the open square hole on the side of the stained tub. Jill shuddered and looked into the cracked mirror. She couldn't remember the last time she had short hair. David loved her long, jet-black locks. For some reason, she could never grow it past her bra line, but she loved how straight it was, compliments of her Navajo ancestors. The sound of the blade cutting away the hair grated to the bone. She thought of David as the long tangled locks fell into the sink. She could see in the mirror that Zayed was curiously watching her, glancing, intrigued by her boldness. But he stayed silent. She looked back, continuing to cut until her hair was spiky short. Angling her head in different directions as if posing for a photo shoot, Jill tried to find any comfort in looking back at herself. There was none. Her body was athletic and strong, and her angular face could pass as a man's with this haircut—a pretty one, but a man nonetheless.

Jill passed the room with the broken toilet on her way out. Something scurried on the floor in her peripheral vision, but she told herself not to recognize it. She became anxious when Zayed handed her his shirt.

"I think it is not a good idea, Jill. David would disapprove."

"I won't get in the way." She snatched the shirt from him and lifted the worn black T-shirt over her head. The shirt fell, covering her fatigues and making her look bulkier. His smell lingered for just a few seconds. Jill couldn't help but notice a man's smell. They all smelled similar, from a stale musky sweat to a sweet musk to her.

"When do we go?" she asked impatiently.

Zayed picked up one of the guns and racked the slide, ensuring a bullet sat tightly in the chamber. Then he handed it to Jill.

"Just so you know, Jill," Zayed warned, "this guy is a member of the Taliban, an unfriendly. We need to be careful. You need to be careful."

Jill took the warning on board but wasn't staying in the hotel. "Do you have a hat in that bag?" Her black fatigues complemented her newfound black ball cap, tilted down over her eyes.

Outside the run-down hotel, and with night upon them, Zayed did his scan. They moved down a side street and were consumed by the gloom of the town. The backstreets were similar to those of Doha, with the addition of battlefield décor, which made them look slummy. A carpenter's shop door was opened wide, the sound of nails hammered into wood escaping into the night. A large pile of timber was stacked neatly until they walked past, giving Jill a close-up of the wood with nails sticking out haphazardly. She wanted to ask about wooden structures in Afghanistan, but that was too trivial. On the left were broken-down vehicles that had been towed there. The front parts of unrecognizable trucks and decades-old cars were missing. A thick coating of dust and dirt indicated that they had been there a long time.

Large neon signs in the local language lit up the dismal streets and shop fronts where they walked. Jill followed Zayed across one small backstreet and then another, their boots clunking on the gravel. Then Zayed stopped fast.

"See over there," he pointed, whispering. "See that café? That is where he is supposed to have coffee in the evenings."

"Do we have a name?" Jill asked.

Zayed didn't answer.

They stopped twenty or so yards from the building when a man in local attire stumbled out of the door, leaned up against the side of the building, and attempted to steady himself. A minute later, the drunk was staggering down the street.

Zayed's hand shushed her as they approached the door. Without hesitation, Zayed walked in. Posturing, wishing she had a testosterone shot, Jill followed. Inside, the café looked more like an old biker bar behind a gas station somewhere on Route 66. The walls were covered in chipped orange paint to mask the cement, which Jill could barely make out through the cloud of cigarette smoke anyway. To the left were a couple of stools at a makeshift bar. A large cracked mirror hung behind it, extending to the right corner where two men sat smoking. They looked up through the smoke. She waited by the door, and Zayed walked across the ten-foot-long room.

He mumbled something in Arabic and then, "Hamrain?" The sound of this name punched Jill in the gut. Adrenaline began to rush through her. The name was on David's notes back at the house. Poker face on, she tried not to show her interest or thrill that they were getting closer to finding her husband. Focus. She rehearsed scenarios while watching Zayed. She scanned discreetly.

Three o'clock. Two Afghans smoked, uninterested.

Six o'clock. No one was standing behind Jill. She began reciting the rules of engagement. You have the right to use force to defend yourself against an attacker. Hostile fire may be returned to stop an aggressive attack. Use minimum force necessary. Check. She knew these rules and studied them. A thought flashed into Jill's mind. She wondered if her potential opponents followed the same rules.

Nine o'clock. A blank wall.

Twelve o'clock. Zayed again. The man who sat in the corner responded in an Arabic-type dialect, slowly leaning back in his plastic chair. An automatic rifle rested leisurely on the man's lap. Two men stood behind him in the shadows. One of the men glanced Jill's way, and she tilted her head down. The sound of a chair slowly scraping across the floor signaled cautious movement. Jill took one small step in the direction of Zayed. The men shifted, and Jill noticed they wore worn leather army boots like hers. The two seedy men turned and walked back toward the wall. Zayed moved in unison, and Jill followed past the man sitting in the chair. They followed the men through a door and stepped into an attached room resembling a store more than a back room. To her left was a long glass door, something you would see in a retail strip mall but tinted black. Bulletproof was Jill's first thought. You could barely see out and most certainly couldn't see in. The two men stood on the right against a cement wall.

The room was virtually empty except for short storage shelves in the middle of the floor and a desk in the corner. The light from a desk lamp failed to illuminate the face of a dark figure who sat behind it. The sound of a grunt greeted them. Zayed stepped toward him, and Jill stood on the left side of the storage shelves. She scanned the shelves filled with army munitions boxes. Reading the text on the boxes, Jill began to head around the other side of them, but their escorts immediately cocked their guns. Jill stopped. Zayed held up his hands, palms facing the man in the shadow. "Marhaba, hello," Zayed said in Arabic.

All eyes now on Zayed, Jill slid her hand into her side pocket and closed her grip on the gun. Zayed said something in Arabic, then slowly pulled out an envelope from the front of his jacket. He placed the thick envelope of cash on the dark table. On top of it, Zayed put David's photo. The room was tense, the air stale.

Jill saw the dark shadow's nod when he looked at the photo. Her stomach flipped. Sliding the money-laced envelope into his top drawer, he shuffled through some papers on the cluttered desk and handed Zayed a torn Post-it note. Zayed read it and then tucked it into the top pocket of his black jacket.

Jill's instinct tapped her on the shoulder. Something didn't feel right. She stood silent. Then it happened, a loud crack. What had to be an armor-piercing bullet broke a sharp hole through the glass.

"Khalas, khalas!" one of the men screamed.

Zayed turned suddenly when one of the men cocked his rifle, aimed it at Zayed, and started yelling. At the same time, the door behind the group splintered open. Jill ducked behind a shelf and pulled out her gun. She heard shouts in what sounded like Russian from the back of the room. Gunfire burst around her. Jill aimed at a figure and shut one of her eyes for focus, but the figure moved out of sight. Ducking down again, she could only hear gunfire and the sound of anguished screams. There were more men in the small room now, different men. Then more gunfire, and she felt shattered glass rain down around her. Struggling to make out anything in the dust from the shattered glass, she looked at the floor where Zayed was lying motionless, not more than four feet away. Tiny glass shards sparkled in the blood pooling around his head. Jill crab-walked over to him with bullets whizzing around her. Full of adrenaline, she dragged him back behind the storage racks of ammo.

"Zayed?" She shook him. She couldn't tell if he was breathing, and there was no time to check in this chaos. Run, Jill, run, and without further thought, she reached into Zayed's pocket and snatched the Post-it note.

Lifting her gun hand above the shelf, she fired, giving her enough time to escape the room. A man shouted in her direction; Jill turned around and shot directly into his belly, gutting and knocking him backward. She could not see how many others remained. "Nyet, nyet," was all she heard. Jill had no time to think as she ran ducking in and around and between cars. She didn't know the direction of the sniper, who was clearly firing to distract the assault coming in from the rear door.

Then a lull—the gunfire had stopped! In a leap of faith, she ran and crouched along the backs of cars until she hit a break between two buildings and sprinted into the dark alley.

Behind her, a man yelled something in Russian. Did he see me? Shit. Her boots smacked the ground hard, and the pace reverberated through her knees. Only the moonlight and a smattering of shop lights were lighting her way.

Ducking into an alley, Jill glanced back between breaths and saw shadows along the buildings across a small parking lot. With that as her cue, she sprinted down into darkness. Rounding two more corners, she stopped fast when she noticed some stairs behind a glass door. Grabbing the handle hard, she shook it open. The door was not locked. She pulled herself in and ran up the two flights of stairs, only to find nothing at the top but a single door. This time the door was locked. She looked at the gun in her shaking hand. She looked back to the door; it had a small window and only darkness on the other side. This door must lead to the roof. Panting hard, she looked back down the dark stairwell, but no one had followed her. Not that she could see anyway. The sound of her heart pounding was loud. Jill let out a deep breath, satisfied she was alone. She put the gun back into her pocket.

She couldn't believe what had happened. One minute there was a meeting going on, and the next second, everyone was shooting. She'd killed a guy. Unless there was a medic on site, he'd bleed out fast. She didn't have a choice. She couldn't believe she had left there or that Zayed was dead too. Who wanted to kill him? And who were those Russians? Chechens? She could swear she heard two different Slavic dialects.

Anxiously, Jill reached her still-shaking hand into the pocket and pulled out the crumpled note. Holding the note up to the moonlight, Jill tried to read it, but the writing wasn't English or Arabic. It looked Russian. The way the words were formatted, it must be an address. There was no mention of David on it; at least, nothing seemed like his name. The feeling of her heart thumping faded as she contemplated what to do next.

She slowly descended the stairs, carefully peering out the windows for any more shooters in the dark. The streets seemed quiet, despite some of the shops still being open. Across the small side street was a dress shop. The illuminated sign lit the dresses cascading like a curtain in the window. She could not see inside, but the lights were on. Suddenly she remembered—she looked like a man! Could I be this lucky? Jill reached the glass door at the bottom of the stairs and looked one way and then the next. No one. There were cars along the main street, but the backstreets were silent. Where were the police? Surely someone must have heard all that shooting and reported it?

Jill fled across the abandoned parking lot, past a mini-mart, and into the dress shop. The bell jingled as she shut the door behind her. She knew no one could see her in here unless they looked closely through the bright garments that served as curtains. Full hangers were squashed with an assortment of different patterns. The walls were lined with long abayas. One wall was piled high with folded clothes in lopsided piles. A bearded older man looked up at Jill from behind a counter. He didn't seem to know whether to smile or yell at her to leave, as she probably looked more like a gay male model.

Thick white eyebrows arched over the man's eyes, and she instantly recognized something she saw in Grandpapa's eyes. She smiled and said, "Hello, Marhaba." The white-haired man said hello back. His accent was thick.

"I need a dress," Jill said, pulling off the cap and shaking her short hair. She spoke slowly in the hopes that he could understand. His arthritic hips hobbled over to where her finger pointed, and he happily began to pull a dress down. Jill shook her head.

Jill wanted a traditional Afghan abaya. The rods bowed slightly with the weight of the jammed clothes. Jill was drawn to a bright blue dress. Although she hadn't seen too many women wearing them here, she wanted to blend in as best as possible.

The old man shuffled through the tight gowns to find the right size for her. He pulled one out and held it up to her. "Good, good, khalas." Jill reached into a money belt under her shirt, pulled out some green paper, and paid for the dress. She then plucked out the treasured paper and asked the old man if he knew what it said.

"Russia, Russia," he babbled. "La la, no Russia, no Russia."

He looked up, said, "Wife Russia, grocery," and walked out the back door.

Before Jill could go after him, he returned with a pudgy older woman. Trustingly, she held the note up for the old woman to see. Her old hands shook slightly as she gently took the note from Jill and held it out far from her face, scowling intently. She was dressed in a drab polka-dotted outfit that fell to the ground, cinched tightly at her overgrown waistline. Her curly gray hair, uncovered, disclosed she was not Muslim. Jill thought that to marry a Muslim, one had to be Muslim, but she quickly pushed the curiosity away as the woman began speaking Arabic to her husband.

"Address, village," he translated back to Jill. His worn, spotted hand pointed at a name on the note. "Petrovich, name Petrovich."

"Petrovich," Jill repeated, and the couple nodded. Jill needed to find a phone. She needed to call Kali and have her run this name in association with LSA. Maybe there was intel on it. Maybe Kali had found information on Zayed? But that didn't matter now, did it? Jill also needed to get to this place written on the paper.

Jill held up her hand and mimed holding a phone. But the old man slowly shook his head. Turning, he pointed to the left window and said, "Typing shop, go, typing shop." Jill stood momentarily, remembering how lucky she had been to have Zayed with her, then pushed the thought away. Right now, she needed to get in touch with Kali. She would have time to think about Zayed later.

Excited and apprehensive, she slipped into the abaya, complete with the burqa over her face. She waved a thank-you to the old couple and moved slowly toward the door. She looked out the glass at a dark and empty street. The door jingled as she walked out.

CHAPTER FIFTEEN

18:33 Zulu Time—Kushka, Afghanistan

Once outside, the part of her dress that crisscrossed over the eye-holes obstructed her view, causing her to miss a stair. Her body lurched forward, and her boot smacked the pavement, saving her from tumbling into a tangled ball of robe. She tried to get some bearing on where to go. From what Jill could translate from the old man's flurry of hand gestures, she was to leave the store, go left down the side road for a ways, then turn right, and it would be there on the right side of the road. He then ended the gestures with "Insha'allah."

"Typing shop," she said to herself. Jill attempted to blend in as a local woman by moving in the direction suggested to her. She rounded the next corner and saw several shops with lights on through her imprisoned view. Jill thought she could see the outline of a typewriter in the shop at the end, but it was still too far away to make out, and the burqa was not helping matters. Intuition stopped her just as she was about to step off the curb. Jill placed her foot back onto the curb and warily looked around. In an effort to appear that she had dropped something, her head tilted slightly down as she further scanned her surroundings—first to her left and then back toward the typing shop. As her eyes passed along the street, she saw it. There, directly across the road to her immediate left, was the café where the gunfight happened.

Instantly, Jill became apprehensive and backed slowly into the closed doorway of an abandoned shop. She patted her right quad to gain comfort from the gun. Could this be the same café?

She peeked out from the dark doorway and looked up and down the street. Two men were smoking in a few shops up to the right across the road. Luckily they weren't looking in Jill's direction. She looked back over at the café, which was now dark. Shattered glass gleamed in the bright orange light of the sign above the café.

It's the same café, she thought and wondered where everyone was. It couldn't have been more than thirty minutes since she escaped the attack. How could it be cleared away so fast? Where are all the men who were killed or wounded? For a second, Jill wondered if she was in a dream, still sleeping, snuggled somewhere between hell and back. In the States, crowds would have gathered by now. Police tape would be up. At least two black-and-whites would hold the crowd back, waiting for CSU to appear. There seemed to be commotion on the backside of the café as several cars stopped in disarray with their headlights on, but it was too far away for her to see any details. Jill mulled over her escape that led her to the dress shop. She couldn't seem to retrace how she ended up so close. "Shit," she muffled under the burqa.

Then her thoughts turned to Zayed. She considered going back to the café to see if there were any signs of his body, but the sound of footsteps stopped that thought short. A man walked past the café, his shoes crunching the shards of glass. Oddly, he didn't glance at the shattered window. He only walked in Jill's direction. His gait seemed harmless enough, strong, but not determined. Out for a night stroll, perhaps? He wasn't wearing army boots, just thick-soled sandals. She stood in the dark, almost holding her breath. Frozen, Jill allowed her eyes to follow him as he passed the doorstep where she stood, crossed the road, and disappeared into the mechanical supply store.

Jill's brain spun. She needed to get to the typing shop, but the only way to reach it was to walk past the café. She hesitated; she needed some nerve now. She also needed to find a damn phone. Another scan. Nothing. She clenched her hands and huffed, then walked out from the dark doorway and started toward the shop.

Down the street, men were moving about, doing their business. She knew it was uncommon for a woman to be out alone at night, but she hoped no one would notice. She suddenly began to feel sweltering under the abaya. Adrenaline mixed with apprehension and intent. She walked toward the first corner of the café and decided not to look inside. Breathe, Jill, breathe. Just a few more steps. Glass crunched under her boots. Shit. She stepped lighter to avoid attracting attention. She had no peripheral vision when she walked past the broken window. Jill let out a long breath at the sound of her boots slapping the clean pavement. She kept moving at the same pace, and her heart rate began to slow.

Three doors past the café, and the typing shop was on the right. Light shone through the bars in the windows. Jill opened the glass door, and a musty smell greeted her. The breeze from the opening door ruffled the edges of the papers tacked to veneer wood paneling. Inside, a herd of old dusty computer screens faced her.

Shelves were crowded with an array of paper, ink cartridges, books, and a round alarm clock that read 20:57. Seated at desks were three men and one woman, heads tilted down, concentrating on the glowing screens in front of them. The wood paneling was warped, the bend forcing a cobwebbed shelf away from the wall. The head of the man closest to her lifted. Jill detected annoyance as he approached her from behind the cluttered counter. Jill noticed a phone/fax machine in a makeshift phone booth to her right. She pointed to the phone and pulled out a one-hundred-dollar US bill. The Afghan man looked at it and then back to Jill. He said something in a language Jill did not understand, then he examined the bill and said, "You call the US?"

Jill nodded.

"Twenty minutes, khalas."

Khalas must mean finish—she had gathered that much on this trip by now.

A small table holding a dirty cream-colored phone sat before a raggedy chair. The numbers on the phone were in Arabic, and she hoped they were in the standard order. Arabic was written in the reverse sequence from English—right to left—so numbers in Arabic were written from left to right. A cloud of dust rose from the chair as she sat down, and Jill suddenly realized that the old woman in the dress shop did not mention David.

She picked up the cruddy phone and dialed zero-zero-one and then the number. The phone ringing reassured her that she might have gotten the number right. The sun should be up by now in Tucson, Jill thought.

"Boy, I sure am happy to hear from you," Kali said.

"Same," Jill replied quietly.

"Jill, you alright?"

Jill's hand had a slight tremor. She was trying to hold the phone away from her head for fear of getting who knows what disease from it. "Five-W," Jill whispered. That was the code for Kali to know that Jill couldn't talk and that something was urgent. Who, what, when, where, why, and how—the fundamentals of clear and concise communication. At least, that's what David's mantra was. And that was precisely what Jill needed.

Focus, Kali. Jill and Kali had rehearsed this over a bottle of wine one evening. They never thought they would ever use it, but they had prepared for this moment. Please focus, Kali.

"You can't talk?" Kali asked fast.

"No."

"Okay, you hurt?"

"No."

"You need something?" Jill sensed that Kali had realized before she finished asking that it was a dumb question. As rehearsed, Kali continued, "What do you need, Jill?"

"Research."

"Where—Kushka?"

"Yes."

"Well, I guess the when is now, eh?"

"Yeah," Jill said with annoyance.

"Who?"

Kali tapped on the keys as Jill answered, "Petrovich." She looked up at the people in the typing shop to see if anyone had flinched with acknowledgment. No one did.

Kali repeated the name and told Jill she would run it alongside LSA and the unknown village outside Kushka. "I'll also run it against your friend Zayed," Kali said as if she just scored a goal. Jill didn't respond. No need to tell Kali she thought he was dead. Besides, she was curious to find out who he was.

Jill twisted her head toward the computer geeks. No one seemed to notice her. She whispered, "The old man said it was thirty minutes from Kushka," Jill said hurriedly. "David?" Jill said with hope. Kali's sigh answered her question.

"Wait, what? What old man?" Then Kali finished her question with, "Never mind. You can tell me later."

After several minutes on hold, Kali returned almost out of breath and sounded excited. "I had to run to the central computer system for this guy since the name sounded Russian. Jill, Petrovich's name is Vladimir Petrovich. If it's the same guy, he is a former Soviet Navy captain who broke into a nuclear storage facility several years back at Murmansk. That's a shipyard." Kali gasped for air. "He took five pieces of a reactor core containing six kilograms of enriched uranium."

"Is there any connection to LSA or David?" Jill whispered, looking through the grate at the uninterested people.

"Well, when I first ran the name, there were over six hundred and fifty responses to Petrovich. But when I added anything with nuclear weapon jargon, I came up with five, and then when I added Kushka, this is the only name that came up."

"He must be the one," Jill whispered excitedly. "Did you get any information on the town outside Kushka?"

"Does the name Towraghond sound familiar?"

"That's the name." Although this word sounded much different when spoken by a woman with a Western cowboy accent than by a little old Russian lady.

"Well, it's about twenty miles past the Turkmenistan border on the side of the mountain. It looks like a donkey trail. I heard they have wild donkeys there; have you seen any? Did you know that the donkeys came from Tennessee in the late eighties?"

Jill grunted at the trivia, a downside of any researcher.

"Never mind," said Kali, who got back on track. "The road is windy, but it looks like a car can drive on it. But a four-wheeler would be better. They have those over there?"

"Kali, focus."

"Right." Kali gave map coordinates. "Not that this will help you unless you have a GPS. You have a GPS out there?"

"No," Jill said between gritted teeth.

"Oh, and Jill, this guy is no boy scout. He was part of the Spetsnaz, the Soviet Special Forces, trained to operate and manage nuclear weapons. I don't get a good feeling from this, Jill. Do you think David was following a story about stolen nukes or something?"

"Not sure. Anyway, thanks; I'll call again soon."

She was about to hang up when Kali said, "Jill—" and hesitated. "Well, um, there is some bad news... well, you'll think it's bad anyway. It's about Matthew McGregor." Jill winced. "He's getting a book written about himself, and I got a call from the writer wanting to interview you. I thought it'd be better to tell you before you saw it on the news. Worst torturer of women before he killed them and all, ya know?"

There was silence for about thirty seconds while Jill wondered if Kali had just said that to her. "Crap, like I need this now," Jill responded ambivalently. And with that, Jill hung up and turned around, hoping no one had been listening. There was no sound of a typewriter, something you might expect in a typing shop. But nobody was looking her way. There was just the odd click-clack of the mouse and keyboard strokes. Jill figured the woman at the desk lifted her head more out of curiosity than suspicion.

Jill exited the shop; her eyes swept the street, and she noted no more headlights behind the café. Jill stood there unmoving. She was in over her head, and she knew it. Damn.

She needed a minute to review her thoughts about Petrovich, David, and what to do next. Jill moved to the closed shop doorway next to the typing shop.

She was no pushover. Well, at least not now, not after Matthew McGregor. Perplexed at what to do next, McGregor now inspired her. She tensed just thinking about those last few hours with him. He had drugged her, she thought, and for that, she was thankful. It distorted her memory of the truth. She closed her eyes and tried to see.

She had to go back to the dress shop. She could trust the old man. That much she knew. As she wandered around, careful not to draw attention, she thought of her belongings at the hotel. The hotel might be easy to get to with directions, but she couldn't risk being seen. It was bad enough that she involved the man in the dress shop. Kushka isn't that big, she thought. Her stuff would have to wait until she could return there, if at all. At least her laptop was impossible to crack. The fail-safe mechanism would erase her hard drive if anyone attempted to break in. Then she thought about her numbers. Her notebook.

The older man smiled when she walked in, oblivious to the danger surrounding her. She lifted off her burqa and smiled back. She walked over and held out five one-hundred-dollar bills. The man looked at the money and then up at Jill. She held the note in the other hand and said "Towraghond" as best as her American dialect would allow. "Driver, need a driver."

He didn't touch the money or the note; his eyes met hers as if searching for a hint of no good. He held up his hands, palms facing Jill—a clear signal for her to wait. Seconds later, he returned with his wife and pointed at the offering in Jill's hands. The old couple's native tongue filled the small shop with a debate. From what Jill could gauge by judging their body language, the older woman wanted the money. The old man was hesitant but relented, and the old lady shuffled out the back door. He shuffled over, and Jill pushed the money in his direction, gesturing that she would keep the cherished note as he motioned for her to sit on an old wooden chair next to the cash desk.

As she watched the old man fumble and fold clothes, her adrenaline began to ebb, and she found herself drifting from alertness to thinking of the past few hours, the past few days. It was the adrenaline that kept her tiredness at bay. Jill wanted to think of David, but thoughts of Zayed took over. Questions about what had happened at the café raced through her head. Who were those men at the café, and were they there for us or the money we paid the shadow man? There was no answer to her questions, just more questions.

The door of the shop jingled open. Jill looked up but did not move. She had put the burqa back on, so she was not too worried. But still, after what had just happened—the recognition of David's photo from the shadow man and the death of Zayed—she knew David had been here, and she was determined to find him. Screw you, McGregor, her mantra continued.

Ducking his head to get through the door, a tall yet stocky young man stepped in and closed the door behind him. He was wearing a dark brown vest over his pajamas.

The old man hurried over to the tall kid, grabbed both his arms, and pulled him close for a hug. The smiles on their faces displayed genuine happiness to see each other when the young man leaned in and touched his nose to the nose of the shrinking man. The similarity of their features, but noticeable age difference, suggested to Jill that these men were grandfather and grandson. Both men turned and walked toward her. As she began to stand, the older man's arms began to flail, and he shared the unusual story.

The tall kid nodded respect at Jill, then pointed his chubby finger to his chest and said, "Is me, Mohammed."

With relief, she replied, "Is me, Jill," and pointed back to herself. An accomplished smile lifted the kid's innocent face, and he motioned her to the door. He looked around outside, and Jill cautiously followed him out.

They moved to the side of the shop, where there was a small walkway between the store and the adjacent building. The alley was dark. Water glistened and trickled on the walls—the remains of someone dumping water from a wash bucket above. She followed him to an empty parking area past the building and over to an old white Toyota Corolla.

So much for the four-wheel drive Kali recommended for the donkey trail; as Jill approached the car, she could see rust holes covering its flank, and one look at the tires made her heart sink.

She pointed at the car and motioned with her hands clasped as if going over bumps. "Do you think the car will be okay?"

"Good, good," he beamed, doing a happy-go-lucky fist pump. "Strong, no problem." Without further hesitation, he signaled her to get into the backseat.

Leaving Kushka was speedy, with little to no traffic. They didn't pass the café on the way out, and after about four minutes of twists and turns, they were out of town and speeding along a gravel road. There were no streetlights on the back road, and ghostly specks of dust floated in front of the headlights. Jill bounced around in the backseat as the rattling car struggled to stay on the trail. She held on to the front passenger headrest, trying to keep steady. It was dark on both sides of the trail, making it impossible to see what was past the edge of the shoulder banks. Mohammed did his best to keep them on the road despite a few near misses when they came close to the edge of the unknown abyss. They passed no checkpoints, making it likely that few traveled this road.

Mohammed appeared nonchalant, driving to nowhere in the dark, and even he, with his size, bounced wildly.

Jill squinted through the abaya when Mohammed pointed at the dark shapes of buildings highlighted by the moon about a mile away. As the forms grew, it became apparent that the village they were traveling to was not a bustling community. They drove into a quiet village that appeared to have only one main road. Jill assumed it must have been close to midnight by then, and there was not one soul on the street. But this town was far from asleep. The town was deserted. Jill sighed. There were two-story, baby-blue-colored buildings on the right side of the road. The only things left in the cracked windows were broken, rusted air conditioners—an old dead tree rested by the steps, stretching up into the deserted shop's landing. One of the flats on the second floor was missing the broken air conditioner altogether.

A bent sign indicating a T intersection dangled on one screw at the end of the main street. Mohammed stopped at the sign, reached back his jumbo-sized hand, and said, "Paper," his tongue rolling on the 'r.' Jill was unsure if it would help him at this point as there were no street signs she could see, but she gave it to him anyway.

To their right was a dirt trail with several abandoned shanties. To their left, the road looked more traveled. Mohammed's door creaked open so he could use the interior light to read the note. He held it close to his face. Farsighted, she surmised. Mohammed closed the door, passed the note back to Jill, and looked around, lost. He decided to turn left. It was as good a choice as any. As they coasted along, Jill noticed something in the distance. About a mile up ahead was the glow of light. The weather had become foggy just before reaching the abandoned village, and Mohammed made another left and drove slowly up the road. He stopped when they saw the light and its origin. Mohammed quickly turned off the headlights and pulled into a field. The car sputtered when he shut down the engine. He did not bother to get out of the lopsided car. He only looked back at Jill, said, "Khalas," and pointed toward the light.

Jill sat quietly, trying to figure out her next move. Every three seconds or so, Mohammed's eyes flicked to hers in the rearview mirror.

Jill decided that whatever came next, she could do it in her clothes. "I need to get this damn thing off," she mumbled. Jill stepped out of the car; her boots crunched on the gravel. She stood behind the back door, lifted the heavy dress off, and tossed it into the backseat. She grabbed her black cap from her pocket and lowered it to her eyebrows. The rusted door creaked as she quietly clicked it shut. She stood motionless for a second and looked around. The air sent a chill through her body as she walked across the lonely road toward the light of the large villa. She felt for the gun, pulled it out of her pocket, and flicked open the clip. She wished she had checked how many rounds she had left when she had light. By her calculations, there should be around six rounds left. "Shit." She pushed the clip back in and pulled back the slide. Clasping the gun in both hands, she hastily crunched across the field toward the light. The place was littered with garbage. Several tires were strewn about, and a small plastic bag scurried across the hard sand in the gentle breeze and flapped when it got stuck on an abandoned car. Jill maneuvered her way toward the house. There was no sound except for a generator humming in the background.

Duck! Her intuition commanded. She crouched down fast and looked toward a dark pink cement house. Square lines and a large arched door held a small dome on its flat roof. Windows checkered the house, with floodlights from the yard bouncing off them. Jill looked up and could see that there was a figure on the rooftop. A bright red flicker deepened; the unknown roof man was sucking on a cigarette. Her feet were frozen to the ground. Jill quickly assessed his line of vision and decided she could see him, but he couldn't see her. He wasn't looking her way, and his stance was one of boredom. He must be guarding the house. Everyone must be asleep. Jill knew she was in over her head, and the slight shake of her hands confirmed this. What was she going to do? A lone USM in Afghanistan?

Hand-to-hand combat. Jill enjoyed this; she liked learning and practicing in the USM training and compliance program. To become a USM, it was only necessary to take the introductory unarmed course, which was rigorous. But after Jill's experience with Mr. Matthew, she wanted more training. She spent additional hours learning Muay Thai. And although the trainers knew she was female, they drove her hard. She had become an expert except for one little problem. She could fight well on the mats, but live with the bogeymen here? What was she supposed to do in this house? Was David being held against his will? What the hell was going on? If she stood any longer, she could not stop the list of endless questions. Jill had a choice. She was still alive, right? Move.

Jill crab-walked stealthily past the entrance to the fence and closed in on the house. Pressing her body against the building, she inched forward, stopped, and waited. She crept forward and then stopped and waited. Jill didn't hear anything but the fast pumping of her heart. She reached the front door, and what she saw made her instantly depressed.

The solid wood door leaned against the jamb, unattached. Some-one had beaten her to the place. She felt like she'd been punched in the stomach. Even with little illumination poured into the windows, it was evident that no one was in the house. Not tonight, anyway. No one had been in this house for some time, Jill thought as she stepped in and moved slowly down the hall. Why the hell is that watchman on the roof, then? He's guarding something... but what?

The shit smell pinched her nose shut from unused drains. Rays of dim light slowly guided her from one room to the next. She found the kitchen. It was small, with plastic cupboards and no appliances. Jill moved out of the room; her foot hit a tin lid. Jill jumped and froze with her back to the wall. The gun was now in both hands and leaned against her right cheek. She held her breath and listened. Did anyone hear me? She waited another moment, released her breath, and sucked in another. She looked up at a large winding staircase that twisted up to the second floor, expecting someone to come barreling down when the sound echoed. But no one came.

Jill tiptoed up the winding stairs, disturbing the dust. Twenty-five steps later, the generator's sound wheezed through an open window, and she reached the second floor. The curdled smell indicated no running water in the house, and the stench was almost unbearable. The stairs continued to a third floor, where the bored man watched. She had no idea how long he would be up there or what the hell he was watching over. Jill needed to search the rooms for something... anything that would help her find David.

As she peered into the last room on the second floor, she noticed it was furnished, unlike the other four empty rooms. The light from outside beamed onto a beat-up desk covered with yellowed papers in the corner. The room looked ransacked, and a surge of hope fueled her.

She swiftly approached the desk and began to rifle through the papers to find something she could understand. She uncrumpled one of the paper balls and saw that it had a drawing on it with Russian words. She folded it and put it in her pocket. She gazed around the dark room. Her eyes panned to the right. Wait! She panned back, and in the corner was a brown leather notebook, open-faced on the floor. She blinked several times and gasped. It was David's notebook! He had been here!

Jill quickly moved to the cluttered corner and picked it up. The world went silent. She lifted the notebook to the light coming through the window. She shoved the gun into her pocket. Her fingers brushed the familiar leather-laced binding. She began to falter when she sifted through the familiar pages, her face smiling back from the cover. Suddenly she felt faint and almost dropped the precious notebook.

She frantically went through the pages; some were torn out, and the ones left had nothing written. The wall's hardness braced her back as she slid to the floor. Her eyes stung as tears pooled. Jill was finally numb. She didn't feel the tears drop down her cheeks. She just sat in silence. She clutched a piece of David and tried to surrender. But something happened that she did not understand, something she couldn't register. She blinked back the remaining tears and chided, "Focus, Jill, focus."

A beam of light penetrated another pile of papers in the dark room. Jill pulled herself up slowly and zombie-walked over to see what they were. The glow had highlighted a yellowed folded newspaper. Jill picked it up and turned it over. She gasped and took a step back. On the back was a picture of someone she recognized. She closed her eyes, but when she opened them again, the figures in the photo were still there.

Stan Brown, David's father, stood shaking a man's hand. Another stood beside them. The paper was written in Russian, and the picture looked as if they were celebrating something. "What the..."

The slam of a door above jolted Jill so hard she almost dropped everything. Jill stuffed the paper and notebook into her shirt, pulled out her gun, and backed up against the wall behind the door. She could hear boots coming down the marble stairs rapidly. She did not move; she did not breathe. She could make out the hallway through the crack of the door jamb. She heard the man hit the landing, and he walked past the room where Jill hid with no hesitation in his steps. The door handle of the room opposite turned, and she could hear the door creak open. The sound of ruffled clothes followed, then a zip. Liquid noise hitting an empty bowl continued for at least thirty seconds, and the man sighed. Zip, ruffle, and he rapidly ascended back to the roof, slamming the door.

Jill heard herself sigh. She needed to get out of there, and now. She took one last look around for anything recognizable, then slipped down the stairs and backed out the broken door.

Outside, Jill looked around and then up. She could not see the guard, and there were no sounds other than the generator. The lights were now her enemy, and Jill contemplated what to do. She had no choice, really. She must make a run for it across the lit courtyard. One deep breath, and she moved to the edge of the gate and slithered around it. She stopped, looking upward in the direction of the guard. He was not there. She waited. Did he hear her leaving? Was he following her? Nothing. No sounds. Nothing. Jill turned and headed toward the car. She stayed close to the solid cement fence that surrounded the other villas. When the lit villa was out of view, she ran across the dirt plot toward the car.

At the end of the lane, Jill could see Mohammed waiting. His king-sized thumbs tapped the top of the steering wheel, fidgeting. Mohammed smiled innocently, and as soon as she got in, he swiftly revved the engine and pulled a U-turn to head back to Kushka. As they quietly left the abandoned town, Jill held the notebook on her lap and thought of David.

Jill remembered the day she had given him the notebook. He had just finished a highly reviewed story on Maslamberg, located two hours outside Chicago, a suspected Al Qaeda training encampment. The smile on his face broadened when Jill pushed the present across the table. It was garnished with a bright red ribbon. A quirky look followed when he saw the picture she pasted onto the inside cover. They had not yet told each other, "I love you." They didn't have to; they knew. David said, "Must be love!" as he lifted his glass of Cab Sav to toast. "Must be love," Jill repeated as they clinked glasses...

The pain in her heart tugged. Why is there a picture of David's father, of all people, on the floor where David was supposed to be? Especially since it was halfway around the world from Texas? Jill had known David's dad had some international contracts, given that he was in the oil and gas pipeline business. Jill was back in the tunnels but could not pull up the file on precisely what David's dad did in that industry. He was always vague about it. She knew this couldn't be a coincidence, as there was no such thing as coincidences, not to this degree anyway. Just as Jill was about to pull up another memory file, the lights of Kushka appeared and guided their descent on the rough, hilly road. Mohammed kept looking back at her; his dark eyes were concerned. Jill's eyes looked dead. It was all she could do to stop letting go when she said to Mohammed, "Vodka?"

Before they crossed into the village's light, Mohammed turned a sharp right, then up a side road to a shanty. A light indicated someone lived in the tin walls held up by two pieces of slanting lumber. Mohammed came back with a bottle of white fire. As he passed the bottle, Jill tried to give a half-baked smile. She placed the warm bottle inside her jacket. With utter despair and not so much as a care, a question entered her brain. I wonder where I will be able to sleep. The memory of the hotel room made her cringe.

As if reading her mind, Mohammed pulled up to the dress shop. He motioned for her to get out of the car. "Come," he said with a smile. She looked down at the abaya crumpled on the backseat. The void streets decided for her. She gathered the abaya into a ball and exited the car. It was too late to wake the old man and his wife, but she needed to translate the newspaper.

Mohammed unlocked the door, and they both entered the gloomy shop. The dead air hit hard. She followed him through the forest of clothes to the back of the shop. He opened the door to a makeshift office with a small cot in the corner. Lighting a candle on the desk, he pointed to the cot. His kind grin outlined the word khalas, and softly closed the door.

The quaint room comforted Jill, for at last, she was alone, and somehow, for the first time on the trip, she felt safe. The brief comfort dissipated when she thought of the notebook and when she thought of David. The candle flickered on the firewater as she placed it on the desk as if enticing herself to drink. She moved the folded clothes stacked on the small cot and spread the abaya. There was no pillow, and she didn't care at this point.

Bitterness hit her stomach when she leaned over and grabbed the bottle. She took a deep breath, unscrewed the cap, and chugged a gulp of hot hell. She almost gagged at the taste but forced it down anyway. And then another chug. The candle lit up the room, and Jill pulled the newspaper and notebook from her pocket. She picked up the bottle and put it back down. She suddenly felt exhausted and laid down on the spindly cot, boots still on. She held up the newspaper article and studied it. The shadow of the candle danced in the background as she looked at the picture of David's father. The delight on his face was notable. She put the paper beside her on the bed and placed David's notebook on its side so she could look at her picture, hoping to feel somehow closer to him. Hoping he was okay. The face in front of Jill began to blur. As her body became heavy, she read the words below her picture:

Remembering our honeymoon, Love Jill....

She didn't notice the extra dot when she faded into the night.

CHAPTER SIXTEEN

02:40 Zulu Time—Kushka, Afghanistan

Sitting around a fire, I see my grandparents swaying. Their eyes are closed, and the hum of meditation fills my ears. My grandmother sits holding the small leather pouch. Beside her is my mother. My body begins to sway as the hum's pitch changes.

The sound of movement in the other room woke Jill. Startled, she bolted upright, nearly knocking over the vodka. The candle was out now, and a sliver of light yawned through the window. Rubbing the sleep from her eyes, she spotted the clock on the nearby desk. 07:10. Jill laid back down, realizing it was nothing but the older man shuffling around the shop, staring at the stained ceiling. She thought of David's notebook and yearned for hers. She always had the best revelations in the morning.

"I have to get my stuff back, and I need to get out of this hellhole," she told herself. "What the hell am I going to do?" Her body posture was one of despair. Lying on the bed, defeated, Jill didn't know where she would go or what she would do next. She needed to jot down her vision. "Again, my family," she whispered. "But why? And why did the hum pitch change?"

Depression crept in now. She had slept all night clutching the notebook. She held it up in front of her. The cover fell open, and she saw herself again. Opening the cover up, she focused her tired eyes on what she read. As she studied the words written below her photo, she blinked. Then hope filled her soul. She could not believe the joy that began to infiltrate her being. Suddenly, she sat straight up and opened the makeshift curtain that hung above the bed. Light splashed clarity to the page. She couldn't breathe. In awe, Jill again examined the notebook and reread what was written below her photograph. It was still there; the words were still there! I never wrote this. I never wrote this. David must be alive! She gasped and said to fill the void in the air, "David is in Hamburg, Germany."

Jill looked back at the notebook; her finger traced the words. David must have written this, but the handwriting was not his. She assumed he had disguised it. But why would he need to do that? Uncontrollably excited for the first time since leaving home behind, Jill heard a rooster crow good morning, and it felt good.

Thoughts gushed in when she thought of Hamburg. David often joked that their trip to Hamburg was their honeymoon. In fact, it was a short assignment where he had to interview the ambassador for a story he was doing on capturing Al Qaeda members with connections to 9/11. Shortly after they got married, Jill had some time off, so she joined him on the trip. Even though the trip was brief, it was one of her favorite memories. Hamburg was breathtakingly beautiful. She remembered when they sat on the patio at the harbor by the river Elbe as the red sunset. How they laughed and chatted as newlyweds often do. They didn't leave the hotel much when David wasn't working. They just lounged and loved.

She regained what composure she could and creaked open the door. Hoping not to see anyone but the old man, she gazed into the store. He was sweeping the floor as the sun started to peek through the hung dresses in the window.

"Good morning," Jill said, and he turned and nodded. His acceptance relieved her.

Jill walked toward him. She pulled out one thousand US dollars and said to him, "Need to go to Kabul." He looked at the money and then at Jill and nodded. Mohammed must have reported that she was safe to be around. But safety is all in how you present it, she thought to herself. She held out the newspaper and asked him to have his wife read it.

"La la, no," the old man said. "Gone to town far, to sister." Disappointed, Jill realized she would have to wait to learn more about the newspaper article. She must get to Kabul airport and then to Hamburg. The article could wait, she decided as she stuffed it into her jacket pocket and turned back into the small room.

Out of the blue, Jill thought about Zayed and wondered if there was anything she should do. She didn't even know his real name to contact his family to make arrangements for his body. After all, it was the right thing to do. That's not feasible, she calculated fast in her head. Not possible at all, she tried to negotiate with herself.

Jill thought of her notebook and precious but limited possessions at the hotel. She needed her laptop and, most importantly, her numbers. After discovering David's notebook, she knew he had to be in danger. She had decided the night before that she would have to find a quiet place with her numbers, and she was damn determined to Remote View. Screw you, Matthew McGregor. The cot squeaked as she sat down on it. She sat silently and thought about the guarded villa, wondering again what the watchman was guarding at a seemingly vacant site. Perhaps she could have Mohammed drive her past the hotel and see if anything looked suspicious.

Nope, she couldn't forgive herself if he got hurt. She'd go herself, and now was a good time. After all, it was daytime with plenty of light to expose anything dangerous. She stood up, walked over to the window, brushed aside the curtain, and tried to get a feel for Kushka.

"Those Russian voices at the café, the Chechen Mafia in Doha, the Russian newspaper article with Stan Brown. What do they have to do with David?" Dust drifted past her nose when she dropped the curtain, and it flounced closed. She needed her numbers, and she needed her notebook—she needed David. And there was only one answer. She must go back to the hotel. One plus one equals two. The calculation was over.

Pulling the wrinkled abaya off the small cot, she pulled it over her head, covered her face again, adjusted, and strode into the stuffed shop. The shrunken man was still sweeping, and when he noticed her, he smiled.

"Mohammed coming, he coming."

Jill said, "No problem. Hotel, where hotel?" Jill walked toward the door. The older man shuffled over to Jill, looked at her eyes through the burqa, then looked out the door window. After a series of lefts, rights, and roundabouts in broken English and hand gestures, Jill seemed to understand where her hotel was. She explained as best she could to have Mohammed wait for her at the dress shop and jingled out the door.

Am I dumb? Jill asked herself. I am in disguise, so I should be able to get into the room. Somehow. She continued trying to reason herself forward. What will I do at the hotel? That was the only question tapping annoyingly on Jill's left lobe. Zayed had the only key, and she was sure he probably didn't use their real names at check-in. She turned left, then into a back alley, then right. She couldn't imagine that they cleared her things out yet, and it was apparent the room didn't get a daily cleaning service. She would have to break in or ask for the key.

After twenty minutes, Jill made a last scheduled left, and the hotel was on her right, about a hundred meters further up. Jill stopped and began her scan. There wasn't much to see on the street. An old, bony man sat on a chair, mumbling while looking at the ground. Across from the hotel was a large field and a small wooden structure. Jill surmised that someone could be hiding in it, and she kept her eye on it as she approached the hotel. Again, she glanced back at it and then back to the hotel. As she approached the structure, she saw a man lying inside. Jill's pace slowed as she tried to distinguish any recognition. He didn't move as she walked by, so she stopped briefly and stared in his direction. What was he doing? The wooden structure looked like a giant covered bed with a bright blue mattress squashed under the man. He was sleeping. Was this his home? Jill decided he was not a threat and continued slowly up the steps and into the hotel. When she entered, Jill determined it was not a hotel but a makeshift office building that had been converted. That's probably why it only had two rooms with a toilet.

She walked past the unaware clerks and down the hall toward her room. Why haven't they noticed me? she wondered. A quick right, and she nearly mowed down the little Indian houseboy before she saw his belt of keys. "Yalla yalla," Jill yelled at the houseboy. She had heard this phrase in Abu Dhabi where a robed woman was trying to get her children's attention at the airport. He watched as Jill lifted her hand palm and touched her fingers together twice, then pointed to the door, mimicking Zayed. "Key," she said abruptly as if he were her slave. The little houseboy trembled ever so slightly while he thumbed through his lanyard of keys. He unlocked the door, bowed slightly, and his head bobbled when he cupped his hands behind his back and backed away.

Inside, the room looked the same. But somehow, it seemed dirtier with the daylight beaming through the window.

Zayed had taken his pack, but the large black duffel was still on the bed. She rummaged inside the geocache only to find a map and nothing more. She didn't recall Zayed taking the grenades. Zayed. She pushed him to the back recesses of her brain, quickly grabbed her carry-on, and glanced inside at her treasures. All clear. She left the hotel.

CHAPTER SEVENTEEN

09:11 Zulu Time—En Route to Kabul

The journey to Kabul was quiet since Mohammed didn't speak much English. For Jill, it seemed easier than going to Kushka. The security guards accepted cash from Mohammed and still waved them through, even without the presence of vodka. The car had no air conditioning, so they sweated in harmony.

The clock on the dash said 13:41. Jill wondered if it was correct. She glanced over at her carry-on and thought of David. Dancing thoughts darted in all directions. She reached in, pulled out her notebook, and reviewed her notes. Why Hamburg, David? Did his big story have something to do with those 9/11 terrorists? Jill knew Hamburg was a thoroughfare for terrorist safe houses. At this point, that was all she knew.

She stared out the window, then back at the notes, then returned her gaze to the view. Jill's foot tapped when she tried the tunnels, but this time nothing. Her hand sank back into the carry-on, and she pulled out the old tattered pouch, paused, and eyed Mohammed, who was studying the road. Looking back at the notebook, she opened it to a blank page dated several days before and placed it on the seat. Where is David? Jill projected. Untying the pouch, Jill juggled the clay numbers on her lap. "Where is David?" she whispered loud enough that Mohammed took a shy glance through the rearview mirror back at her and then hastily back at the road.

She hummed inwardly, then stared at the numbers, moving them zombie-like on her lap. Jill could feel herself entering the vortex of peace. If she thought of McGregor, she did not know it. She was determined to overcome her fear and anxiety of facing him again. After what seemed to be many miles flying past, Jill wrote the number 2762, and then after a few more miles, her hand began to scribble. She began to write phonetically what she heard and what she tasted. Then she wrote how she felt. Hum. She was in stage three now as the scratch of the pen on the paper was frantically sketching.

The car lurched to the right when an old pickup truck roared past, bringing Jill back to this location, the unconscious to the conscious. It was called bi-location. A moment when the Viewer was in two places at one time. Like being unstuck in time without going anywhere.

She blinked. Mohammed was doing his best in the rattletrap to get them to Kabul. She adjusted herself and looked down at the notebook. She examined what she had just drawn. It was something she had seen before. It was a star. Not just any star. Scribbled in black ink before her eyes was the Star of David. Beside her sketch, she read the words: Wood. Cold. Pretty. Doom. Then she saw something strange. Underneath, Jill had written the word "Ochrana."

The airport looked even grimmer than she had remembered from only two days before. It was almost midnight now. She thanked Mohammed. She had wrapped the gun in a plastic bag, and when she got out, she motioned Mohammed to open the trunk. As she placed the gun down, she opened the bag slightly and gestured for Mohammed to look. His only word was "Shokran. Thank you." He blushed, sheepishly smiled, got back into the car, and rattled away.

Upon entering the airport, she found a bathroom and gratefully removed the hot abaya. Jill felt more at ease not having to think about sticking out like a sore thumb in upper rubber-boot Afghanistan.

The check-in clerk advised her that although the next flight was in less than one hour, it would take over twelve hours to get from Kabul to Hamburg. Even more troubling was that she was headed to Baku in Azerbaijan, both places she had never been to before. Jill questioned the clerk further to find out where Azerbaijan was. Through broken English, the clerk explained that it was on the other side of Iran, near the Caspian Sea. She made a mental note to learn more about that part of Eastern Europe. Jill looked at her tickets and confirmed what the clerk had attempted to tell her: after Azerbaijan was a two-hour stop in Vienna, Austria, and then on to Germany some twelve hours later.

"Jill, you're in Germany?" Eric said excitedly into the receiver. She looked around the airport. People were bustling to catch their planes, the rain was sliding down the large-paned windows, and German was being spoken into the PA as she stood at the payphone.

"Yes, I'm in Hamburg."

"Well, I'm glad you're okay," he said. "Kali told me you have some information on David's whereabouts."

"Well, it's more of a hunch than anything right now, but I feel he may be here in Hamburg. I..."

"Jill," Eric interrupted. "We have been working closely with the GSG 9 der Bundespolizei. You know, the counter-terrorism unit of the German Federal Police. You remember the unit over there?"

"Yes, how could I not? They're considered one of the best counter-terrorism units in the world. Kali said they think Petrovich is now in the US?"

"Or still in Germany," Eric said firmly. For a second, they both were silent. "We don't know for sure, but I have a close acquaintance at

GSG. Johan Rhein. I met him at an anti-money laundering conference in London several months ago. He has a team working on the Petrovich file. I'll get Johan on the private line and tell him I've got the agent following a lead on Petrovich on the line. That will get his attention. Jill, did you find anything out about Petrovich?" he queried. Then he interrupted with, "Standby, Jill."

"Guten Tag," Eric said to Johan. "Yes, she's on the other line now, and Johan, she hasn't briefed me why yet, but Jill has just landed in Hamburg. Yes. Okay, standby, Johan." Eric resumed talking to Jill. "Jill, he said he wanted to debrief you regarding Petrovich. Johan said he could send a car to pick you up. Since it's official business, he offered for his department to foot the bill for a hotel."

"Danke," Eric said, thanking Johan, and he hung up. The line muffled, then Eric came back. "Jill?"

"Yeah, I'm here," she said wearily. "I didn't really find out any information on Petrovich, Eric. But I'd appreciate any help on the ground here. This may sound over-the-top, but would they let me use some of their resources?"

"To locate David?" he asked. Jill told Eric about the ambush, about Zayed and his death.

"I wonder why, when shown the picture of David, you got the name Petrovich?" he asked. "What makes you think David is in Hamburg?" He seemed perplexed, but still, he considered the possibility when Jill told him about the written line in David's notebook.

"I think he was sending me a message," she said, full of hope.

Suddenly Jill felt a bit uneasy and turned to look around. Many people were moving about the airport. She studied her surroundings, and she found the cause of her uneasiness. A man was standing, dressed in black pants and a black turtleneck. He stood about one hundred feet away from Jill and stared at her. There was something sinister in his stance. Jill stared back, and the man looked away. "Eric, this isn't a secure line. I'll try to get one when I meet with Johan to give you more details."

"Is everything okay, Jill?" he queried. She turned around to look at the man, but he was gone.

"Yeah, you'll understand when I call you back." Jill didn't want to tell Eric she viewed it. Well, not now, anyway. She thought of the star she had drawn and the strange word below it. Kali and I will make this our little secret.

Eric gave Jill the details of the driver coming to pick her up. "Johan said he had someone close to the airport. He should be there by now, Jill."

"Thanks; I appreciate all the help I can get. Will they give me a security clearance?"

Borderline annoyed, Eric said, "I'm sure they will give you what they can, within reason, Jill. I'll arrange clearance for you there. Who would have expected you to be back on the job but in a different country?"

Jill hung up. His last comment resonated with her. What the hell, back on the job? She did another scan—no sign of the staring man—and walked across the terminal into the rain. The smell was fresh coolness. It wasn't long before a car and the driver pulled up, and a sign saying "Oliver" was shoved under the windshield wiper.

The man was dressed in slick charcoal Armani, guiding her out of the rain into a small black Audi sedan. A little chilled, Jill sat as the driver sped away from the airport. Looking past the rain-covered windshield and fast-moving wipers, she couldn't help but feel she was somehow closer to David than she had been in the past week. The lump in her stomach had faded, or maybe she was just used to it now. She missed him immensely, and she couldn't help but feel sad.

Reading the note given to her by the driver, it had specific instructions to be ready three hours from now, at nineteen hundred local, to
provide her with a briefing on Petrovich. Works both ways. Jill was
thankful to find a shower and perhaps some clean clothes, hopefully.
The smell of airplanes still permeated her skin, and a hot shower would
be like a long-awaited orgasm. She closed her tired eyes for only a brief
moment and thought of the word Ochrana.

CHAPTER EIGHTEEN

13:43 Zulu Time—Hamburg, Germany

Rain streamed down the oval window of the plane as it landed in Hamburg, and the pilot stated over the PA system that it was 15:43. It looked the same as it did when David and Jill were last there. She welcomed the rain and wondered what the temperature was since the captain did not say this in his last PA—not in English, anyway.

The flight out of Kabul had Jill on an airplane similar to a Boeing 727. It was old and rattled, but it was clean. Even so, she was happy to sleep most of the way. Vienna was a blur of waiting people, and it felt good to be in Hamburg, at least half-rested anyway. Hamburg airport felt safe and civilized. Feeling blessed that the airport had all the amenities she had missed this past week, she approached a gift shop. Her first quest was to find a calling card and contact Kali; she should just be getting to the office now if Jill calculated right. She walked directly over to the private phone booth, sat down, and dialed the extra-long calling card numbers on the back of the red card.

"I am glad you finally called in! Where are you, and what is going on?" Kali asked excitedly.

"I'm all right," Jill said, then updated her on her latest activities. "And Kali, I found David's notebook."

There was a pause. "You mean, the one... Jill, news has broken out confirming that the missing reporter is David." Jill's heart sank. "CNN is sending a team over to Doha to catch up to Time, who are already on the ground scouting for any new information on his whereabouts. It doesn't sound like there is much in the way of leads for them. They've called here several times a day for you, Jill. We keep telling them you have no comment."

"Shit," Jill said. Her heart began to hurt. "Kali, I think I've stumbled across a message from David. It's in the notebook."

Jill described the verse to her, and Kali asked, "Honeymoon, but you..."

"He means Hamburg, Kali. I am in Hamburg."

"You mean Germany; God bless. I have a lot more questions. While you were out of touch, we have followed any intel on this Petrovich. You're not going to believe this, Jill. Hang on to your hat. It turns out the German police GSG has sent out a bulletin about the former Russian. It came from Eric's office. I called Eric to tell him you had asked me to pull information on the same guy. Jill, you need to speak to Eric. He has assembled a team to review the case because the Germans think this terrorist may be in the US. Stand by, and I will transfer you to him. Don't you think it is strange, Jill, that you are in Germany too? I guess you are right. David must be there."

"Jill, you're in Germany?" Eric said excitedly into the receiver. She looked around the airport. People were bustling to catch their planes, the rain was sliding down the large-paned windows, and German was being spoken into the PA as she stood at the payphone.

"Yes, I'm in Hamburg."

"Well, I'm glad you're okay," he said. "Kali told me you have some information on David's whereabouts."

"Well, it's more of a hunch than anything right now, but I feel he may be here in Hamburg. I..."

"Jill," Eric interrupted. "We have been working closely with the GSG 9 der Bundespolizei. You know, the counter-terrorism unit of the German Federal Police. You remember the unit over there?"

"Yes, how could I not? They're considered one of the best counter-terrorism units in the world. Kali said they think Petrovich is now in the US?"

"Or still in Germany," Eric said firmly. For a second, they both were silent. "We don't know for sure, but I have a close acquaintance at GSG. Johan Rhein. I met him at an anti-money laundering conference in London several months ago. He has a team working on the Petrovich file. I'll get Johan on the private line and tell him I've got the agent following a lead on Petrovich on the line. That will get his attention. Jill, did you find anything out about Petrovich?" he queried. Then he interrupted with, "Standby, Jill."

"Guten Tag," Eric said to Johan. "Yes, she's on the other line now, and Johan, she hasn't briefed me why yet, but Jill has just landed in Hamburg. Yes. Okay, standby, Johan." Eric resumed talking to Jill. "Jill, he said he wanted to debrief you regarding Petrovich. Johan said he could send a car to pick you up. Since it's official business, he offered for his department to foot the bill for a hotel."

"Danke," Eric said, thanking Johan, and he hung up. The line muffled, then Eric came back. "Jill?"

"Yeah, I'm here," she said wearily. "I didn't really find out any information on Petrovich, Eric. But I'd appreciate any help on the ground here. This may sound over-the-top, but would they let me use some of their resources?"

"To locate David?" he asked. Jill told Eric about the ambush, about Zayed and his death.

"I wonder why, when shown the picture of David, you got the name Petrovich?" he asked. "What makes you think David is in Hamburg?" He seemed perplexed, but still, he considered the possibility when Jill told him about the written line in David's notebook.

"I think he was sending me a message," she said, full of hope.

Suddenly Jill felt a bit uneasy and turned to look around. Many people were moving about the airport. She studied her surroundings, and she found the cause of her uneasiness. A man was standing, dressed in black pants and a black turtleneck. He stood about one hundred feet away from Jill and stared at her. There was something sinister in his stance. Jill stared back, and the man looked away. "Eric, this isn't a secure line. I'll try to get one when I meet with Johan to give you more details."

"Is everything okay, Jill?" he queried. She turned around to look at the man, but he was gone.

"Yeah, you'll understand when I call you back." Jill didn't want to tell Eric she viewed it. Well, not now, anyway. She thought of the star she had drawn and the strange word below it. Kali and I will make this our little secret.

Eric gave Jill the details of the driver coming to pick her up. "Johan said he had someone close to the airport. He should be there by now, Jill."

"Thanks; I appreciate all the help I can get. Will they give me a security clearance?"

Borderline annoyed, Eric said, "I'm sure they will give you what they can, within reason, Jill. I'll arrange clearance for you there. Who would have expected you to be back on the job but in a different country?"

Jill hung up. His last comment resonated with her. What the hell, back on the job? She did another scan—no sign of the staring man—and walked across the terminal into the rain. The smell was fresh coolness. It wasn't long before a car and the driver pulled up, and a sign saying "Oliver" was shoved under the windshield wiper.

The man was dressed in slick charcoal Armani, guiding her out of the rain into a small black Audi sedan. A little chilled, Jill sat as the driver sped away from the airport. Looking past the rain-covered windshield and fast-moving wipers, she couldn't help but feel she was somehow closer to David than she had been in the past week. The lump in her stomach had faded, or maybe she was just used to it now. She missed him immensely, and she couldn't help but feel sad.

Reading the note given to her by the driver, it had specific instructions to be ready three hours from now, at nineteen hundred local, to provide her with a briefing on Petrovich. Works both ways. Jill was thankful to find a shower and perhaps some clean clothes, hopefully. The smell of airplanes still permeated her skin, and a hot shower would be like a long-awaited orgasm. She closed her tired eyes for only a brief moment and thought of the word Ochrana.

CHAPTER NINETEEN

15:27 Zulu Time—Hamburg, Germany

The room at the hotel was sparsely decorated—small but clean, and it warmed her from the chill outside. The European walls were uniquely tailored in teak lines with black and silver grout. The room doubled as a mini-office equipped with a computer and printer. The clock blinked 16:27. The bed was more straightforward than the beautiful comfy one in the obscure upscale Moroccan-style hotel in Kabul. This bed looked tightly made, and a starch smell perked Jill's nose when she sat on it and laid down her carry-on.

She walked into the bathroom and sighed with delight. It was a stark difference from the dark room where the bed and office were. Baby-blue walls surrounded a large stainless steel Jacuzzi in one corner and an oversized shower stall in the opposite corner. Stainless steel bowl sinks sat atop white marble. Fluffy towels were rolled up in tight tubes and piled neatly on the shelf that divided the shower from the tub. Jill glanced in the mirror and saw the effects of sleep deprivation on her tired face.

Back at the desk, Jill placed the German mobile phone the driver had given her beside the computer and lifted the side of the printer. She was pleased to see a scanner. Undecided at first as to whether to take a shower or continue in her current condition, Jill knew she would not regret her decision.

After twenty minutes of hot rain massaging her muscles, she dressed in the thick cotton robe and headed to the mini-office. On the way, she stopped and opened the mini-bar. There was no scotch, just the usual beer, wine, and soft drinks; somehow, she felt relieved. As the computer warmed to life, she called the hotel for express cleaning of her clothes.

Jill unfolded the article she had taken from the abandoned house in the hills of Kushka. She stared again at the picture of Stan Brown. She had analyzed this several times since she recovered it, still asking the same questions: What are you up to, Stan? Why is the article in the same place as David's notebook? Why was it in the middle of nowhere in the same location as a lead to Petrovich? What are you up to, Mr. Brown? She was determined to find the answers.

Too restless to sleep and hopeful to rest, she opened her laptop and fed it some juice. The desk was equipped with a wattage adapter for North America. Jill checked her emails and then prepped the printer to scan. The brush of light studied the article and the schematic drawing she had found in the abandoned house, and she sent them off to Kali to translate. No emails from David, but there was one from Leila:

Where are you, Jill? Call me. L

Jill glanced at the time, thinking of calling Leila. But she needed information about Stan Brown, and she needed it now. She needed to understand what the hell was going on. Leila, my friend, you'll have to wait. Jill Googled the search term that had nagged her on this last leg of her trip:

"Stan Brown Russia Afghanistan." Putting these words in quotes would narrow down the search results.

Most of what she found about Stan was small news clips and website content reiterating what she already knew about him—an oil man from Texas. There were several articles about a fight he was having with regulatory bodies about increasing standards, which would cost his business a significant amount of money, and how US companies were forbidden to hire slave labor, even if the work was being done outside of the US.

Jill leaned back in her chair, pulled the plush towel from her head, and threw it onto the couch. She began to flick at her spiked hair as she mused how Stan always seemed to find himself in the thick of things. Narcissistic was his method as a husband and a father. Jill remembered him bragging about a frivolous run-in with a waiter in a restaurant. The waiter accidentally spilled a glass of red wine all over David's mother, who was wearing a crisp white pantsuit. David's father took offense to such a substantial degree that he had the waiter fired.

David's mother always backed up Stan's ridiculous actions. She managed to imitate Stan's arrogant attitude, likely due to being married to a man of great wealth for so long. She did not care for basic humanity; that was Jill's impression, anyway. Her body and face displayed a woman trying to be much younger than she was. Being around either of them was hard, as common sense was the missing ingredient in any discussion. Or was it morality? Talk always revolved around money. For Jill, money was just a means to exist. Jill thrived on helping others and saving others. Ironically, Jill's career ultimately would save David's parents if there were any incidents in the US. If she did her job well, that is. Jill's and David's family were like oil and water. She often wondered why David was so different from them.

The secure mobile phone rang as she clicked through all of the propaganda. "Jill, it's Kali. I got that article translated and am waiting for that drawing, but I wanted to call you and let you know I sent it to your VPN account. Jill, it wasn't in Russian, as you had thought. The article was written in German. The schematics, though, are in Russian, so it's taking longer to translate. I am working on the logistics of you assisting GSG, and I think I can get your airfare covered too."

"Thanks, Kali," Jill replied, but she wasn't interested in that right now. "Can you research any companies or groups that use the Star of David as a logo? Can you also correlate this with David's name, and for that matter, Stan Brown?" Jill said, all business. Kali would never get offended by this. She knew her job, she knew her place, and still, they remained good friends.

"What's this Star of David?" Kali queried.

"Just a hunch," Jill replied, remembering her oath.

"I don't like when you get those types of hunches."

"Also, Kali, the name Ochrana. See what you can find on it. Cross-check everything with Petrovich. Okay?"

"Ochrana, what the heck kind of name is Ochrana?"

After a brief goodbye, Jill hung up, logged in, and downloaded the transcribed text. The article chronicled a contract awarded to Stan's company, Marksman Oil, LLC. It was for an oil pipeline between Turkmenistan and Pakistan that ran through Afghanistan. Many oil companies from the US were involved in oil production in the Middle East. That would explain why he would be in this article. But why was it in German? She half-heartedly supposed that it would be news for Germany, given its political position on the US-occupied forces in Afghanistan. After all, the article was written from a negative point of view. "US contractor receives a reward while American troops continue to keep the peace in the country." Yadda, yadda, yadda.

From Jill's involvement in profiling and with all the 9/11 terrorists coming from the Middle East, she knew parts of the area were very corrupt. Even the recent trilateral meetings were frayed by the current

US drone attacks on deep tribal regions of Pakistan. Contracts were not just given without some under-the-table negotiations—not in today's climate, anyway. There was also blood money, which exchanged hands regularly and financed the extortion of oil companies when their employees ended up in a desert jail for being drunk in public or flipping the bird.

Stan would fit right into such a place, Jill thought. David sometimes called him an "evil little ferret of a man." David didn't care; after all, he did not want to be a puppet in Stan's little show, and Jill had to agree. But she knew in her heart that Stan must love his son. Blood is thicker than water and all. And if he had any information about David, surely he would tell her. Surely?

She typed "Star of David + David Brown" in quotes in Google. Nothing. She typed "Star of David + Stan Brown" into quotes. Nothing. "Shit." She'd have to wait for Kali. She picked up her notebook and plopped herself down on the lime-green couch. Germans, she thought, feeling how uncomfortable the hard couch was.

When she opened her notebook, the Star of David tried to speak, but her sketch had no voice. Jill flipped through the tattered notebook, came across one of her mind maps, and noticed the word "Family" circled. Is the Star of David symbol a coincidence, even though David bore the same name? Jill jumped off the couch and headed to her laptop.

Without further hesitation, she picked up her mobile phone and dialed. Voice mail. "Stan, this is Jill. By now, you must have heard the news about David. I need to speak to you urgently. I am in Hamburg, Germany." She left the number at the hotel.

She walked over to the bed, pulled the leather pouch from her bag, and then sat back on the firm couch. Her heart was mixed with excitement and apprehension by the time she had the clay numbers displayed. "Star Gate," Jill said aloud. It was the CIA Star Gate project; she learned during her training at the RV department at the FBI. They attempted to teach Jill that her ability was more scientific than clairvoyant. With all intel gathered by the intelligence research department—the ones that spent countless hours sifting through endless streams of data—and now with RV, data was to be verified by more than one source. While the SGP attempted to justify that the science of RV was authentic, all it did was invoke what they called the "giggle factor."

But Jill knew differently. From an early age, with her grandparents' teachings, she knew what she could do was very real, and most times, no giggles were involved. It sometimes kept her awake at night. She remembered when she saw herself walking in her town, deciding whether to cross a desolate rocky area where a dried-up riverbank was. She was late that day and didn't want Grandpapa to worry. He always worried too much.

The day after her vision, Jill, all twelve years old, was late for a playdate with her friend. She knew she could cross the dark shrubby area easily. She'd done it numerous times, but not at this late hour. So she stood at the edge. It was dark out, and she was about to step into the abyss when she saw headlights. It was Grandpapa. Jill felt relieved that he had come to look for her. Then the very next day, the news spread quickly all over town. A boy, eleven years old, was stabbed to death in the exact place where Jill was headed. She didn't quite understand her gift at that age, but she knew now that SGP would not change who she was and would become.

The RV department had helped her to understand her gift and contain it. Now she was more determined than ever to use it again. If it took a hundred Remote Viewing sessions, she would do it. She was going to find David, and she was going to do it now. She wanted to harness her gift in this Remote Viewing session. She was damn determined to let it all go. Fly.

As a human, your brain thinks about petting a dog before you actually do it; the truth is in virtually everything that humans do. Now, as Jill sat, she swayed; she chanted. Her chant was simple. "Oooommmmm, David, oo oom mmmm, where are you, David?" More chanting, and then, without skipping a beat, deep in trance, Jill whispered, "Ochrana."

CHAPTER TWENTY

The fat man stood in his long white gown in a circle of replicates of himself. His head was tilted downward as he stared at what appeared to be an old Star of David on the floor. The hum of low voices filled the dark room like an eerie men's choir. The putrid smell of incense floated around them. The men did not exchange glances during this time; all gazed upon the star carved into the old wooden floor. After a time, the chanting abruptly stopped, and they chanted a word in unison: "Ochrana."

The arrogance in the room shifted from calmness to loud slapping on each other's backs and odd handshaking. Voices began. Hellos, in a strange "Hail Mary" sort of way. Robotic:

"How are you? Good. How are you?"

"How are you? Good. How are you?"

Six men moved around each other, careful not to step on the symbol on the ground, and one by one, they walked through a dark door and up several creaking wooden steps into a meeting area. Careful camaraderie bounced around as they disrobed and placed the black cloaks in six separate wooden boxes on the wall. The hinges scraped like fingernails on a chalkboard as they shut the doors.

The elected leader, a fat man, took his spot at the head of a table. "Sit, please sit," his gravelly voice commanded, moving his arms outward in reception. The dark green room featured dim lights highlighting the dark pine wooden table. The chairs chirped as the fat man's colleagues took their places around the table. To the fat man's right were two men who appeared to be of Eastern European descent. Slavic, of some sort. To his left, the first man was clearly of Arab descent, with his nose hooked down. The next, a wispy, grayed man sat ramrod straight in his chair. At the very left of the table was a bald man with dark skin.

"Gentlemen, we have our work cut out for us. As you know, Ochrana was set up to counter the Russians' hold on the oil back in the early nineteen hundreds. Today, as the only members left of Ochrana, we must focus on our target and ensure no one discovers our strength. NATO has found nothing during its visit to Chechnya. This is good." He grunted as he flicked his cigar on with his Zippo. "We must keep it that way." The American pulled another drag, sucking heartily on the cancer stick.

The group nodded haphazardly. "My Arab brothers agree," the hook-nosed man lisped. The fat man looked around the room one by one. The thin man beside the Arab did not appreciate the stern look for agreement. "Agreed." His German accent was strong. The bald man nodded an unrecognizable affirmation, and the two men on the right did the same.

"They have not discovered anything more because of their incompetence?" the fat man croaked.

"Or was it because of Operation Silhouette?" The man to the right spoke in broken English through his Chechen accent.

"We are not to speak of this operation," the fat man insisted, annoyed. "Our people are in place. I have confirmation the money has arrived in the bogus financial firm's account in Cyprus. Our mule will be bringing it here via a Turkish ship to a port in Georgia."

"How will this mule get the money into Germany?" the staunch man asked.

The bald man shifted in his chair at the other end of the table. "This, my brothers, I have taken care of." Except for the tongue curl on the r, his accent could pass as American. But he was Arab. His eyes beamed bright blue, and his skin was slightly tanned. "I have someone on the inside at airport security. The mule will pass through customs and security; he will not be checked." He leaned confidently back in his chair, slumping to the right.

"Who is this mule?" asked the quiet man beside the Chechen. It was the first time he had spoken in this meeting. The fat man's cigar was squashed in the ashtray, remnants of smoke floating skyward.

"He's a contractor. Experienced. Trustworthy," the Arab answered abruptly. "I have used him in Afghanistan; he will do the job well."

"My brothers are ready," the Chechen bragged in broken English. "We are always ready."

"Brothers," the fat man spoke, "when this transaction is complete, we will have what we need to secure more than just the Russian oil." Shoulders around the table shifted to relax. Blatant smirks abounded when the fat man lifted his arms and roared, "Ochrana."

"Ochrana," they replied in unison.

Jill blinked back in disbelief as she looked down at the clay numbers. She heard her mobile ringing, but she did not answer it. She just sat there and stared; her jaw dropped. This was different from any viewing she had ever had. The page in the notebook was blank. Screw the phone, she thought as she grabbed her notebook and splashed what she had just Viewed onto the page.

Ochrana, Russian oil, Operation Silhouette. "What the hell is Operation Silhouette, and what the hell is Ochrana?" As she sat back, she contemplated what this viewing could mean. She did not see David in the viewing, and she couldn't see the face of the fat man as her view had been from behind the man at the head of the table. All she could see was his shadow, his silhouette.

"What did you get yourself into, David? What did you get us both into?" Jill was pissed off. She was mainly pissed off at David for not disclosing more of what he was doing. She was also pissed that her search for him took her into dangerous territory. She had killed a man, Goddamnit! That realization haunted her. She killed him trying to find David. Kill or be killed; she'd have to reconcile herself to that fact. But she was more pissed off than ever that her vision did not contain David or anything recognizable to help her find him.

She stood up fast and marched over to the mobile, picking it up. The call display was showing a number she didn't recognize: 00.

She was still holding the phone when she heard a ringing. But it wasn't her mobile. It was the black handset beside the printer on the desk.

"Oliver here," she barked into the phone.

CHAPTER
TWENTY-ONE

It was Johan's assistant, summoning her to the brief at HQ. GSG's HQ was in the heart of Hamburg, and it was no wonder the city was called the Gateway to the World. A few hundred kilometers upstream from the North Sea, sizeable deep-sea vessels would anchor at the port here, one of the biggest and busiest in Germany. Jill could hear David giving her the rundown: "Hamburg is Germany's most influential city. It houses Germany's most prominent media houses, the oldest stock exchange, and has Europe's highest cost of living." She thought she could hear the national anthem of the US playing on a loudspeaker as they drove along the Elbe on the way to HQ. The driver sensed her curiosity. "Each vessel performs its national anthem when they sail toward the port, like a welcome salute," he said.

They drove over so many bridges that Jill thought of Venice; then, at last, they parked in front of GSG. The barren gray building exterior did not hint at the beauty of the high-tech briefing room. The glow of technology blipped around the dim room. A bright screen depicted a world map punctuated with smatterings of glowing red dots. At the top left of the screen were what appeared to be two live, closed-circuit television (CCTV) video cameras that transmitted a signal to a particular set of monitor feeds. The cameras in the feeds were focused on two different locations. One looked like it was covering the outside of a warehouse, but it was dark out now and hard to distinguish from the angle where Jill stood. The other feed was a shot of a deserted street where a lone white van was parked. On the right of the briefing table sat a group of computers that formed a large circle facing inward toward the middle of the room. Empty chairs sat in front of their screens.

A straight-backed man spoke English clearly for Jill's benefit and directed her to sit in the last open chair. Four men and one woman were dressed in form-fitting black suits surrounding the round table. The man, annoyed by her interruption, stopped and turned in her direction. "Team," he said half-heartedly, "this is Jill Oliver. She is on special assignment from America. She is familiar with this level of terrorism and is renowned for her profiling skills." He then continued as he turned back to the group.

"As you know, an Egyptian named Ibirham Akhmed is trying to sell two bars of enriched uranium. We've heard from our NOC, non-official cover for GSG, and it appears the sale will happen tomorrow night." The stocky man's black suit matched the rest of the staff sitting at the table. He stopped speaking when another man walked into the briefing center. Heads turned as he approached Jill.

"You must be Jill." He extended his hand. "I am Johan Rhein, but you can call me Chief." He had no accent. "If you need anything, please let me know personally."

Taking a step back, he addressed the team with a nod. "Jill was recently in Afghanistan, and I am told she was given the name Petrovich by an informant there. I haven't had time to speak to her in detail." He looked over in Jill's direction. "Jill, can you tell us what you know?"

"Well, I was in Afghanistan working on an unrelated assignment and was given an address in Kushka..." Jill trailed off when the team's eyes began to glass over. The lone woman was clicking her pen as if to speed Jill up. "Kushka is in northern Afghanistan. I followed the lead to a smaller town. It turned out to be deserted. However, I did find a large villa with a power generator running. A watchman guarded it, but I got inside without being noticed." The lone woman sighed loudly, egging Jill to move on to her next point. "The villa was empty; there was nothing there. Sorry, I couldn't be of any more help. But I will say this: somehow Petrovich must be connected with LSA." Just then, all eyes came to attention. "I was in Kushka based on a lead that had something to do with the Lost Soviet Arsenal. I just don't know why I was given his name. You see..."

One of the men was about to say something when Johan interrupted.

"Petrovich." Johan reached over, shuffled some folders, and handed one to Jill. "We think he is behind the sale of the uranium, and we feel that deal is imminent." Jill opened to a photo of Petrovich. According to the file, he had weathered skin with a strong jaw—and maybe a broken nose in his past—aged fifty-two: dark eyes, deep cold black eyes. Jill slightly cringed as she looked at the pictures of his buffed, tattooed body and skinhead look. She wouldn't want to meet him in a back alley, or anywhere else for that matter.

"How sure are you about this?" Jill inquired. "Is Petrovich working with Matta Al Jazzeria or Al Qaeda?"

"We don't think they are connected. Petrovich is Russian, and the Russians regard Al Qaeda as kleine kartoffel."

"Kleine, what?"

"Small potatoes." There was a slight chuckle in the room.

"Do you have any information on Petrovich's whereabouts?" Jill asked. "Was he in Afghanistan recently?"

"We believe he was," Johan said. The sound of rustling pages began anew, and he handed out folders to everyone seated at the table.

Jill looked down at the gray folder and flicked it open. They collectively reviewed the list of potential buyers and their backgrounds. Ibrahim's thin file told Jill that he was a new player in the terrorist game. To have a pending sale of this magnitude meant there must be someone with more clout higher up in the organization pulling his strings. The exposé detailed the evidence of connections with East Germany's Secret Police, who, until the fall of the wall, regarded the Soviet Union as a loyal partner. That would make the Petrovich connection possible.

She didn't know much about the Stasi. "The Stasi was run using an estimated 300,000 political informants," Johan said. "Although known for a thriving underground record-keeping system, the Stasi disbanded in 1989. Since then, all the people under surveillance records have been released and published. We have matched two of these names from this open-source database. We believe the buyers may be from one of the Arab countries currently suffering unrest, but we don't have anything further." Pages rustled again as the agents flicked through the lists of people.

As unsettling as it was to Jill, America was not so different these days. Wikipedia, Wikileaks. It's all out there for people to find. You just have to look hard enough.

"It's going to be a long night, folks. In your folders is your assignment. It must be completed before twenty-three hundred," he commanded. The sounds of chairs scraping across the floor indicated the briefing was over.

"Chief, can I speak to you in private?" Jill asked, feeling the glares of the others burning a hole in her cheek. He paused, allowing her to join him beside the empty computers. He was over six feet tall, and his pale face looked down at her. His hair would put him in his early fifties, but he had no wrinkles to match. He crossed his arms, and slight creases in his black suit bunched the inside of his elbows.

Jill began impatiently, "I am sorry to interrupt, but I think this may be important. Eric said you would give me access to your resources."

"Yes, Ms. Oliver, you have been cleared to our level of security, equivalent to the CIA in your country. We need as much insight on Petrovich as possible before tomorrow night, and you are the first to have recent information."

"I am unsure if Eric told you why I am in Hamburg?"

"Yes, he said your husband is the missing reporter, and you think he is here."

"I can't explain this, sir, but I think these names may be related to Petrovich. Can you run them?" Jill pushed the Post-it note toward him.

"Americans, David and Stan Brown. Highly unlikely." He looked back at Jill. "But I will run their names." He was humoring her.

"When is the sale happening? Do you need me?"

Resting his right butt cheek on the table, he said apprehensively, "Jill, this is a very sensitive operation. We've put too many staff hours into this to have anything go wrong. A female American law enforcement officer would potentially raise a red flag. You could be part of the communications team." He explained that she could be in the surveillance van and watch the take-down. "But that's pretty much it."

Jill didn't insist. Frankly, she wasn't much interested in German policing. If it hadn't been for Petrovich, she wouldn't give a rat's ass about it all and would be doing her investigation on German soil.

"I'll have the driver take you back to your hotel. Report in at thirteen hundred tomorrow," he said, a little too gruffly as he walked away.

CHAPTER TWENTY-TWO

21:09 Zulu Time—Hamburg, Germany

Food sat on the plate, picked through. Back in the comfort of Jill's hotel room, she clutched a glass of Cab Sav and lay on the bed. She thought she would be hungrier than she was since it was past eleven o'clock in the evening. She nursed a long sip and attempted to digest her day. Without resolve, she gulped down the rest of the glass and laid her head back. Her thoughts swirled around David and Petrovich.

Why Petrovich, David? The sale of uranium—man, that's a great story. Her heart sank just a bit as she wondered why David had not taken the time to contact her, and now it was international news that David was officially missing. Maybe that was why she hadn't heard from him. He must be undercover. She knew she was getting closer to David; she could feel it. But where would she start in Hamburg? If Petrovich were David's story, selling uranium from Petrovich would explain why David was in Afghanistan. Based on Jill's experience, she couldn't imagine that Petrovich would be in Germany, where the sale was about to take place, unless Petrovich's group was thin. Then he'd have no choice. Jill's mind was racing in the tunnels. There would be no sleep tonight.

She sat up, walked over to the desk, opened her computer, and then walked over to figure out the cappuccino maker.

After twenty minutes of fiddling, Jill sat and sipped the cappuccino while she checked her emails. The one from Kali had two important words only.

Call Me.

No matter what time.

An alarm stung Jill, and she quickly dialed Kali.

"I couldn't find any connection to the Star of David," Kali said. "Are you sure it was the Star of David?"

"Well, it's a drawing, Kali. A scribble in my notebook, you know, the kind." The caffeine had a kick to it, her answer coming out fast.

"Is it a six-pointed star? Does your drawing have six points?"

"Stand by." Jill walked over and grabbed her notebook. She sat back down, propped up her feet, picked up the phone, and held the notebook open on the desk. "Yup, it has six points. Why?"

"I did a lot of reading regarding the Star of David for you. People today relate it to Judaism. Did you know that the Star of David was not truly a Jewish symbol before World War II?" Kali skipped a beat, excited that she had some information of interest, as trivial as it may be. "The origins are quite vague, Jill, and Christians and Muslims also used it. The six points represent the absolute rule of God over the universe in all directions. The north, south, east, west, up, and down are all under one God's rule. It may also symbolize the dual nature of good and evil and could be used to protect people against evil spirits."

"Interesting... I guess." Jill was only slightly intrigued.

"Do you think your drawing is about protecting yourself, a warning maybe?" The vocal vibration and the slight voice pitch told Jill that Kali was worried.

"Maybe, but I doubt it," she said, trying to ease Kali's fears. However, Jill felt a nag tickle her brain.

"There's more, Jill. This star is called a hexagram, dating back to 922 BC in Egypt. It was also known for its role in Arab magic and was used by Freemasonry as early as the seventeenth century. Jill, Hitler used this as a symbol of shame to the Jews in the Holocaust, and today's version of the hexagram is used as a proud symbol of Jewish honor on Israel's flag."

"Arab magic. What is Arab magic?" Jill shifted her feet off the desk and sat up.

"I thought that would get your attention. So far, I can't seem to find much on it, but strangely, you have been pretty much in the Middle East. There has to be some sort of connection."

"Hmm, I will see what I can find on the net; maybe I will ask around. But people will look at me like I'm a nutcase if I ask about magic, never mind Arab magic. But I guess it's worth a shot," Jill negotiated with herself.

"Well, that's about it to report. I can't find any information on Ochrana, if that's even a word. It's as if it doesn't exist, just like Zayed. Speaking of Zayed, I gave his alias to Eric. He said he'd make a few calls to see who he is."

"No need, Kali. He's dead," Jill said with a tired sigh.

"Dead, how?"

Jill gave Kali the Coles Notes version of what happened in Kushka. "Anyway, let me know if Eric finds anything on him. It may help us figure out where David is. And Kali, I think there may be a connection between that car I thought was following me in Tucson and the Chechens here. Did you get any info on them?"

"I haven't heard from Eric about it. When I speak to him next, I'll ask. Wow, Jill, this is getting crazy. Oh, I almost forgot. Take this number down. Leila keeps calling. She said she hasn't heard from David but needs to speak to you." After rechecking the number, they hung up.

Leila, finally. She's probably just worried about me. Jill got up and brewed another cappuccino, then returned to the indented seat in front of the computer to Google "Arab+magic."

"No Arab magic wiki, that's gotta tell you something," she uttered to herself. She needed to stay focused on Ochrana, but somehow she was pulled to find out more about what this Arab magic was, more out of interest than any relevance to finding David.

Looking at the scratched number on her pad, she dialed.

"Sorel," a groggy voice answered.

"Leila, this is Jill." She glanced over at the time. "What time is it there? Wait, where is there?"

"Don't be pissed at Kali, Jill. She told me you were in Hamburg. I was in Brussels and hopped on the train. I got into Hamburg around midnight. Jill, where are you staying?"

Silence. Jill realized she did not take notice of the name of her hotel. Was she losing her touch? She felt comfortable in Germany; after all, it was Europe, with more CCTV cameras than one would hope to encounter.

"I—I don't know. It's a long story, Leila. Hold on." She rifled through the top drawer of the desk to find a letterhead. "Fairmont on Neuer Jungfernstieg nine-fourteen."

"Are you okay?" Leila asked. "Why are you in Hamburg?"

"I'm okay, but, well... I can't talk about this over the phone. Why did you go to Brussels? Have you heard from David?"

"Not exactly."

Jill's heart skipped. "What do you mean... not exactly?"

"Like you said, Jill, not over the phone. But I need to see you. I have been doing my research, and I've found some interesting information. I'm on my way over to your hotel now."

CHAPTER TWENTY-THREE

Jill's stomach started to ache as she sipped on her third cappuccino. The lobby café was grand, and while she waited for Leila, she began to notice the splendor of it. Elegant and regal, the gold and burgundy walls set off the parquet-checkered floors. It was dark outside; it must have been at least two a.m. by now, and Jill was thankful for the twenty-four-hour lobby café.

There was a light mist on the windows, and combined with the dim streetlights, Jill could see a large body of water across the road. She'd had to think twice about where she was, which troubled her. Usually, she'd know exactly where she was and what time it was, for that matter. Another Navajo trait. But she was exhausted to the point of weary.

Jill sprang to her feet when she saw her. As Leila approached, there seemed to be a hint of despair in her eyes. Jill couldn't control herself any longer. Seeing Leila, David's longtime friend and colleague, was too much. The women, who loved the same man but for different reasons, squeezed each other tightly. Floods of tears spilled down Jill's cheeks as they hugged. Leila pulled her close, nearly squeezing the breath out of her. After minutes of standing there in a hug, Leila whispered, "It's okay, Jill. Let it out; it'll all be fine; God doesn't give us what we can't handle. Shh, it's okay." Leila's voice hummed, and Jill's brain didn't recognize the slight hint of amusement.

Jill squeezed back hard and breathed like a child after a long cry, trying to catch her breath as she ended the embrace. They sat down kitty-corner at the small table in front of a large glazed window. They had not realized that a German waiter was standing there, shuffling.

"Ma'am, can I get you a café or something? Scones?" he questioned politely. "American coffee?" he offered as he held up the steaming carafe.

Moments later, Leila sipped the hot brew, glanced around the room nervously, and then back at Jill. Jill took a final sniff and listened to Leila attentively.

"What happened on your trip besides your new 'do?"

Jill shrugged and self-consciously ran her fingers through her spiked hair. Leila's head tilted quizzically while Jill gave a brief overview.

"Chechen mafia, Jill. Are you kidding me?"

"It's what Zayed told me; he said they were Chechen." Jill's hand trembled slightly.

"Who is this Zayed again?"

"He said he was a friend of David's; have you ever heard of him?" Jill looked directly into Leila's dark eyes. Leila blinked down into her steaming cup.

"Jill, has David ever talked to you about his Pulitzer story? He has been working on it for some time now." Leila returned the direct stare.

"What story? Which one? The one in Doha?"

"Well, sort of." Leila paused. "Jill, what I am about to tell you... please don't react until I'm finished." Jill leaned forward, her head starting to spin. Leila continued, "The last time I spoke to David was the day he left to go back to Doha." Leila paused as Jill's anxiety rose.

Jill's stomach began to bubble, remembering the morning David said he was speaking to his editor. "Yeah," was all she could muster.

"He was telling me that he was getting close to figuring this story out and how he would angle it. It was the last time I spoke to him." Leila's face dropped slightly. "Have you ever heard of something called Operation Silhouette?" It was almost as if Leila was studying Jill for the first time and not the other way around. Leila leaned back and placed the hot mug on the table. Jill followed. Even under stress, Jill was habitual in using submodalities. This technique was used to build rapport. Mimicking someone's actions made them feel at ease. But today, Jill didn't realize she was doing this. Her foot began to tap the leg of the table.

Jill looked at Leila, scanned the files in her brain, and after thirty or so seconds, she thought intensely about telling Leila about her Viewing. After all, she trusted Leila, right? But why hadn't David told her he was talking to Leila? This thought pricked Jill's torn gut. Leila shifted uncomfortably in her chair and scanned the café.

Sure enough, they were alone. Leila straightened her short bangs that somehow made her look like a character in the Kill Bill movie and said, "It's what David believed to be—" Leila lifted her arms and finger-quoted David's words, "the story of a lifetime." In one of his interviews with a soldier from Iraq, you know, the one that was a double agent? Planted. I can't remember his name; do you remember the one I am talking about?"

"Yeah, I remember the story. Not the name, but the story. What's this have to do with David missing? What was he working on?" Jill was beginning to feel irritated and didn't like that. Not now, not with Leila.

"Well, this person told David about this Operation Silhouette. At first, David thought he was delusional, post-traumatic stress disorder

or something like that." Jill nodded in understanding. "Then he started to ask about his sources, good sources. I think one of the sources, a
mercenary, told David that a group was working together. The kind of
group you don't hear about in the media getting along in the Middle
East. Jewish Israelis, Saudi Muslims, American Christians, and the
Chechens."

"Chechens?" Jill echoed, stunned. "As in the Chechen Mafia?" Jill
thought about the Star of David and what Kali had said about absolute
rule under one God.

"I don't know, Jill, but after your experience, I would guess yes. The
last time I talked to David, he didn't know much more than this. It was
why he went to Doha, to figure it all out."

She leaned back uncomfortably. They sat in silence and sipped.
Both women looked out the rain-soaked window. Jill was embarrassed
by her first thought. Why did Leila know more about David's assignment than she did? The question rolled around, touching her with
envy.

"Let's be frank, Leila. Confidentially, okay?" Jill looked directly into
Leila's eyes for confirmation, but even with the unshakable stare back
from Leila, she couldn't help but feel a bit paranoid.

"Of course! Always," Leila responded.

"You remember I told you about my Navajo visions?"

"Yeah."

"Well, there is something I have not told you. I am sworn under oath
not to. I've never even told David about this."

Leila's eyes lit as she listened intently. Jill hesitated as she thought
she saw something in her eyes. It was a hint of amusement.

Jill hesitated, then decided she was just disheveled and continued.
"But I know because of your background that you will understand
this. Leila, I was a Remote Viewer for the FBI," Jill confessed.

"Remote Viewer?" Leila's dark eyes looked like they were scanning her brain for comprehension. Her eyes bulged, signaling she must have found the answer.

"You know, like the psychic department of the FBI, and it's public knowledge now that it exists. I was part of a Remote Viewing team. We used our psychic ability as a tool to solve cases."

Leila intently watched Jill reach into her carry-on bag and retrieve two notebooks and the pouch.

"That's David's notebook, isn't it? That's the one you found in Afghanistan?" Jill didn't have to say anything; she didn't need to.

Jill placed David's notebook on the table before Leila and flipped the worn cover open. "See this writing, Leila? It's not mine." Leila stared at the page with the picture of Jill and said nothing. "He left this notebook on purpose. Somehow he wanted me to know he is in Hamburg." Leila was silent as Jill told her the story of their trip to Hamburg just after they married.

"How would he know you would get this?"

Jill shrugged. "Don't know; maybe it's not even for me? Maybe I am just on some goddamn goose chase. But I don't think so. I told you about Petrovich, right? It turns out the GSG is working on a case that involves him. I believe that this is why David is in Hamburg."

Leila didn't ask about the case; she knew Jill couldn't tell her about it. Jill reached for the leather pouch. "I swore not to use my Remote Viewing tools, but I had no choice." Jill didn't want to mention that she hadn't viewed it mainly because of McGregor. Confessing this would be too demeaning. Leila's eyes followed as Jill opened the pouch and scattered the clay numbers. Leila said nothing as her sights stalled on Jill's hands with a look of curiosity.

Jill opened her notebook and placed it on the clay numbers. Leila snatched the notebook when Jill turned the page to the scribble of the Star of David and gasped.

"Where did you get this symbol from?" Leila showed Jill the drawing.

Jill was bewildered. "I drew it. I drew when I was Remote Viewing."

Leila's jaw slowly dropped, and her eyes bulged a little. She looked at Jill squarely. "On the call that morning when David left, he asked me... he asked me if I knew anything about a group that uses the Star of David as their symbol. I didn't." Leila reached into her top breast pocket, pulled out a photo, and laid it on Jill's notebook. "But I do now." A picture of the Star of David stared back at them. It was a picture of an old wooden carving. Jill grabbed the photo and jumped up from her chair.

"Where did you get this, Leila? What is this a picture of?" Adrenaline dripped into Jill's veins.

Leila stood, towering over Jill. "Sit, Jill; let's sit and try to figure this out." Leila nudged Jill back into her seat with her hand on Jill's shoulder and leaned in. "In the past week, I have been working on trying to find out what David's story is about, from what I know. The Star of David," Leila glanced around the room, slightly nervous, and resumed, "It's used in many fashions, cults, religions—even on the Israeli flag. But then, when I was in Brussels, I was led by an informant to an old church. Down the stairs, in a separate room, was this star. It was carved into the floor."

Jill recalled her Viewing but wasn't ready to share this information yet. She remembered her conversation with Kali. "Freemasons?"

"That was my initial thought, but after interviewing one of them from a lodge there, on the sly, of course, I changed my mind," Leila smirked.

Leila's gift, her beauty, managed to get her where she needed to go in life. Somehow, Jill was comforted that she was using this gift to help find David. "After looking at this picture, he said it was not a symbol they used. He warned me, Jill." Leila's eyes narrowed. "See how the wood carving is beveled? Three points of the star lay on top of the other three points. The man told me that this hexagram is carved in a fashion worshiped by evildoers."

"Evildoers—what are we, George Bush or something?" Jill sniped. Leila leaned back, and Jill mimicked the gesture. They looked at the photo next to the star drawing and sat silently. Jill's brow furrowed as cloudy thoughts swirled in her head.

"What the hell was David working on, Leila? What the hell?"

"Let's write down some facts; let's put this on paper. It's easier that way." Leila lifted Jill's notebook and clicked on a pen. Abruptly she stopped. "What is this?" she asked, looking at a page full of scribbles.

"It's my vision notes. Since David disappeared, I have been having visions. Like dreams. This page—" Leila perched up and looked to where Jill was pointing, "is my decipher notes. Sometimes they are hard to figure out; I still haven't found this one. Anyway, wh—"

The screech of Leila's chair startled Jill.

"What?"

Leila's eyes bugged out. "Jill, why do you have the word 'family' circled?" She pushed the book to within four inches of Jill's face.

Pushing the book back, Jill said heavily, "I think my visions have something to do with my family."

Leila was about to continue but stopped when she saw a man in a suit approaching the table. "Ladies, pardon my intrusion." He bowed slightly. "I noticed on our system that you had signed for these coffees." Jill and Leila looked at the man and wondered why he was bothering them. "Miss Oliver?" he queried, looking from Jill to Leila and back.

Jill looked up at the young man's striking blue eyes. "Yes, that's me."

"I have an urgent message." The gloved man nodded and handed Jill an envelope. "Pardon my intrusion." With a click of his heels, he swiftly turned and walked away.

Jill opened the small ivory envelope and pulled out a folded piece of paper. "Anything interesting?" Leila said, watching curiously. Stan Brown's name popped off the page, and Jill's posture sharpened. Along with his name was a phone number and the time the call came in—eighteen minutes ago.

Leila stared at the note in near disbelief. She hesitated and then confidently said, "Jill, did you know David's father has an office in Brussels?"

"Wha..." Jill muttered, trying to connect the dots.

"I went to see him, Jill, the day before yesterday."

"How did you know he was there?"

"I called his skank sister." Leila shot a look toward Jill. "Yeah, they don't like black people either. Pfft, but she gave me his number; I think she was high on something."

"So she's out of the loony bin again," Jill meowed mockingly.

"It's what led me to Brussels; that and a call back from one of my sources."

"What did Stan say?"

"Not much. He hadn't heard from David, blah blah. He's still a mean bastard of a man," she meowed back scornfully.

"Did you tell him I was in Hamburg?"

"No, I ah, didn't know you were here when I saw him."

"I left him a message on his mobile earlier today," Jill continued. "He's probably just returning my call. Not sure what the urgency is, especially since you just saw him. Maybe he's heard from David?" Jill began to fumble through her pack for her mobile, then stopped before she pressed send. Intuition tapped her again, and she said, "I think I will call him from the hotel phone. You can never be too careful with mobiles."

It was time to find out what Stan wanted.

CHAPTER TWENTY-FOUR

"Nice digs," Leila said as she plopped onto the bed. She watched Jill pick up the desk phone and dial.

"Stan Brown," a raspy smoker's voice answered.

"Hi, Stan. It's Jill." She hesitated with a tinge of guilt.

"What is going on with David?" A warning tweaked her brain when he asked her, in a tone too matter-of-fact, "I have not heard anything, have you?"

"I got your message; it said it was urgent."

"I was surprised to see that you were in Hamburg. What a coincidence, Jill. I am in Hamburg too. We need to meet; I need to speak to you. My driver is close to your hotel. I will ask him to come there and pick you up."

Before she could respond, the phone line went dead.

"There is no such thing as coincidences," she said to Leila.

"Do you think the word 'family' you circled meant David's family and not yours?" Leila asked. "After all, taking away any coincidence, Jill, you are in Hamburg, and so is David's father."

Soon after, Jill was waiting in the gold-flushed lobby, its blinding gaudiness outlined in thin strips of bold purple. She plunked down onto a firm, square sofa. David would be livid if he knew Jill had met with his father without him. But she had no choice.

She walked over to the lobby door to distract herself, nodding at the porter as he opened it. Perhaps sitting on a bench outside in the crisp night air would alleviate this helplessness that made her feel she wanted to sleep forever. The rain had stopped for some time now; the only evidence left was the lingering smell of it.

Hamburg at night was bewitching. Two young men dressed in designer suits strode together down the wet sidewalk hedged with blossoming white lilies. The shorter of the two was moving his hands about like a girl, excited about some new gossip.

The fresh sweet smell of the lilies floated past her nose and sailed her consciousness with it. Leila had offered to wait in her room, and Jill found herself in the tunnels of her mind, the hum of the chants taunting her. She stared blankly into the air, her brain filling with the faces of people she knew—familiar people—hovering before her and then gliding away. The sand painting, she reminded herself. Her trained mind only interrupted when she heard herself talking. "Family," she softly uttered.

Jill had to focus. What did her Viewing of the Star of David have to do with that photo Leila took? Jill was good at Viewing, but she needed to understand its context, and now with Leila's photo, the men in the viewing seemed eerily relevant to figuring out where David was. Leila had always had a nose for a story and best captured these stories through the camera lens.

She would talk to Leila more about her viewing when she returned from meeting Stan. She would tell her what she knew. She had to trust her—she had to trust someone.

A black Audi limo crawled up the short, busy driveway in front of the hotel, and the back window, squeaking slowly, rolled down. A fat face stuck out.

"Hello, Jill," Stan rasped. He opened the door and stepped out closer to her. His blue suit tightened when he leaned forward to give her a shallow hug as he nudged her into the backseat of the car. She began to ask him why he was in Hamburg. Jill noted his agitated finger tapping his knee as she quizzed him.

"I have some business here, and I wanted to make sure it was done correctly," he coughed.

"Your oil business? What type of oil business are you in exactly again?"

"Oh, Jill," his voice said with a hint of a growl. "My business is much too boring to talk about. Boardroom meetings, contract negotiations, and things of that nature. Let's discuss what I know you're actually interested in. I am planning to leave Hamburg tomorrow night and wanted to see you before I leave. I guess you are working on a case of some sort. Are you helping to find David? Do you think David is in Hamburg? Why would he be in Hamburg, Jill?"

Jill stared at Stan and wondered why he was asking all these questions. It was difficult trusting a man who shared little to nothing with her husband. David didn't look like Stan, and Jill had difficulty seeing any resemblance between father and son. David had a full thick head of hair, and it would be doubtful that he would ever go bald as Stan was. "Ah, I don't know. I think he is working on some story, and I am genuinely worried about what it is?" Jill thought of telling him more, then remembered the schematic, article, and David's notebook. She blurted, "I heard you got a new contract in Afghanistan. Have you been there?"

"It's business, Jill. Let's discuss how we can find David."

"We?"

"I'd just made some calls to some informative people to see if they could find out any information on David's whereabouts when I got your message. So far, nothing, but I'll let you know when I hear back from them. Why do you think David is in Hamburg, Jill?"

"I'm not sure," Jill was dumbfounded and sat quietly, trying to decide if she should ask him about Kushka, about Petrovich. She wanted to see his reaction. She wanted to see his eyes, the blinks. But it was too soon; Jill needed more information. They sat in silence as the driver sped along the straight canals.

Stan seemed to be uncomfortable with the silence. "Well, if David didn't lead you to Hamburg, what did, Jill?"

"I ah, it's work-related. Where are we going?" Jill snapped, feeling slightly uneasy. He turned towards her like a lazy bulldog.

"You know, Jill, sometimes David can be impulsive, and when he gets that way, he makes stupid decisions." Jill thought she saw a slight sneer. "Has he left anything for you? Any word or documents of any kind?"

"What are you talking about, Stan? What documents? And are you saying David is stupid? You think it's impulsive because he is working on a story undercover?" Jill's anger began to boil.

"You don't have to raise your voice, Jill," Stan said snidely.

"Pull the hell over," she yelled to the driver. She didn't have time for this bullshit right now.

"It's a long walk, Jill. We'll take you back to the hotel."

"Pull over now," Jill yelled louder. "I knew this was a bad idea, Stan." The car jerked to a stop, barely long enough for Jill to jump out of the backseat and slam the door shut.

"Shit!" She landed in a pothole and looked back at the car. She thought she could see Stan smirking as he drove away.

She stood silently as a mist of rain threatened to open its floodgates. It would figure! It was pissing alright, but she could not bear another second with Stan. She should have trusted her instincts. She should have trusted David. What the hell documents was he talking about? Asshole. She began to shiver but couldn't determine if it was from anger or the cold. She needed to get her bearings.

There were scarcely any cars on the road, but she could swear that the last one on the left side of the next intersection was Stan's Audi. Is he following me? There was little movement on the streets and no noise except a small oompah-pah-ing pub across the road. Her pace hastened as she dodged past a parked car on the narrow road and into the pub.

Inside the small pub was a man playing the accordion. The smell of smoke and beer hit her like an invisible wall blocking the door. She entered anyway.

"Phone," Jill asked the bartender. His handlebar mustache was so long and twisted you could hang keys on each side. He pointed to the back of the pub. Jill rushed to the back past the men who stared into their beer glasses, unmindful of what her night had brought her. There, between two bathrooms, the payphone hung, covered in grunge. She lifted the receiver and then stopped. Who was she going to call? She had no numbers, and she had no Euros on her.

She walked back past the remainder of the drunks in the late-night pub to the bartender and gave the man a look. She imagined she must have looked like a beggar—wet, her spiky hair laid flat on her head.

"Please, sir. Please call the Fairmont Hotel for me. Please."

CHAPTER TWENTY-FIVE

12:51 Zulu Time—Hamburg, Germany

Jill sat in the corner of the pub and watched the door. The smell of cigarettes made her nauseous. She lifted the full ashtray on the red checkerboard tablecloth in front of her and placed it beside her. Despair filled her eyes. She was so deep in thought; she didn't notice Leila walking through the smoke-hazed doorway.

Tall and strikingly beautiful, Leila stood dressed in dark green khaki pants that somehow matched her Asian green eyes. Her pants were the kind that David would wear. But these pants were apparently built for a willowy, sleek body. The legs of the pants had the usual side pockets similar to Jill's now-soaked fatigues. But Leila's were tapered down her legs and hugged her calves before trailing into her black stiletto boots. Jill felt rumpled and defeated as she stared at this black beauty. Jill was athletic and regarded herself as no pushover. A beauty, most times, she could hold her own. Leila could hold her own too, but somehow she exuded raw beauty. Class.

Her picturesque stature turned in Jill's direction. In the dingy light as Jill stood up, Leila abruptly stopped and stared at her. Drenched and shivering now, Jill pushed towards Leila.

"What happened to you? It's almost three a.m., for God's sake?" She stopped short of touching Jill on the arm.

"Let's talk in the car. I need to get out of these clothes. Is the taxi waiting?" Jill's lips quivered.

In the taxi, as they sped along the dark road, Leila squeezed her hand quickly, then let go and said, "We need to get you warm, Jill. I don't think we should return to the Fairmont; my hotel is closer." Leila nudged Jill's pack on the floor between them with her left boot. "It's all here."

But somehow, this did not give Jill comfort. All she could say was, "Yeah."

"Marriott," Leila said to the driver. He nodded, pulled into the right lane, and merged off the main highway. Leila was always abrupt. She was no-nonsense, which annoyed Jill some days, but today she didn't care.

At least fifty streetlights had whizzed by the windows before anyone spoke. Jill was too busy looking at the driver as he peered back at Leila, a hint of admiration in his glances. Jill looked past the peering eyes in the rearview mirror. She was getting colder now, and her body had begun to shiver uncontrollably. But even the constant shivers that attempted to keep Jill warm didn't stop her from watching to ensure they weren't being followed. I'm paranoid. It probably wasn't Stan's car that she had seen. After all, why would he need to follow me? There were few headlights on the road at this hour. Jill finally sighed in relief and looked over at Leila. "I saw Stan. We were just talking about David and stuff. We got into an argument. He called David impulsive and dumb." Jill sat miffed. "He asked me if David had been in touch with me or left documents of some kind."

"Documents? How could he have left your documents?" Leila sounded interested.

"The only thing I can think of is his notebook. He did leave that on purpose. It's why I am in Hamburg. But all the pages were ripped out of it."

After a few minutes, Jill wondered why Leila didn't say anything. Jill felt a niggle. Something wasn't right. But what was it? Jill looked at Leila, who looked like she was scowling. Annoyed maybe, Jill did not know. They sat in silence before either of them noticed they were leaving the heart of Hamburg.

They had heard it before they saw it. The fierce roar of the engine came up behind their taxi fast, and then without notice, high beams flicked on and lit up the inside of the taxi. The glare almost blinded the driver as he looked in the rearview mirror, and the car slightly swerved in reaction to the right.

Their bodies lurched hard as a large truck hit the left side of the taxi's rear, spinning it. Exhaustion left Jill and was replaced with adrenaline.

"Hold on, Leila," Jill yelled. The taxi spun in circles. Instinct again tapped as if begging for Jill's focus, trying to communicate, like an action movie trailer flashing in front of Jill's eyes.

One word came out of Jill's mouth: "PIT." Jill instantly knew that these pursuers, whoever they were, were not trying to kill them. They were not trying to run them off the road; they were trying to stop them.

Jill knew the PIT well. During training, she had enjoyed the thrill of chasing Tom's car, pushing him into that fateful spin. Tom was not unlike the driver of this taxi, who was attempting to control this spin in the goddamn wrong direction.

"Leila, when you can get out, run. Okay, run!" Jill commanded. For a split second, she caught the fear in Leila's eyes. Then the car stopped so fast that Jill hit her head on the car door window. The whack dulled her senses for only a moment. And a moment was all they needed. She heard the footsteps, then the shouting. A man yelled something in what seemed to be Russian. Both car doors opened. She saw Leila's back arch and convulse before Jill felt the Taser rip through her nerves.

CHAPTER TWENTY-SIX

The sound of water dripping woke Jill. The smell of wet earth pierced her nose. Groggily, she grabbed her head. She opened her eyes, but it was pitch-black. Jill tried to sit up and feel around the floor, but she almost fell over when she attempted to get her bearings. Drugged was her first thought. The cold cement floor was dry, and so were Jill's clothes. How long she had been in this dark room, she did not know. She felt around the concrete. Something ran over her hand, and Jill yelped. "What the...?" It must have been a rodent. God. Where the hell am I?

Confusion filled Jill. She'd been in a place like this before, drugged and cold. She thought for a moment that she could smell her fear. Flashbacks of her time with McGregor shook her. She didn't know how long he'd had her in that cold cave. Being drugged provided her only relief, numbing the pain he inflicted.

"Leila?" she whispered aloud. Nothing. "Leila?" Again nothing. "Leila, hello, anyone?" Thirty seconds had passed before she heard something. Movement. Muffled movement. Then Jill heard a moan. "Leila?"

Jill waited in silence. Then she heard a scream. It wasn't far away. But it wasn't in the same room. The scream sounded more like a surprised cry, like something you would hear in a horror house at an amusement park.

"Freakin' rats," Leila yelled as the click of her stilettos tapped the cement.

"Leila, where are you?" Jill stood up and immediately bumped into a wall. Feeling around the wall, she discovered that it wasn't cement. "Leila," Jill repeated.

"Jill?" After several back-and-forth callings, they found each other; only the wall separated them.

"Where are we, Jill? I hate effing rats."

"I don't know," Jill replied. "We need to get out of here fast. There were two men. I think they would have killed us if that was what they wanted, but they'll be back. We need to get the hell out of here now," Jill tried to devise a plan. "I think this wall is just drywall. Stand back; I'll see if I can kick through it."

After a series of knocks, Jill figured out where the studs were and lifted her leg to do a front-snap kick. Jill raised her right leg, the stronger of the two, and aimed her boot squarely between the studs. Her boot thudded against the wall before her knee snapped back at her. The reverberation was so strong that her knee hit her right boob.

"Ow, mother—! It's not drywall. Crap," Jill spewed as she tried to regain her balance.

"Jill, can you hear that?"

Jill stopped and listened. It was the sound of boots hitting hard cement in the distance, smacking in their direction. Then Jill blurted to Leila, "If they come to me first, wait. When you think it's the right timing, make a distraction. Some sort of distraction, anything," Jill said desperately. And before Leila could answer, the key twisted in Jill's door. The lock clicked open, and Jill could see the silhouettes of two men.

A light flicked on, and its harshness burned Jill's unaccustomed eyes. She squinted while holding her hand up to shield herself from the glare. A shorter man stood in front of Jill. He looked as gruesome as the photo she had seen of Petrovich. He had short brown hair, and his tight black turtleneck met his full-face beard, an attempt to cover a large scar. Jill assessed his body language fast. He stood in an attack stance and held a Taser in his right hand.

"Where is he?" His Slavic accent was thick. The big man stood by the door like a bouncer in a dark bar. He was blonde with an American Marine buzz cut. He shifted from one leg to the other. Getting ready for something, Jill thought.

"Who?" Jill stalled. They know who I am. She profiled as fast as her brain could manage, but it wasn't fast enough. The left hook hit her square in the jaw. Blood splattered from her lip as she fell to the ground.

Dazed, Jill's head spun hard. She spat out blood. "You know where he is, you bitch. Think you can get away from us? You know he is here in Germany. Why else would you be here?"

Before Jill could say anything, she felt the pain of his boot landing directly into her rib. It was her rib that saved her liver and her spleen. Jill cried aloud in pain. The short man grabbed her hair with his left hand and lifted her head. His breath smelled like rotting teeth. His throat growled again as he pulled up phlegm and said, "Piece of shit, American," then spat in her face. Jill's head hit the ground and clunked. "You think he can stop us, that stupid piece of shit." And just as he was about to crack another rib...

"David! David! Help me, David!" Leila shouted.

That's all Jill needed. She was trained in HTH. Hand-to-hand combat is what you do when you don't have a weapon when you need to survive. She'd communicate with him alright. She was used to the pain after Matthew McGregor.

Still on the floor, the crescent kick—a defensive maneuver where one kicks the left foot in a clockwise swing—disarmed the short man with the Taser while looking over in Leila's direction. That landed the Taser beside Jill. She grabbed it fast as the small man lunged toward her. His back arched when Jill zapped his calf. She rolled quickly towards the bouncer and jumped up directly before him. As slow as he was, all it took was a split second for Jill to front-snap him straight in the groin. He fell to his knees in agonizing pain. Jill winced as she turned her body sideways and thrust her foot into the side of his head.

Jill screamed as she grabbed her side, the cracked rib reminding her of her beating. The men were both down in the tiny room when Jill turned the key and pulled it out of the door. She didn't look back before she closed the door and locked it. She knew she had only bought them about three minutes. But three minutes was all they needed. Tasers could last up to ten minutes, but she didn't want to assume the best just yet.

"Leila. Leila." There was a hint of panic in Jill's voice.

"In here," Leila yelled. Jill scrambled with the keys. The first didn't fit, but the second one did. She flicked on the light, and Leila almost leaped onto Jill.

"Let's go." Jill spat blood and hobbled alongside Leila, her arm holding her side. As they pushed through a steel door, the hallway opened into what appeared to be a warehouse. The contents of Jill's carry-on were sprawled out on a stainless steel counter. The numbers from her pouch were in disarray across the gleaming metal. Leila's camera was open, and the memory chip was gone.

They heard yelling and boots on cement. "Shit." Jill winced as her arm swept the collection of stuff back into the pack. They hit the exit door and ran out into the street.

The fire exit door slammed behind them, and they found themselves on an empty cobbled side street. Tall buildings surrounded them at least six stories high, and it looked like the sun was just starting to set.

"This way!" Jill yelped as she headed towards the sound of traffic. She could see cars passing fast on the street in front of her.

"Ouch," Leila hissed as her ankle twisted and the heel of her left boot cracked off.

"Come on," Jill ordered. Although every slap of her boots on the pavement jolted pain into her body, she had to keep going. When they hit the main road, they stopped at a taxi letting off its fare. An older woman was counting change when Jill jumped into the backseat. Leila hobbled behind her in a panic, nearly knocking over the woman.

"Go, go fast," Jill said frantically. The driver looked back with a questioning lift of his eyebrow and then squealed the tires as they merged into traffic. Both Jill and Leila looked out the back window. No one followed.

CHAPTER
TWENTY-SEVEN

8:23 Zulu Time—Hamburg, Germany

The elevator bell spoke, "Twenty-first floor." Jill's head lifted from her gaze on the dark tile floor where she sat waiting. She looked down the sterile hallway towards the elevator. Leila and a tall, thin man stepped off. Leila was no longer wearing her sleek boots and no longer hobbling. Instead, she wore what appeared to be Adidas runners that resembled black shoes. Jill knew they were runners because the rubber soles squeaked toward her.

"Sorry it took so long, ma'am," the man apologized with a glance at his watch. It was 10:23. The thin man presented Leila to Jill.

"Who knew they could run fingerprints that fast? They even found a match for my iris." Leila sounded impressed. "You must be a VIP here or something," Leila said to Jill with a no-nonsense stance. Most VIP offices in governmental operation centers were on the top floors for security reasons. Leila followed Jill's gaze to her shoes. "Ah, yeah, while they were checking me out to get this security clearance," Leila's finger flicked the new shiny card clipped to her right breast jacket that proudly stated GSG Security Clearance Class 3, "they sent for my things at the Marriott. A real shame, those Jimmy Choos!"

"Follow me, ma'am." The German guard gestured. Jill stood up and grimaced; her taped ribs still jabbed when she moved. They followed the guard along a glass corridor and into what looked like an interrogation room.

Jill and Leila sat in silence, Leila shifting uncomfortably in her chair. Jill watched her as she looked around the tiny room to see if there was any surveillance. She was paranoid now too. After Matthew McGregor, something was constantly tapping on her shoulder—the hair that stood on the back of her neck. Somehow, McGregor seemed to own her. Her senses would never let her rest. The PTSD doctor told her about heightened senses, but today, watching Leila, Jill knew something was not quite right with her. It was Leila's body language that Jill recognized that made her suspicious. Maybe it was the security checks that put Leila off-kilter. It couldn't be the loss of her Jimmy Choos that was bothering her, could it?

A knock on the door intruded on the silence, and the chief walked inside. "Jill... oh, hi," he said. "Can I have a word with you, Jill?" A glint filled his eyes as he looked at Leila. She was beautiful, after all. "In private?"

Jill looked at Leila, and it was evident she wasn't moving. "I'll wait here," Leila said.

Outside in the corridor, the chief opened a file. "I have some intel for you. But I wanted to speak to you first." He looked at the pages in the file and then quickly closed them. "Leila has passed the security checks, but what I am about to tell you is personal. Private, Jill."

Jill paused, and for a brief second, she felt relief. "It's okay; I trust her," Jill told the chief. Jill couldn't help but feel hope when they walked back into the room.

Leila tilted her head as she held out her hand. "I'm Leila Sorel." She was flirting again, and this time it annoyed Jill.

He shook her hand, holding it a second longer than he should. "Johan, but you can call me chief." He flipped through some pages and began to read out loud. "Leila Sorel, thirty-two, born American in Freeport, Louisiana. Mother and father Brazilian. Current job, a photojournalist for Time." His robotic voice changed when he flirted back. "Nice to meet you, Leila."

His face turned serious when he looked back toward Jill. "I see the swelling on your lip has gone down."

"No worse for wear," Jill said. "Did you go to that building? Did you find anything?"

"We couldn't find it. Sorry, Jill." Johan flipped a page in the file. "We also searched our databases for any gang-type members that fit their description. Chechens, Russians, so far, we've got nothing. But we did run those names you gave us. David and Stan Brown with Petrovich, and there was a blip." Jill's eyes widened. She waited for Johan to continue and wondered if they could hear her breathing speed up. He glanced at Leila. She sat seriously. "I had to get special authority from the US to access these files and get special permission to share them with you both. They're highly confidential. But first, I need to ask you both some questions, which," he shot his glance back to Leila, "which is why you are here, Leila."

Leila didn't flinch. "I'll help if I can."

"Leila, how long have you known David?" He looked at her squarely.

"Ah, about three years, give or take."

"Have you ever been on assignment with him?" he asked more pointedly.

"A couple; why?" Was that annoyance Jill detected in Leila's reply?

Johan returned his eyes to Jill and continued, "Jill, do you know what a NOC is?"

Leila began to shift nervously.

The drip of newly spawned adrenaline started to fill Jill, and she said, "NOC as in the NOC you spoke about in your brief?" Johan nodded. "You mean spy?"

The non-official cover is what most countries' governments call them. Operatives who've assumed roles as everyday citizens but remained in specific locations gathering information for one operation or another. Sometimes the NOC would stay dormant for years before being called upon to duty. Other people would refer to NOC as black ops or covert operations. There were no records of these types of operations except at the highest security levels in each country. It was sort of a gentleman's agreement, something unspoken. Plausible deniability between countries was the spy game. It often called for extensive arrangements that hid the details, the evidence, hiding the fact that the goal or target of such black ops ever occurred. WMD, weapons of mass destruction in Iraq, was one such operation. And if something went wrong, the NOC was on its own.

Leila shifted again and was about to say something to Jill. Her hand reached over, and she laid it across Jill's forearm. Her eyes pleaded. "Jill."

Johan interrupted, "Jill, I said we discovered new information, a blip when we ran Stan and David Brown's name." Leila looked at Johan knowingly and nodded affirmation to him. Not that Johan needed it. Courtesy was all he offered.

He blurted it out fast, "David's a NOC for the CIA," he paused and looked back to Leila, "and so is Miss Sorel."

Jill sat silently, feeling like she'd received another kick to her gut. All she could do was blink, and with every blink played a flashback. She had only known David for just over a year. Late nights, long assignments, the hush between them that just existed but was never spoken. That's why her instincts were like salt and pepper together in one mill over the past year. Jill knew she loved him; she'd dismissed anything else. Her instincts were so jumbled that she couldn't make any semblance of them when she was around him. Jill's shoulders slumped, and she exhaled too loud to be polite.

After several minutes, it was Leila who broke the silent spell. "David loves you, Jill; he truly does."

"Stop it, Leila. Just shut the fuck up." Hearing her words echo, Jill was almost embarrassed at what she had just blurted, but what else could she say? What else could she do? Jill grabbed her hair with both hands and leaned her tired head into her palms, elbows perched on the cold table. What was Jill supposed to think? After all, this was her lover, her best friend. Best friends tell the truth, don't they? Fear and anger circled in her head, and Jill suddenly felt exhausted.

"Do you want me to leave you two alone?" Johan asked.

Jill didn't answer. She didn't lift her head. Strands of short, tight hair pushed between Jill's fingers, and she felt like pulling it goddamn out.

Finally, Johan gave a slight huff, apparently German displeasure. "There's been a sighting of David, Jill," he finally said. He flipped another page insensitively, and before Jill could react, he continued, "What gets even more interesting is Stan Brown. He's David's current assignment."

CHAPTER
TWENTY-EIGHT

Jill bolted up and started to pace in the tiny room. Her head was beginning to pound from the confusion. "Where is he?"

"He's working on an op. It's called Operation Silhouette."

Jill stopped and stared at Leila. Leila's eyes continued to plead. "What the heck is going on, Leila?" Jill stood with her arms crossed and stared into Leila's eyes. Blink, goddamn it, you bitch, blink.

Before Leila could answer, Johan held up his palm towards Leila. "Jill." He paused for a split second, then flipped to another page.

Jill looked at Leila, then back at Johan. "What else does it say, Johan?" Jill demanded as if she was his commander.

"They think David is in Dubai, United Arab Emirates; funny thing... he left Hamburg a couple of days ago. They can't be sure, as here it is written that he's undercover. That's the latest on him." Jill and Leila both heaved a breath of relief.

"Do they know this for sure? Can they verify that it's David who is in Dubai?" Johan shook his head.

"I, ah, I...." Jill stammered. "I need to get to Dubai, chief. Or at least I need to speak to David. I know you said he is still deep undercover.

But did the brief state anything about David's whereabouts or how I can contact him?"

More pages had flipped before he confirmed no. "Also, Jill, when those bruisers held you, I received a call from Eric. FBI. We discussed searching for a man. His name is Zayed Saleem." He flipped a page. "Zayed Saleem. Age thirty-seven. NOC. Undercover Middle East PRO for Time. Target: Jill Oliver."

Jill's jaw dropped, and she looked squarely at Leila. "You know Zayed?"

"No," she insisted. "David mentioned him, but I've never met him. What else does it say about Zayed?" Leila questioned Johan.

Johan looked down at the page again and read out loud. "He was extracted from Kushka by special ops for the Russian Foreign Intelligence Agency. He was airlifted to Dubai. Neck wound. Prognosis positive."

"I thought I heard two different Russian dialects in Kushka. Does it say why I was the target?" Jill questioned.

Johan looked back at Jill with an odd look on his face. "Seems like a no-brainer to me, Jill. Whoever is targeting you knew that David was on to them; of course, they'd have had you followed."

"Then I was Zayed's target for what? To protect me? From the Chechen Mafia? Why?"

"Maybe that's why David is in Dubai," Leila interrupted. "To see Zayed."

Johan shrugged and then continued. "Operation Silhouette," he read, "suspected to be a front for Al Qaeda. Perps go into foreign countries where there is civil unrest, where a tyrant rules, and go all social networks in the country. It's a new form of terrorism," Johan continued. "Syria, Yemen, Egypt, Bahrain." He paused and took a breath. "Iran. We've been following this, as have the US and the UN.

Practically all the original EU five have too. The GCC, Arab League, you name it."

Jill looked at Leila and identified that this was the first time Leila had heard this based on her posture. Stiff and straight, Jill asked the question anyway. "You knew about this, Leila, didn't you? You told me that David's Pulitzer was about Operation Silhouette. What do you know, Leila? I want to know now. NOW!" Jill pointed the finger at Leila, its tip nearly touching Leila's nose.

"I, ah, I don't know anything more than what we spoke about, Jill." There were no excessive blinks and no REM when awake. "David told me this; that's all I know."

The room was hushed for a moment, and all that could be heard was a distant ring of a phone in another room. "Did you know he was a NOC?"

Leila's eyes lowered. The gentleman's agreement with a governmental NOC was non-disclosure of information, and Leila again looked around for surveillance.

Before she answered Jill, Leila asked, "Are we being recorded?"

Johan confirmed "no," and continued, "I don't care about your US government breach. Clearly, you two need some time alone so we can continue. There's a lot to cover yet, ladies. Ten minutes." His chair chirped as he stood up and closed the door behind him.

Jill was treading the floor; her arm squashed into her armpits when Leila walked over and attempted to hug Jill. "No, Leila." Jill stood squarely. Pools of distrust filled Jill's eyes. She lifted her left shoulder and slightly turned as she repelled Leila, wincing at the pain.

"Jill," Leila said with reverence. "Jill." Her voice grew louder. "Please, Jill, please sit down. I'll explain everything."

Jill did not move, stubborn as a mule.

"Jill..." Leila looked carefully as she trailed off, her head averting downward. "Please, Jill, there is more you need to know about David."

Those words sliced through Jill and grated against her bones. A look of shock and something unrecognizable shone in her eyes as she slowly took her place back at the table and stared blankly at Leila. Leila sighed heavily. Jill blinked back, and then Leila began.

"Are you familiar with the Patriot Act?" Leila said rhetorically. "Well, it isn't really like how it is described in the media. There was more communication between federal agencies, but since the act was introduced, they've tightened the screws. Ever since 9/11, NOCs have been under strict NDAs—non-disclosure agreements." Leila reached over and pressed her hand on Jill's. "NOCs are ordinary people that move around, so what better cover than a journalist? Besides, I am not what you would call a mainstream NOC. I'm not trained in field ops. My job is to take pictures. Pictures of what the NOCs discover. I'm more like an assistant, the photog that takes pictures of crime scenes. Except my backdrop is the spy scene.

"He is a great writer, Jill, and his job is real." Leila began to sound bothered, but Leila always seemed bothered. "Ya know, Jill, it's not like he screwed around on you or something. It's just a career choice. Like everyone else, that doesn't fully explain what happened at work. Like if you were married to a doctor and he didn't tell you how many patients he lost that day," Leila appeared to try and reason.

"I thought husbands and wives didn't have secrets; it's what a good marriage is built on. It's called trust, Leila."

"Do you tell David details on a nuke move? Do you tell him about threats, terrorists, and forthcoming events? For God's sake, he didn't even know you were a Remote Viewer."

Jill had no choice but to admit that Leila had her on that one; all she could do was grunt and surrender.

A few minutes passed in silence. Jill thought hard. Leila was right. In the law enforcement game, nothing was ever as it seemed. So Leila and David are NOCs. She could understand Leila not breaching the confidence of her NDA. David—that one she'd have to think about more soulfully. But despite the secrets and the large stone in her gut, she needed Leila's help right now, and she had no other choice. The pity party shit she'd figure out later.

"Leila, about my viewings, I need to tell you something. I had a strong one—something I had never experienced before. I drew the Star of David a few days before this viewing. The one you saw in my notebook, remember?" Leila sat slightly forward. Jill began to relay what she had seen. "The next time I tried viewing, I saw something I had never seen before. This viewing was vivid, like a movie or something. There were men around a table, six men that all seemed like they were from different countries. They spoke of this Operation Silhouette. They even talked about controlling more than just the Russian oil." And then she stopped. "And here is the weird part, Lei. I saw these men in black gowns, and they were circling a wooden Star of David. It was the exact one in your photo. They were standing around it chanting. Chanting the word Ochrana."

"Ochrana," for a second, Jill thought she saw recognition in Leila's eyes. "What the hell kind of name is that?" Leila blurted.

"I've got Kali searching, but so far, nothing. The leader said something that Ochrana was formed to control Russian oil. Have you heard this word before?"

"Ah, no."

They sat in silence. Leila spoke first. "Can you call Kali and see if she's found anything? Do you know the GSG very well, Jill?"

"I'll call Kali when we're done. As for GSG, they are the top CTU counter-terrorism unit in the world. I think it's because they also have direct access to Interpol. Given their proximity to the European Union, they have particular pull in these agencies that the US doesn't have."

"Then why not tell Johan? It's worth a try," Leila hastened. "He said he didn't care about US breaches, so your oath won't matter here, right?"

"Can you imagine what he'd say if I told him I have psychic powers?"

The door opened, and Johan popped into his head. "All clear?" He eyed one, then the other. "Did you kids kiss and make up?" Leila shot him a 'whatever' look, and Jill noticed that Leila instantly did not like him.

"Okay, where were we?" He sat back down and shuffled the pages. "Stan Brown, age fifty-two, CEO of Marksmen Oil."

"Why was David's target Stan Brown? He's his father, for God's sake."

"Well," Chief began as Leila and Jill perched on their chairs, "it appears our Mr. Brown had some blips on the screen himself when we ran his name. Good call on that one, Jill." He flipped to the next page. "He hasn't left Hamburg, not by air anyway. It seems our Mr. Brown has a thing for oil. Russian oil, to be more precise. It seems as recent as two weeks ago that large amounts of cash had been transferred, well should I say laundered, based on the number of times it's been rerouted." The ladies exchanged a glance, mesmerized. Leila seemed the most impressed as she connected the dots of Jill's viewing with the report.

"Some people are stupid," he said as he shook his head and read silently. "I think he needs to fire whoever is managing his transfers. No wire transfer information is safe anymore. Jeez," he chuckled. "He even sent money through Cyprus." He paused at the bewildered looks on their faces. "You do know that Cyprus has one of the biggest banking wormholes in this hemisphere, right?"

"No," Jill answered.

"What else?" Leila urged, growing impatient. Leila was brash most days but was bright, and the reading pace appeared to grate on her nerves.

Johan shot a look back at Leila. "In the sidebar notes from the analysts ... when running Petrovich and Brown's name, it states that Petrovich and Brown were in Afghanistan approximately the same time, just over two months ago. There's a high probability they know each other."

He closed the file when Jill asked, "It just doesn't make sense, Johan. Why would David work as a NOC tracking his father?"

"Oh yeah," he said nonchalantly as he flipped the file back open and thumbed to the last page. "David Brown, age thirty-two, NOC for CIA, cover, freelance journalist. Born Robert Barnes, adopted by Stan Brown at age one week." He looked up at Jill's stunned face. "David is not Stan's biological son."

CHAPTER TWENTY-NINE

The porcelain clinked as spoons stirred coffee. Jill and Leila were alone now in the small, stark room. Johan left to take an urgent call. He said something about new intel, and they waited in anticipation, sipping the hot brew. It had to be well over 1900 hours by now. Five hours and counting for the uranium buy is what Johan had said before he left the room.

"I had no clue, Jill." Leila broke the silence. "I wonder if David knew Stan wasn't his biological father. It sounds like he's okay, Jill," Leila tried to reassure her.

Jill sat befuddled. What is okay? she thought to herself as she gulped her coffee. She was thinking, all right. Her mind sped fast through her tunnels. "He must have known; that's why he was working on his target. Stan." Leila looked at Jill and waited for her to say something.

Silence hung. Then Jill said, "I found a card in David's pocket. I can't remember the doctor's name, but he specialized in DNA testing, Glen, or something. Could be a story he was working on, I guess." Jill stopped herself. "Story—did David even write any stories?" she asked with an intentional sting for Leila. The jibe was ignored.

"Jill, a NOC is not an active agent, you know. They do their regular jobs, waiting for the call. Sure, they're in specific locations for a reason, blending in, watching, and learning. If the CIA wanted Stan, David would have been a perfect NOC for the case. It's probably why he was recruited. David must have known Stan is not his birth father. They also must have known they didn't get along. I guess listening in on a few calls would have determined that. Jill, your viewing, did you see what they looked like, these men?"

Pondering, then reflecting on the mental images, Jill answered, "Yes, all except the fat man."

"The fat man?" A pause. "How old was he?" Leila questioned.

"Don't know; all I could see was the back of his head. He smoked cigars, though."

"What?" Leila's voice leaped with recognition. "Could you see the brand, Jill, the name band on the cigar?"

"It's not like that, Leila. Sometimes you can see details, but most of the time, it's just impressions. Words can be full sentences or just impressions."

"You said this viewing was different, like a movie?"

"It was, but it's not an exact kinda thing. A viewer has to be careful not to fill in the blanks. It could skew the viewing." Another pause. "Why?"

"Stan smoked cigars right in his office and didn't even ask if I minded when I was there. The jerk." Leila grabbed a pen and the notepad that sat on the table. She wrote the words STAN BROWN in all caps and underlined it. Then she started her journalistic scribe. Operation Silhouette. She quickly underlined it with several fast strokes.

"Brussels," Leila spoke as she wrote, and Jill followed her writing on the page. "I ended up in Brussels on assignment for Time. The CIA is well aware of these new ways of spreading terrorism—Al Qaeda disguised as activists, using social networks to enrage people for control of countries or oil, and its resources. In my assignment brief, they mentioned what Johan said. Social networks were hard to control. The US is concerned about it, Jill. Well, anyway, I was sent to Brussels with another NOC as there was supposed to be a meeting of people who controlled this Operation Silhouette. I think it was the meeting you saw in your viewing. Was David in your viewing?"

Jill frowned and hushed, "No."

The chair creaked as Leila shifted back, flipping her pen deftly through her fingers. "If your viewing was accurate, Jill, then that picture of the star I took meant something. That must be where they meet. Does anything else come to mind? Have you shared this star theory with anyone?"

"Johan said Cyprus, right?" Leila nodded. "In my viewing, the men were talking of transferring money from Cyprus; I think it was by boat to Germany."

They both stared at each other, but Leila said what Jill thought. "Do you think the fat man in your viewing was Stan?"

Jill's tensed body language affirmed yes.

Johan walked in, and before he could sit down, Jill asked, "Have you ever heard the word Ochrana, chief?"

He stood, apparently thinking. "Ochrana, no. Sounds Russian." Och-ra-na, he wrote in his notes. "I can run the name. Why? Where'd you get that name?"

Jill looked at Leila and was surprised when Leila said, "I heard it from an informant in Brussels. Jill and I were just discussing this, and we think it may have something to do with Operation Silhouette. There's more, Johan. This informant also said there's a large shipment of cash being moved. It's coming via Cyprus, and it's coming to Germany. Maybe it's the same money that Stan is moving?" Johan's mouth drew open. "I think whatever is happening with Operation Silhouette has something to do with Petrovich and the buy tonight. What's the new intel?"

"The analysts are still analyzing." He rolled his eyes. "Who is this informant?"

Leila made up a half-cocked story, and the chief raised his brow in disbelief but said nothing. With a swift brush against his arm, Leila flirted just enough to settle his suspicion, and he rushed toward the door.

"I find it hard to connect an American businessman with purchasing nuclear devices. What would Stan want with anything like that? Moving cash to protect himself from US taxes, I could understand." He didn't sound convinced.

Jill said, "Run Ochrana with the Star of David." He gave her a funny look and closed the door behind him.

"I think we're getting close now," Jill said with renewed hope. "Stan Brown, that bastard!"

CHAPTER THIRTY

The sounds of the clay tiles splattered across the table. "I don't know, Leila. If the chief walks in, he'll think I'm a loon," Jill said hesitantly.

"Who gives a rat's ass," Leila said as she clicked the lock on the door. She hurried back to the table as Jill began moving the numbers. "What can I do?" Leila offered.

"Nothing. You just need to be quiet."

Leila zipped her fingers across her lips and leaned back in her chair. After several minutes of humming, Jill chanted, "Ochrana." More chanting and then "Operation Silhouette...."

"Shukran, thank you," the fat man said as he sucked on the shisha pipe. The bright blue hose coiled into an Arabian bong. The small Bangladeshi man scurried away after setting down the tray. The tent was grand. Majestic billowy strands of maroon fabric fluttered as the air conditioners breezed cool air. The tent walls heaved in and out as the wind outside swirled sand into the air.

Bright red cushions lay on the sand, and the fat man's legs splayed, too big to crisscross as he sat. A normal-sized man would not have squashed the eight inches of cushion into the ground as he did. His heels touched what looked to be an intricately woven Iranian carpet. The flecks of gold that stitched the sides were flattened under the weight of his shoes. The wash of color from the hanging lanterns kept the backside of his head a silhouette.

Two men dressed in black fatigues stood guarding each side of the door flaps that opened to the hot desert. The long coil hissed as the fat man sucked before puffing out the smoke.

It was Petrovich who spoke first with his thick Slavic accent. "We finally meet again." His dark eyes glared as he looked at the fat man. "Why are you here? There is no need to take such a risk."

The fat man took another pull on the pipe, this time slower. "Some things I need to take care of myself." The fat man patted the sizable black suitcase that lay beside him.

"I've been told your lab rats have inspected the package and that everything is as we've promised," Petrovich said as he leaned back and rested his right arm on the back of the bright cushions.

A mousy waiter scurried back, smiled widely, and said, "Another flavor, sir? We have apple, cherry, and—" The fat man's fingers lifted together in annoyance as he dismissed the servant.

"Only one thing left to be confirmed," said Petrovich. "As we've agreed, you will not use this technology in my homeland. Mother Russia does not need your capitalist pigs there; your country has done enough damage." Petrovich leaned forward and shot a menacing look toward the fat man. "If I hear anything like this, I'll kill you myself, and then I'll kill your family one bone at a time." The guards stirred as they cradled their AK-47s.

"You need not worry, my brother," the fat man drawled. "I have better uses for it."

Jill dropped the pen onto the newly scribed pad and exhaled. Leila stared blankly at her. Jill blinked several times as clarity faded back in. She couldn't decide if Leila was looking at her in admiration or if she thought Jill was a goddamn freak. They both gazed down at the pad. "What the hell is it?" Jill said as she studied the drawing.

"I was wondering that myself as you drew it. Man, that's some spooky shit to watch." Leila flicked the pad and turned it towards herself. On the page was a large thin triangular shape that seemed too large to fit onto the page.

Jill grabbed the notebook back and began to write below the odd shape. Fat man, silhouette, Petrovich. Then she took a sip of her cold coffee. Leila read her notes upside down; it was a journalistic skill that Jill knew she cherished.

"Did you see the fat man's face?" Jill shook her head no and began to put the clay numbers back in their pouch. Jill was tired after this viewing, more so than usual. It took more energy on a cellular level, primarily when she was concentrating on a particular subject. But again, this viewing was not a typical Remote View. She could see even more vividly than the last time.

"Tell me everything," Leila demanded. "What did you see?"

"A fat man in a tent talking to a man that looked like Petrovich." Jill shuddered and continued, "There were also two men guarding the doors—ya know, the kind we had the pleasure of meeting here."

"Chechens," Leila added. "What the hell did those men want with David anyway?"

All Jill could do was shrug, as she did not know. "There were Chechens in Doha, in Kushka, and now Hamburg. It has to do with me, Leila, not you."

"Well, somebody really wants something from you, Jill."

"What's odd is that I could swear I was being followed in the US even before I left for Doha." Leila's brow arched.

"Anyway, in this viewing, they were meeting in a tent. I think the viewing was in a desert, Leila, 'cause it looked like an Arabian tent."

"Desert? Do you think it could be Dubai?" Leila gently tapped the notebook. "What does this look like to you, Jill?" Leila questioned, examining what Jill had drawn.

Jill looked at the thin triangle-type shape on the page and began to run her fingers along the sketched lines. It seemed like a blueprint drawn by a child. Jill's finger continued to move along its lines, and the tip of her finger brushed the needle-nosed tip of the triangle at the top of the page. Inside the triangle were rectangles that looked like vertical cubes of ice stacked end to end, forming the triangle.

Jill looked swiftly towards Leila in recognition. "I've seen this before, Lei. It was in a flash I had when I first found out David was missing. See this line here?"

As Jill traced it, Leila looked down again at the page; her head tilted to the right when she echoed, "Flash?"

They both studied the bumpy line that stretched horizontally across the page.

"I call it a flash card that I sometimes get. It was this picture as if I was watching it from above. It was like a needle shooting through something fuzzy, like pillows, like a cloud."

The lock door handle jiggled and clicked as someone attempted to open it. Johan's voice came through loud. "Ladies, open the door, please. It's GSG policy not to lock the doors." Defiantly, Leila rolled her eyes and unlocked it.

"We haven't heard from our man on the inside," he said as he rushed in, shut the door, and sat down. "He's missed his last two checks." Johan's head lowered. "All indications are that the buy will not be happening tonight." He made an inaudible grumbling.

"Do you think it has to do with our capture earlier? We spooked them, maybe?" Jill asked.

"Leila. Anything on Stan?"

Johan shook his head. "They're running more intense intel now, but at first glance, there has been no apprehension of large sums of cash or deposits into German banks. Not yet, anyway. We ran the word Ochrana. It seems you have a fascinating informant." He glanced slyly with half a giggle towards Leila. She didn't return the flirt. "Ochrana didn't pull up much, but when the analysts ran Ochrana with the Star of David. Not much, but with Ochrana and star alone, it nearly started our computer systems on fire." Johan began to read faster. He was apparently trying to keep his cool; after all, he was German.

"Ochrana, the Star icon," he continued in a forced monotone, "has been sporadically reported over the years. He seems to be an old legend and has never been taken seriously. Like those conspiracy theories you read online or listen to on the late-night radio. One world power, the world is ending, you get my drift. I think your informant might have had a few too many whiskeys. But here is something you will find of interest, Jill. Stan Brown just landed in Dubai approximately five hours ago."

CHAPTER
THIRTY-ONE

Jill and Leila exited the black Audi and entered the Hamburg airport. They practically ran to their gate as Jill held her rib cage with her right arm, only allowing herself to wince a few times.

"I understand that Germany has substantial ties to Israel, but seriously, they are not able or willing to help us in the UAE? He didn't believe there was a connection with Stan either. That's bullshit!"

"We've got the contact for the intelligence broker he trusts. I guess that's all we can expect. Frankly, based on what's been happening, he's vetted, and right now, that is all I care about," Jill huffed. "I don't think he believed anything we said after he ran Ochrana anyway."

The A340 was run-down. The carpet reeked of grunge as they walked back down the soggy aisle towards the emergency exit row. As the flight hit cruise at thirty-nine thousand feet, Leila said, "You were right about Johan. He would have laughed us out of the GSG for good if you had told him about your abilities."

"There's more that I haven't told you," Jill said, her gaze fixed on the bulkhead before her. Without legroom in the exit row, it was awkward and uncomfortable. Leila sat in silence, with only the sound of the dishes clattering in the galley to be heard.

Before Jill continued, she looked around the airplane. There was an older man seated by the window across a row of empty middle seats, and no one sat in the seats behind them. Only when she felt comfortable, she began to speak again. "In the viewing at GSG, the fat man appeared to be buying something, or it seemed that way anyway."

"You mean what was supposed to happen tonight at GSG?"

There was a pregnant pause, and then Jill hushed, "Yeah." It was only one word, but Jill already knew what Leila was thinking. Minutes passed, and then the inevitable question came.

"Err... don't take this the wrong way, Jill, but these viewings that you do—is it possible to project what is happening in your life into viewings? It seems over-the-top to think you see Stan Brown buying uranium from this guy Petrovich. As you said, Jill, filling in the blanks?"

"I know..." Jill tapered off and started into the tunnels. She wasn't sure how long she was in there when Leila spoke.

"Where's that trolley dolly?" Leila said snidely. "Guess we have to help ourselves." Leila fidgeted in her seat. Ten more minutes passed before they were finally served wine in plastic wine glasses. "This ain't no first class," Leila continued to grumble, trying to keep herself occupied while she waited for Jill to say something.

"I suppose it's possible," Jill said as she sipped from the plastic glass.

"The thing that gets me, Jill, is why Stan? It just doesn't make sense. What would he want to do with uranium?"

"Yeah," Jill said halfheartedly.

Without notice, Leila jumped up, clicked open the overhead, stuck her hand in her bag, and pulled out some paper. Leila clicked her pen on and began to write. "Okay, let's assume the fat man is Stan. So far, we have him in Afghanistan winning a contract. We also have Petrovich there around the same time. Then today, you have a viewing of Stan buying something from Petrovich in some Arabian tent." Leila scrawled.

"That would make sense of why David is in Dubai then. But David wasn't following Stan. Stan just landed there," Jill added.

"Also, David went missing just over a week ago, not two months ago when Stan was in Afghanistan." Leila started tapping her pen on the page. "What are we missing?"

"So David's a NOC, and his target is Stan."

"Stan's not David's birth father," Leila interjected. She paused, and the domino pieces began to fall into line. "So the question is... why is Stan David's target if David went to Dubai ahead of him?"

"What hospital did Johan say Zayed was at?" Leila questioned.

"American International, I think. Something with the word 'American' in it. What, you think we should visit him?"

"My bets are he knows something. Maybe David went to see him. David would have vetted me, Jill. If he knows something, he'll talk to me. It's called HUMINT. I'm sure he's up to speed on it."

"HUMINT?"

"HUMan INTelligence; refers to intelligence gathering, you know, sharing secrets from one human to another. It's spy shit, Jill."

The silence between them was deafening, both trying to come up with the answer. "Well," Leila said at last. "It's clearly got something to do with Operation Silhouette."

Jill sat up and winced at the lingering pain in her ribs. "What did Johan say it was again—Ochrana? A conspiracy theory?" Jill mocked.

"One world power and all," Leila quoted with her fingers in the air. "That guy hasn't been laid for a century. Wound tighter than a drilled screw in hardwood."

"You know he was right, though, Lei. I've heard this before too. One world power, the Freemasons, is well known for this term. Even the likes of Hillary Clinton referenced it. One God's rule," Jill whispered.

"One president of the whole world—my colleagues and I have joked about that so many times," Leila chimed. "But it's usually after a few drinks and a discussion about our overbearing boss."

The thrum of the engines helped move their thoughts forward. Then it came fast, like an epiphany. Based on her SOG work, Jill knew what it was instantly when the idea entered her mind. "What if my viewing is accurate and Stan was buying uranium?"

Leila listened intently. She may be beautiful and bold, but Jill had the gift, and Jill's brain was ticking fast now. "There is only one reason someone would be buying uranium, Lei. And if that someone wants to dominate with a one world power..."

They sipped again, silently trying to digest this thought.

Jill's foot tapped, and their glasses were empty after another sip. Leila lurched upwards, hit the call button, sat down fast, and said, "Operation Silhouette, what does this have to do with Stan and him buying uranium, Jill?"

"Don't know, a distraction maybe, but I do know David thought Stan was evil." Jill saw Leila slightly stiffen. Most people wouldn't have caught the move. But Jill was a profiler, and she knew something was weird about the movement. But Jill almost felt guilty for saying Stan was evil. "If David was right, then he can pretty much do anything. But Leila," Jill sighed hopefully and watched Leila, "one thing I do know. If Stan is in Dubai, then so is David."

CHAPTER
THIRTY-TWO

13:42 Zulu Time—DUBAI, UNITED ARAB EMIRATES

The day was almost over when they landed in Dubai. They had passed through immigration painlessly enough, and after Jill had done her scans, they jumped into the first of a long line of idling taxis.

The city beamed, bright sunshine reflecting off modern glass buildings. The time on the dashboard read 18:12. The taxi driver honked his way through construction site after construction site before he sped along the main road. The odd-shaped buildings glimmered beside Starbucks, Pizza Hut, and a Waitrose supermarket.

"So this is Dubai," Leila said as they passed another cosmetic surgery billboard. "Not really an Arabian experience, is it? And who names a hotel The Address?" Leila snorted.

Jill shrugged. "Johan recommended it, so I am sure it'll be nice." They merged right towards a large off-ramp, crossed over a long bridge, and watched a high-speed subway train pass over ahead.

There, towering over the city, was a colossal structure. The driver noticed their wide eyes through the rear-view mirror and explained, "World's tallest building." His head bobbled. "The name is Burj Khalifa, after an Abu Dhabi sheik, you know. The hotel where you are staying is at the base of it just over there." He pointed with a crooked brown finger. "Abu Dhabi had to bail out Dubai since the real estate bubble burst," he babbled.

The car popped over several speed bumps before trailing up the drive to the doors. Jill noted that there were no security checks, just bling bling bling everywhere she looked.

"Holy shit, Jill," Leila said as she kicked off her shoes in their hotel room, plopping down onto a comfy bed. Jill was already looking out the window and stretching her neck hard to view the top of the tower. Leila walked over and mirrored Jill.

"Hocus pocus my ass," she said. "This is real shit; that's your sketch, Jill."

"Yeah." Jill was disheartened. The realization hit her the moment she saw it. Jill knew now what was happening. She was in Dubai to find David, and her viewings were guiding her every step of the way. But it was more than that now, and Jill knew that too. Find Stan, and I find David. Find Stan and stop a major catastrophic event. It was her job, after all. Survive!

"You're in Dubai?" Kali murmured, annoyed after being awoken by Jill's unexpected phone call. "Cool." Jill could hear her stretch.

"Yeah, sorry to call you so early, but it's important, and I was sure Eric would be in the office, that he is in Virginia. We believe David's here somewhere too." Jill briefed Kali, saying, "Right now, I need you to translate my RV to Eric."

"You sure that's a good idea, Jill?" Kali queried.

"Right now, I have no choice. I'll take the hit if there is one. Just do it, okay, Kali?" There was no fussing from Kali, so Jill continued, "Tell Eric that I believe that Stan Brown has just bought, or is going to buy uranium from Petrovich—the transaction I believe was supposed to happen last night in Germany. But it didn't happen. Tell him that I think Stan is behind Operation Silhouette too. I don't know where the bars are now or how he plans to fuse the WMD, but get Eric to run Matta Al Jazeera—Al Qaeda's leader. Kali, I think Stan is playing his big-boy game, and Al Qaeda is not involved. Oh, and also find out the last known whereabouts of Dr. E.—the uranium doctor. Get a list of available labs that can test uranium. Tell him to do a sweep of them. And Leila is with me—let Eric know. You can call her phone since you have her number." Jill hung up the phone.

"We need to go see Zayed," she said, turning to Leila.

"Ever heard of a shower first?" Leila moaned.

Jill gave Leila an eye roll. "Come on, Leila; we don't have time."

Once outside on the curb—still unshowered—Jill hailed a taxi. "American International Hospital," Jill chimed to the driver. He sped along the main road, and Jill began to think of Zayed. It was strange that her first thought was of Zayed meeting Leila and what he would think of her.

The traffic was a bumper-to-bumper parking lot of vehicles. While they chugged along, they had time to appreciate the scenery. The buildings were tastefully designed for the most part. There were giant pictures of what appeared to be royal family members decorating the glass fifty stories high. Tall points shot up to the sky on some buildings, and there was even a building with a large round ball on the top. Their taxi honked its way for miles before it pulled off the main road and headed over an overpass leading to the hospital.

The large brown building sat alongside a wide river. Inside the hospital was a scene that Jill had never experienced before.

"This is a hospital?" Leila exclaimed. "Nice!"

It looked more like a glamorous hotel than a medical facility. Over-sized wing-backed chairs were scattered around. Oversized plants gave a homey appeal, along with a fake fireplace. A uniformed man walked around the chair area, asking the waiting patients if they wanted something to drink.

After a stop at the reception desk, they found Zayed's room on the third floor. "Hello?" said Jill hesitantly before they walked through the door. There was only one bed in the posh place, and Zayed's eyes peeled open as they stood before him.

"Hello, Miss Jill. I was hoping to see you again." His right eye twitched. "I was told that you might visit me. Guess you have the right connections to find me so fast." He caught his breath and then looked at Leila. "And who is this?" Zayed purred.

"Leila Sorel." Leila pushed forward past Jill. Zayed had a bandage around his neck and an IV drip stuck in his left arm. Besides his bandaged state, nothing about the décor would have given a clue that this was a hospital room.

Jill's brow furrowed at the introductions and got to the point. "Have you seen David? Have you heard from him?"

"I haven't seen him. Little hard to get around these days." Zayed looked up at the bag of fluid.

"I know why you couldn't tell me when we were together that you were goddamn babysitting me." Jill's anger spilled. "Was it fun watching me, or did you actually care about David's well-being? I know you're a NOC, Zayed." Jill's stance shifted.

Zayed rustled beneath his bed sheets. "Don't take it personally, Jill. It's just a job. I was hired to monitor you while attempting to find David. That's all. Oh, and for the record, they may call what I do a NOC. But I don't work for any particular agency. I like to call myself a free agent. An independent contractor of sorts."

Leila seemed perturbed about how the conversation was going and pressed for details. "Who were you working for? Who hired you to manage Jill?"

"Miss Leila, they told me about you, the people who hired me. You're a NOC, just like David. How long have you worked for the OGA, other government agency?"

"Look, Mr. Zayed," Leila spat, "we need information, and we need it now. There is more at stake here than just finding David."

It took a minute, and then Zayed said, "I know."

"Why were you extracted from Kushka? Why were Russian ops there in the first place?" Jill demanded.

"Oh, I don't know, Jill. They didn't bother to tell me when you left me there bleeding to death." Zayed glared at Jill squarely. "My guess is they were there for the same reason as David. Look, ladies, I gather information for the people who pay me. One of my best clients is the US. They pay very well. This client gently asked me to share what I know because someone you know has wasta."

"Wasta?"

"It means someone with clout. You know, a big shot at the CIA. I'm not happy about it, but I've been paid, so who cares." Zayed motioned for Jill to close the door. "My client," Zayed continued, "and its allies have a concern. So do the Russians."

"With what?"

"Grozny."

"Grozny?"

"Grozny is the capital of Chechnya. It has a significant oil pipeline. It's currently under the control of the Chechen Mafia. The Russians want control back. They need the export energy to catapult them into a complete resurgence to regain their position as a world power." Zayed looked out the window to the water below and then back at them. Jill wondered if he was doing his surveillance scan. "The Gulf states are getting worried. There's been intel that the Chechens are getting ready to do something with the pipeline." Zayed's mouth crinkled on the right side when he said, "The Russians think they are working with the good old US of A, but I know different. Oil is money, ladies. And money is power."

Leila looked at Jill. Jill could almost read her mind.

"What does this have to do with David?" Jill probed.

"Two words," Zayed snidely said. "Stan Brown."

"That's just stupid," blasted Leila. "What drugs do they have you on? If they wanted Stan Brown, they could easily pick him up."

"Well, that's the forty-three-million-dollar question, isn't it?" Zayed mocked. "I get paid to gather information, nothing more. Our Mr. Brown is clean. He's been interrogated before, and I don't mean the cute little girl kind of interrogation. Still, no agency has ever been able to get anywhere. He's protected."

"No one's protected, Zayed," Leila asserted, clearly ticked off. "The CIA can pluck him anytime they want."

Zayed just smirked.

"You think he has something to do with the Chechen Mafia?" Jill asked. "Do you think that has to do with why the Chechens were following us, Zayed?"

He lifted his hand and brushed the bandage on his neck lightly. "Not me, Jill... you."

"What... why?" Jill thought out loud. "Because they believe that I know where David is? If they are following me..." Jill thought of Hamburg and looked at Leila.

"If they were following Jill," Leila interrupted, "they would know that David wasn't with her."

"But they would not know if he'd been in touch. If he'd said something or given you something, Jill," surmised Zayed. "Do you have something of his, Jill?" Jill didn't answer that question and could only think back to the question Stan had asked her regarding the possession of some documents.

"David must have something, something on Stan Brown or something about Grozny, and it seems an awful lot of people are in the race to find it." Then a flash of the schematic passed Jill's vision.

"I heard that David might be here in Dubai. Strange, Stan had just arrived too, if it's true, don't you think, ladies? So how long have you known David," Zayed peered in Leila's direction, "Miss Leila?"

"Two and a half years or so. David recruited me." She sounded proud. This news pricked at Jill.

"Not a long time to know someone well, is it?" Zayed mocked.

CHAPTER THIRTY-THREE

"I don't think it was such a good idea to tell Zayed where we are staying." Leila voiced her concern to Jill as they walked through the hospital lobby. "We can't trust the little prick. I wonder if he has ever met David. And what was all that smoke and mirrors bullshit? We can take care of ourselves from Mr. Hotty Pants. You said you shared a room with him. Yummy!" Leila exaggeratedly licked her lips. "Anyway, ignore what he was saying about David. The guy's an idiot, all that independent contractor crap." They had walked a few more steps before Leila asked, "Where are we going now?"

Jill stopped abruptly. "Let me see your phone. I need to call Kali."

"I don't think she's up yet." Leila pointed to the clock on the wall that read 7:13 p.m. Jill sat down on one of the bright blue chairs, and Leila found one next to her. "Why do you need to speak to Kali suddenly?"

"I found a drawing in Kushka. It was in Russian. Kali was having it translated."

"What was it a picture of?" Leila sat up fast.

"It could have been anything. It had boxes and arrows and Russian words. It was a computer printout, I think."

"You found this in that guarded villa? Why would they leave some-thing if it was that important?"

"Well, David's notebook was there. The schematic was crumpled up like it was trash." Jill squished her hands together, miming a snowball, and continued, "Maybe David left it as a clue, like the writing in the notebook."

Jill hesitated. "Maybe." But she really didn't know what to think. Her mind was on Zayed. Her mind was somewhere else. Could she have been so stupid? After seeing Zayed and hearing what he had to say, she felt something when she stood in his room. The nagging feeling was doing more than annoying her. A shot of pain pulsed in her head. She needed to get back into the tunnels. She needed to think this through.

"Why would someone guard an empty villa full of trash?" asked Leila.

"I wouldn't call it guarding; he was more like a watchman."

The two sat for a few more minutes before deciding they were hun-gry. They needed to wait until Kali could get into the office anyway, and Jill couldn't handle Kali when she was tired and grumpy. She likely had to contact the translation department, which didn't open until nine o'clock.

They walked outside. Jill hadn't realized that the hospital was in a construction zone. They needed to hail a taxi, but there were none in sight. In the distance beyond the construction site fence was the main road. The streetlights were already burning brightly.

"Shit, it's like breathing in water," Leila complained in the humidity of the evening air.

"It's hot, but let's walk over there." Jill pointed towards the road past the construction lot. "We might be waiting here all night, and the sun is almost down." Jill's stomach grumbled. She hadn't eaten much in the past week, and her clothes began drooping.

"Your rib okay?" Leila asked, casting a worried look at Jill. Jill just nodded.

They turned the corner, walking past large tin signs, then further past tall tin-paneled fences that housed the construction site. Leila saw it first. Dust flew as a black SUV screeched to a stop fifty meters before the curb. Coming up fast behind them was a white Land Cruiser with dark-tinted windows. Two men jumped out of the first car and shouted at them.

Before Jill could think or plan, she yelled, "Run!" She turned and darted in between the two pieces of a metal fence. Her shoulders brushed the metal, and Leila followed.

Jill's heart raced, and adrenaline overcame her tiredness. She had to hold her stinging side as she jumped over pieces of concrete. They were zigzagging through the construction obstacle course when Jill heard the second car squeal to a stop. She heard someone yell in a Slavic language. A bullet whizzed past Jill's head, even with a good head start. It was too dark for her to see the water before she tripped over the bank's edge and fell in. The putrid water met her nose as she spat it out of her mouth. Her feet hit a rock in the waist-deep pool. What the hell... and where the hell is Leila? "Shit!"

Jill crouched further into the water when she heard more yelling. Chechens. Jill could swear she heard a car racing away. She concentrated on her heavy breathing; she had to be silent but needed air. Will they listen to me? Can they see me? She had no way to defend herself. She was a sitting duck in the water.

She had to move; she had to find Leila. She had to survive.

All she could see was the darkness of the land. She was no more than five feet from the water's edge. Shouting. They were getting closer.

Think, Jill, think! She looked around and hoped for some recognition of her surroundings. She saw streetlights at a short distance, but the bank she fell from blocked her view of the men with the silent guns. Jill slowly turned around to scan her perimeters, and as she looked behind, all she could see was a large body of water, a river, or a canal. Maybe she could feel a current. There were lights on the other side of the shore. She couldn't swim with her rib; it was too far. Jill searched her brain for answers—where was she, and what should she do next?

Jill was about to swim closer to the bank when she was startled by the sound of pebbles tumbling and plopping into the water with her. She dared not move as she crouched in the water. Then she heard a whisper. "Jill?" It was Leila who squatted below the four-foot bank. Jill stood, showing herself to Leila. Then she silently lowered back into the water. Inch by inch, she began to move in Leila's direction. Time moved in slow motion.

As the sounds of boots smacking dirt grew louder, she thought her heart had stopped—Am I breathing? The fear was maddening; she felt she would burst out of her skin.

And then there he was. He stood atop the bank and looked out in Jill's direction, only hesitating momentarily before scanning the rest of the water. He was standing only three feet to the left above Leila. He couldn't see her. Can he see me?

Even in the dusk, she could tell he was dressed in black with a black cap, just like that guy in Doha and like the man at the Hamburg airport. He moved slowly and turned. It sounded like he was swearing and definitely swearing. He began to walk away and then abruptly stopped. More swearing before he turned and looked back in Jill's direction. She did not move. She did not breathe, and for a moment, Jill thought she should close her eyes. The man hesitated and continued to walk away. It had seemed like an eternity before she noticed Leila waving her hand. Even with the moonlight, Jill thought not even Leila could see her. Minutes passed, and upon hearing nothing more, Jill slowly continued to inch her way back to the muddy, rocky bank.

"You okay?" Leila whispered.

"Yeah," Jill whispered back. "Come on." They waded along the shore's edge, their feet half in the water and half on the rocks trying not to make any noise. An eerie feeling surrounded Jill's soul, and she stopped and held her breath, listening for the slightest sound that would ignite a sprint.

"What?" whispered Leila. All Jill did was lift a finger in front of her shushing lips. They heard only the silence of the night and a hint of the city's hum in the background. Where were they? They began to walk again, punctuating their steps with frequent stops, hoping for continued silence from the men. The shoreline seemed endless. They needed to climb the bank. Jill motioned Leila to look over the edge. Leila stood, peeked her head, and gave Jill a thumbs-up. They dug their feet into the walls of hard sand and pulled themselves over the ridge.

The construction site was meagerly lit by moonlight. Dark shadows cast gloom everywhere. She didn't know if any of them were the men. Then Jill heard shouting and the crunching sound of gravel underfoot as the men moved towards them.

"Come on, Leila." Her waterlogged boots were heavy. She tried to move her hesitant legs, but her surroundings were hard to see. They were running now, and Jill found a makeshift path amongst piles of pipe and concrete. No time to think, no time to plan. Just run.

The sound of boots was getting closer; they were gaining on them! With only the moonlight as their guide, they fled as fast as they could. Jill's only saving grace was that their pursuers couldn't go too fast on the treacherous slope, which would risk a hazardous fall—but neither could they. Adrenaline flowed quickly. She didn't feel any pain; she didn't feel anything but raw fear. The men were gaining on them. She had to think; she had to be innovative. She prayed for inspiration, and it came.

Jill and Leila took the corner. Jill darted an immediate right and saw stairs leading up from the pit to the street. She dog-paddled up the concrete stairs, Leila following.

Reaching the top, they sprinted across a dark street and crossed the road into another construction site. Jill was startled when her feet hit piles of garbage—bags full of litter. The sounds, she knew, would alert them. They kept running left and left again, then right, then zigzagged in the maze of dark side streets. At last, just as Jill's lungs felt about to burst, they ducked into a door well and huffed for air. They waited for any sign of the trackers dressed in black. Silently, Jill fumbled through her wet clothes to get Leila's phone, but hope faded as her numb fingers pushed the powerless buttons on the waterlogged phone.

"Shit!"

They stood catching their breath, and Leila snapped, "More friggin' people trying to capture us. This friggin' time they wanted to kill us, Jill. Hanging out with you is just so much fuuuuunnnn."

Jill didn't retort. She needed to figure out where they were.

"Well, I guess they know you're in Dubai."

"They were probably watching the hospital," Jill pointed out.

"Ya think?" Leila mocked.

Jill held up the phone, her breathing starting to slow. "We need to get one that works. Sorry." She handed the phone back to Leila. The edge of adrenaline was beginning to fade as her torso began to throb. The air had a humid haze as Jill looked down the dark street. The streetlights were about a mile away.

"They'll be looking for us still," said Leila. "Two chicks in a construction site? Seriously. And how big is this effin' mafia? They got cronies everywhere." Leila took a final huff before sticking her head out and peering down the street. "Clear."

They began to move in the direction of the streetlights and decided to cut across a construction lot to get off the street. They ducked in and out of the darkness around large piles of dirt and rock. They stopped when they heard a car slowly pass on the other side of the fence behind them. After it had passed, they continued. They were almost to the gate that crested the well-lit street. Between them and the entrance sat a large backhoe. On the other side was a small guardhouse that could only fit a chair. Jill could see by the streetlight shining down that no one was in it. They stopped, and Leila looked between one of the tall tinned panels. Large cement blocks held up the space between the panels. Leila stuck her head through and then glanced back at Jill.

"It's clear, Jill, but the road has streetlights. It'll be easy for anyone to see us. There aren't any sidewalks, so we'd be right on the road. And it doesn't look like a place where taxis would be trawling at night."

Jill looked through the break in the fence. "Maybe we should try and stop a car or something. Hitch a ride to a taxi stand." The wall was about ten feet from the road. "We can watch from here."

Leila was taller than Jill, and they watched the first car coming up the road. A white Land Cruiser with tinted windows. They ducked back as it passed. Within seconds, a second white Land Cruiser drove past.

"Is that all people drive around here—white Land Cruisers?" Leila said. The next car was a white Toyota pickup truck with brown stripes and no tint on the windows. It had a round orange hazard light that wasn't glowing on the roof.

Leila leaped in front of Jill, through the panels, onto the lit road, and waved to the driver. Jill scanned up and down the street and followed her. A bald white man in his early fifties rolled down the passenger window.

In a British accent, he said, "Been dragged through a hedge backward, mate?" As he looked in Jill's direction, she looked down at her soggy pants that were now stuck to her legs and the dirt on her belly. Jill did another scan while Leila pitched their quest to find a taxi. There were no other cars. Not any that Jill could see, anyway.

They squished into the front seat of the small-cabbed truck and sped out of the construction site. Jill concentrated on watching the quickly passing scenery to ensure they weren't being followed.

"What are you two birds doing on a construction site?" Leila gave him some song and dance about getting lost while trying to find a taxi.

"Why didn't you just get on with the concierge and get a taxi from him?" he asked.

"Hospitals have concierge services?" Leila replied.

"Spot on; they do, even valet."

As the two continued to chat, Jill tuned them out. She looked out the side mirror; there was more traffic now that they were on the main road. Nothing seemed too suspicious to anyone else. But to Jill, everything did.

She thought of what Zayed had told them. About the pipeline in Grozny. About the Chechens. What do they believe David has told me or given me? She did not know. It must have something to do with that schematic, Jill decided. Then another thought entered her mind. What if it doesn't? Then what? Chechens chased her around this goddamn hemisphere, and she'd had enough. But what was she to do? Ignore what she knew, or thought she knew, about Stan? Ignore her viewings? She could be wrong. She hoped she was.

"Can you drop us off at a mall?" Jill abruptly asked the driver. "We need to find a phone."

"You can use mine." The pudgy driver held up a Blackberry.

"It's an international call. We need one anyway."

Several traffic lights later, they approached a flyover and saw a sign: MALL OF THE EMIRATES. The mall looked vast and had a massive odd-shaped structure protruding like a bulky arm. The driver noticed they were staring and said, "Indoor ski slope." He giggled. "It's quite the picture seeing Arabs in their dishdashas with a jumper over the top, skiing." He finished his sentence with the words, "Only in Dubai." After what seemed to be endless speed bumps, they pulled in front of the bling doors and thanked the driver with a grateful goodbye.

CHAPTER THIRTY-FOUR

"What? What do you mean they came and took the schematic?" Jill said to Kali. Jill sat in the food court, watching Leila saunter towards her with a tray of subs.

"Yeah, when I got to the office this morning, they had confiscated my computer," Kali said with an annoyed edge. "They grilled me too. But I didn't know what was in the drawing. I told them, do I look like I can read Russian?"

"Are you sure it was Russian, Kali? Could it have been Chechen?"

"Ah, I, ah, dunno. I suppose. The clerk just said it looked like Russian. So I assumed it was. Aren't they the same anyway?"

"Chechen is a form of Russian, but it has its dialect. If I remember correctly, I think Chechen was a form of Arabic. Before Russian authorities attempted to ban it, that is," Jill recalled.

"I'd call the translation department for you and ask, but they were grilled harder than me. I think they'd give me a no-comment kind of gesture if you know what I mean. Did Eric reach you, Jill? He called to tell me that he couldn't get through. I tried you, too, and nothing. The phone just went to some lady speaking Arabic, I think."

Jill told Kali about the phone but omitted the part about being chased by the Chechens. She gave her a new number and hung up.

"What is it?" Leila asked, noting Jill's frown.

Jill told Leila what had happened to Kali at the office.

"The CIA, what the...? She's sure it was CIA?" Leila said, puzzled. She placed the tray of subs onto the shaky metal table and sat down. They silently thought until Leila asked, "Can you remember anything about that schematic?"

Jill thought momentarily, and then Leila flipped over a napkin and clicked on a pen.

"I can't Remote View here, Leila." Jill felt utterly defeated.

"I know that. Just see if you can remember anything. You're not a grandma. You still have a memory, don't ya?" Leila teased with a half-smile.

Jill faked a chuckle and grabbed the pen. "Funny, ha ha." Her left index finger pressed the napkin to the table as she drew. "Well, it had a large box that took up most of the page, and then inside," Jill ripped a bit of the napkin when she pressed a little too hard, "inside were smaller squares like this. They were all the same size," Jill described as she drew the smaller boxes. When she finished outlining the boxes, she said, "There were lines, maybe arrows like this." Jill dragged the pen, drawing several lines from the small boxes to outside the large boxes, and then printed X X X. "These were the words in Russian or maybe Chechen." She finished putting the three Xs at the end of each arrow outside the large box.

They sat momentarily, looking at what Jill had just drawn before Leila piped up. "Do you see what I see?"

Jill looked up at Leila and then back down to the drawing. "A bunch of boxes with lines leading to words." Jill sighed.

Leila huffed. "Look again, Jill. It looks like some sort of site plan." She pointed to the large square. "See, this looks like a compound of sorts, and here," Leila then touched the small squares, "this looks like buildings inside the compound. The words could be the name of the buildings or perhaps people's names."

Jill stared at the napkin. "Maybe..."

Something gave Jill a shiver. She scanned the food court. A man sat eating his food with his hand, staring at them before licking rice off his fingers one by one. He seemed harmless enough. Then Jill looked to her left. The food court was packed with an eclectic melting pot of nationalities. Jill snatched the napkin, and the chair scraped across the floor as Jill said pointedly, "Let's go," and walked towards the food court exit. Leila grabbed the subs and scrambled after her.

"What's the rush? We didn't even eat," Leila said with hurried breaths. They briskly walked through the glamorous mall, past branded stores. Past Louis Vuitton, past Montblanc, past Paris Gallery, and outside the mall doors. A long line of patrons was outside, most carrying large paper shopping bags, waiting in a taxi line.

As Leila and Jill stood at the end of the line, Jill did her scans.

Three o'clock. Three Arab teenagers dressed in dishdashas laughed loudly while playing on their mobiles.

Six o'clock. A lady in a bright green hijab bounced a crying baby in her arms, shushing it.

Nine o'clock. A white couple that looked to be at retirement age slid into the first taxi.

Leila watched Jill. "You're being paranoid."

Jill glared at Leila before hailing a cab. She stepped into the backseat of a bright pink taxi, the female driver of which matched her vehicle, in head-to-toe pink. The pudge of her cheeks pressed against the pink hijab. The music was blasting Bollywood. She punched on the meter, then turned down the music.

Jill commanded, "The Address Hotel," without so much as a please.

"Music, okay?" the driver asked. Jill just nodded.

The sounds of Bollywood again streamed throughout the vehicle, and Jill's brow furrowed as she looked at Leila. "Look, Leila; I've been chased halfway around the goddamn earth, been shot at, beat up." Jill attempted to grab her damp clothes and then held up the crumpled napkin still in her hand. "And now the CIA goes AWOL with this drawing, and you think I'm being paranoid." Jill leaned back into the seat.

"I guess you have a point." Then she grinned inconsolably and threw a sub onto Jill's lap. "Eat!"

It was hard to concentrate on eating, with the crazy lady taxi driver weaving hard in and out of traffic. At one point, Jill considered banging her on the back of the head with her sub when she drove onto the shoulder, too busy texting on her mobile phone.

Jill scarfed down the last bite of her sub when her new mobile rang. Eric's voice had to bellow to get above the loud music. After a few minutes of discussion about what Kali had told him about Stan, Eric said, "You sure about this, Jill? 'Cause if I call the Central Intelligence Department of the UAE, there's no turning back. They will apprehend him. They take their laws very seriously. They don't need to justify pulling him in, or even if he disappeared."

"I know, Eric, but I can't worry about that now. If something harmed many people, I look at this as if I am working on a case. I'm trusting my instincts," Jill yelled back.

"We've verified most of the intel you gave Kali. It seems Stan Brown has been on a low-priority watch list for some time now. They suspect him of money laundering. Nothing more, Jill. I'll have to move this up the chain of command before contacting the CID there."

"My father-in-law, how ironic is that."

"There'll be an extra investigation because of that, Jill," Eric warned.

"I expected that."

Beside Jill, Leila silently watched and listened to the one-sided conversation, then mouthed the word D-A-V-I-D.

"Have you heard anything more about David?" Jill's body lurched to the left from a too-fast approach at a large roundabout. "According to Johan, he is here in Dubai and has been for a few days now." Jill gushed hope. "There's more, Eric." Jill thought of Zayed and what he had told her. "Stan's plan may have something to do with control of a pipeline in Grozny, Chechnya. It's a long story, and you can probably tell I'm not in the best place to discuss this right now. Did Kali tell you about the confiscation of that schematic I found?"

"Yeah, I'm going to have to pull a few favors to get to the bottom of that, Jill. You know the drill."

Sure enough, Jill remembered the politics, but couldn't these two agencies put their testosterone aside and cooperate for once?

"Jill, I'll put in my report, but I think you should try contacting the US CIA department in Dubai. It's the largest in the Middle East. They operate out of the US Embassy there. Just in case something goes haywire with the CID. I'll put you in touch with someone I can vet. Stand by." Eric put Jill on hold.

"What?" Leila said as she lifted her hands, palms up in the air, before grabbing the handle to steady herself. "Bitch!" The driver merrily pressed on and off the gas pedal with music blaring, unaware of the complaints in the back.

"Okay, his name is Frank Wells," Eric said, returning to the line. "He'll be waiting for your call. But Jill, they are going to want the facts. I'll brief him about your background and Remote Viewings so he doesn't throw you out on your ass. I'm not sure they'll take this seriously. Your viewings were done independently and were not part of any official viewing group. There's a high probability that they are inaccurate. Remote Viewing must be done in a group; you know that, Jill." He gave Jill the number for Frank Wells, and they hung up.

Jill sensed that Frank was her last chance.

CHAPTER
THIRTY-FIVE

The US Embassy in Dubai looked brand new. Jill and Leila paid the taxi driver and scrambled out of the car. "You shouldn't have given that crazy bitch a dime," Leila scolded. They brushed themselves off, shaking the sand out of their hair. They stood in front of the three-story marble building. Several white floodlights lit up the sides of the beige structure. A security hut sat before the doors, and a chiseled, no-nonsense guard asked them why they were there.

"We're here to meet with Frank Wells," Jill said before he buzzed them in.

More security guards manned the embassy anteroom—it looked like one you would find at an airport. "Passports and mobile phones," the Filipino guard was curt. They obliged by placing their mobiles and passports in the tray before walking through the metal detector. The guard locked their stuff into one of the several dozen small compartments on the wall and handed Jill the key.

"Frank Wells," Jill said to the receptionist through a slot in the bulletproof glass. "He's expecting us." They signed in, were buzzed through a door, and had to wait several seconds for it to close before a second door opened into the embassy offices. A casually dressed woman, whose glasses slid up and down her nose, greeted them crisply, "Please follow me, Miss Oliver."

She led them through a series of corridors and finally into a large office with floor-to-ceiling windows covered with metal blinds; fluorescent lights brightly lit it.

A youngish-looking man with red hair sat at one end of the table. He wore blue jeans and a green golf shirt with an alligator logo stitched over the top left breast.

"I'm Frank." He stood, reached out to shake their hands, and gestured for them to have a seat before offering them a glass of water from the jug sweating on the table. He sat down again, glanced at his laptop, then looked back at Jill.

"Thanks for meeting us so late, Frank," Jill offered.

"I just got back from the airport and was wrapping up a rather lengthy report when I heard from Eric. I read the brief he sent me about you, Jill." He smiled genuinely. "So you're a Remote Viewer. I've heard of this type of intelligence. To be honest, I've read quite a lot about it. Ever heard of Ewin Sands?"

Jill nodded. "Yeah, he's a pioneer in the field of RV."

"I thought they called it virtual viewing now?" Frank replied. Jill shrugged. "Eric says you're in Dubai because of the information GSG gave you. Is that right?"

"Yeah, David and Stan Brown," Leila piped in.

"David is my husband," Jill said, then recounted the highlights of her search for David, including her misadventures in Afghanistan, the Chechens that were chasing her, and what Zayed had told them about Grozny. Jill watched Frank for a reaction or hint of his thoughts. He was apparently listening, but his relaxed body language reflected mild disinterest until Jill said, "I think all of this is somehow tied to

Operation Silhouette and Ochrana, but I haven't been able to connect the dots yet."

"What did you say?" Wells sat a little more upright and seemed to stiffen a bit.

Leila repeated the words back to him. His eyes shifted to her for a split second. "Sorel," he said, looking back at his computer screen. "Leila Sorel." He tapped on the computer keys and, without looking at them, said, "Where did you ladies hear these terms?"

Jill waited for him to make eye contact before she said, "In one of my Remote Viewings."

Frank leaned back in his chair and crossed his arms. "What exactly was in the viewing?" The question was more of a demand than a question.

"Well, in my first viewing, I saw what appeared to be a group of men meeting secretly for some reason. They were discussing controlling the Russian oil. And after what Zayed told us, it makes sense that it might have something to do with Grozny. In my second viewing, there was a man who I believe may be Stan Brown, buying uranium from a guy who looked very much like someone named Petrovich."

"We believe they're going to use Operation Silhouette as a ploy," Leila added. "You do know what Operation Silhouette is, right, Frank?"

Wells gave her a sharp look and circled his hand for her to continue. "Go on."

"We think Operation Silhouette and Ochrana are related, and we believe Stan Brown now has the uranium in his possession. Well, maybe not on him personally. That would be unlikely, I think," Jill finished and waited to see Wells's reaction.

He said nothing, just stared at them blankly. He was thinking, but Jill couldn't figure out by his body language exactly what. She reached into her pocket and pulled out the crumpled napkin. "We believe whatever is going on has to do with this." She flattened the napkin on the dark wood table.

It only took a nanosecond for a wave of recognition to race across his face. "Where'd you get this?" Wells sat up a little too fast.

"When I was in Kushka, Afghanistan. I found a schematic like this. Maybe it was in Russian or Chechen, and it was being translated in my office back in Tucson."

"That's before your goons showed up and confiscated it," Leila said snidely.

"My goons?" Wells parroted.

"As in CIA," Leila answered. "They took the schematic before Jill could have it translated."

"I see. Was this schematic the only one you found? Were there others?" His red sideburns moved as he ground his jaw.

"Why would the CIA confiscate the schematic Jill found?" Leila demanded softly.

"Well, Miss Sorel, based on your security level, I'll give you two words: It's classified."

Leila glared at him. He ignored her.

He looked back at the screen and then at Jill. "And as for Stan Brown, Miss Oliver, I highly doubt this story of yours is accurate."

Leila jumped up, "Come on, Jill, this asshole is wasting our time."

"Now, now, Miss Sorel," Wells was smug. "In Dubai, you can be arrested for insulting behavior." Leila turned around, flipped him the bird, and stormed out the door. Jill picked up the napkin from the table, stuffed it in her pocket, and followed her.

"That guy's a jerk-off," Leila huffed minutes later as their taxi swerved around a roundabout. Jill kept her mouth shut. She was too deep in thought to worry about Wells. He didn't believe Jill's theory either. First GSG, then Eric, and now this guy. Who was she kidding? Maybe she was off on her viewings. After all, they had been her first since McGregor. How accurate could they actually be? Jill began more than ever to second guess her gift. Second guess herself. Maybe she did interject her thoughts and feelings into what she viewed. She had gotten the Burj Khalifa building right, but who wouldn't think of the world's tallest tower when they went to Dubai? For a moment, Jill felt stupid.

She reached into her pant leg pocket and pulled a scrap of saturated paper. "What are you doing, Jill?" Leila queried.

Jill squinted at the note, found the number, and punched the keypad of her mobile. "Hello, Nasser? This is Jill Oliver. Johan Rhein from GSG gave me your number. He said you could help me. Can we meet?" There was a pause. "When?" Another pause. "Okay," and Jill closed the phone. She said to the taxi driver, "Take us to Madinat Jumeirah."

"Where are we going now, Jill? Haven't you had enough for one night, for one week? No one believes us. Hell, I'm starting to wonder if I even believe us," Leila's eyes glossed over as she gazed out the window.

"It's the IB that Johan gave us, remember? We have to try, at least." But Jill was starting to feel the same hopelessness.

Leila tilted her head back and yawned. "Better not be any Chechens, or I'm going to kick your ass this time."

The city seemed busier than earlier; like a Middle East Vegas, it was alive at night. Café-lined streets seethed with a hodgepodge of colorful hordes.

Madinat Jumeirah stood rock solid like an old Arabian fortress. Massive, thick, sand-colored walls with timber-like dowels protruding from the rooftop protected a labyrinth of shops, restaurants, and bars.

A couple laughed as they stumbled out the front door of the high-end marketplace as Leila and Jill walked in.

"Wow, impressive." Leila whistled. The inner souk boasted high ceilings supported by massive, darkly stained wooden beams. Little shops littered the sides of its maze of walkways. The heady smell of Arabic perfume mixed with incense wafted in the air. It was as if Jill and Leila were walking in an old Arabian market—but inside instead of out.

"Where are we meeting this guy? And how will we recognize him?"

"He said he'd be smoking shisha under a pergola in an outdoor courtyard on the water canal. And Leila, follow my lead. I'm not going to ask him to find Stan at this point. All I care about is finding David."

"Good call, girlfriend," Leila agreed. "And Jill, even if your viewings were accurate, I don't think anything can be blown up that fast. These things take time. Find David and then save the world. In that order!"

Jill marveled at how Leila could think so nonchalantly about nuclear devices detonating. But what did she expect? Leila didn't know what Jill knew.

Jill scanned the surroundings. But what was she looking for? The Chechens were not here. There was no way they were followed. But Leila was right. She was paranoid, and something about meeting this guy felt seedy.

They walked along the canals full of people partying. The turquoise water reflected glowing lanterns, and small boat taxis ferried passengers to the dock. The canal was lined with restaurants and bars. Music thrummed and competed with laughter. There were people everywhere. Jill and Leila threaded their way through the milling crowds and eventually reached the pergola about twenty-five feet in diameter. A young couple quietly chatted on the left side of the structure.

To the right sat a well-dressed man in a shimmering gray suit. His long hair flounced onto his shoulders. He was definitely an Arab. Jill profiled him as Leila inhaled sharply and whispered, "Man candy."

Jill gave her a sidelong glance as they approached the low-cushioned seats. "Nasser?" Jill said.

He sucked on the tip of the bong's coiled hose, causing the water to bubble and gurgle, then puffed out a cloud of smoke and replied, "Miss Oliver, come, please sit down. Shisha? It's apple," and he offered her the hose tip.

"No thanks," Jill politely refused, trying not to snub him.

"After you called, I spoke to Johan. He vetted you. But what he said about Miss Leila does not do you justice," he said as he moistened his lips and looked appreciatively at Leila before returning his gaze to Jill. "How can I help you? Johan told me you are looking for your husband. Is this what you need my help with?"

Jill nodded. "Yes, Johan said he had intel that David was in Dubai. We need your help to find him. His name is David Brown, and he's a journalist. I don't have a picture of him. Sorry."

Nasser sucked another hit, then answered, "In my business, we don't need pictures. All I need is cash. Dubai is rampant with spies, contractors, and all sorts of people willing to help in such matters. But everyone wants a piece of the pie."

"How much?" Jill had expected his answer and counted out the five thousand from her money belt that Nasser had requested as a down payment.

"You'll bring the other half when I give you his whereabouts." His voice was slick.

"How long will it take you?" she asked. Leila looked at him so intensely that she was on the verge of gawking. Jill nudged her foot to break the spell.

"I'll call you when I find him. Don't worry, Miss Oliver. If he's in Dubai it won't take me long," he promised.

CHAPTER THIRTY-SIX

21:13 Zulu Time—DUBAI, UNITED ARAB EMIRATES

"I've made a decision," Leila said as she kicked off her shoes in the swanky hotel room. "Emirati men are yummy. I think I'll have one for dessert when this is over."

It only took Jill ten minutes to shower. It was well after two a.m. now. Her hair was spiked as she walked barefoot across the room and shoved the mouse, pulling the computer screen from sleep mode. "Nothing," but Leila didn't hear Jill as she was softly purring, now cocooned in the overstuffed bed.

The sound of the phone ringing startled Jill alert. "Oliver," Jill said instantly, still half-asleep. On the other bed, Leila opened one eye and groaned.

"Miss Jill," Nasser whispered confidently. "I have what you need. Meet me back in the same place we met last night. Six p.m." Then he hung up the phone. Jill looked at the clock on the nightstand, which blinked at 15:18. "Shit." She whipped off the covers and jumped out of bed. Her movements were so fast it startled Leila awake.

"What?" Leila grumbled.

"Look at the time. Did we sleep all day?"

"We didn't get back here until two, so by my calculation, we still have a few more hours of sleep to make up." Leila was sitting up now, her long hair tangled from the sheets.

"That was Nasser," Jill said excitedly as she headed towards the bathroom. "We have to meet him at six o'clock today. Same place." She could hear Leila ask about David as she shut the bathroom door behind her. David. He hadn't mentioned David but said he had found what she had been looking for. Jill's heart began to pound harder. Had he seen him? She could only hope. But she wasn't up for hoping right now. She was done with that. She was done with caring about everyone, everything. After showering, brushing, and flushing, she exited the bathroom and tag-teamed it to Leila.

She sat in front of the computer screen and heard the familiar chime of... you've got mail. There was only one message, and it was from Kali:

No news on the schematic. Been hard to reach Eric, which is strange.

Be safe, O

"Enough of this already." Jill marched over to her carry-on and grabbed her notebook and pouch. She thought she heard a faint "what?" from the bathroom. Jill didn't respond. She pushed the computer back, squashed down her notebook, and opened it to a blank page.

She felt herself going fast after the five-minute chant. She was moving quickly through an energy channel. And there she was... viewing.

The bright light with a yellow hue lit up a ten-meter radius. Men were moving jerkily in the light. They were shouting and shouting in Arabic. A silhouette of the fat man blocked most of the view.

To the left of the silhouette knelt a man on the sand. His hands were tied behind his back. He was naked from the waist down. His head was lowered; his hair covered his face. The fat man said something in

Arabic, and the bound man slowly lifted his head and looked in his direction. The look on Zayed's face was one of betrayal. Vile malice. His face was swollen, and it was a wonder he could see.

The desert was pitch dark. The fat man tilted his head slightly to get a better look. It was just enough of a movement to see a headshot of a man. A headshot of David Brown. His look was one of forlornness. His face dawned a week of hair growth.

The fat man jerked his head back when a man suddenly grabbed Zayed by the hair. David was no longer in view. The man tilted Zayed's head back and stuffed a mitt-full of sand down his throat. It only took a second before Zayed was engulfed in flames.

"Jill, Jill!" Leila screamed as she shook her. "You okay? Jill! You're crying. What happened?"

Jill blinked herself back from the bio-location and looked down at the page. There before her was a sketch of the Star of David. It had the same points and folds as the one she had drawn before, but somehow it seemed smaller.

"I, ah, I viewed," Jill said, now a trembling mess.

Leila took the pen from Jill and lowered it onto the page. Then she guided Jill to her bed and gently nudged her onto it. "Sit here. Tell me what you saw."

Jill sat and swallowed hard, trying to understand what she'd just viewed. "It was horrible, Lei. It was in a desert at night. I connected so vividly that I thought I was there standing, watching. I felt things I have never felt in a viewing before. This time I felt it; the feeling was so strong."

"What? What did you feel?"

"Evil." Jill shivered and wiped her nose on the sheet.

"Your hands are shaking." Leila, now sitting beside Jill, clasped her hands around them. "Tell me, Jill, what did you see?"

"I viewed men in fatigues. They were torturing a man."

"Chechens? Who was being tortured?" Leila held her breath.

Jill recalled the military men. "They didn't look like Chechens. They almost looked... well, American. And the man being tortured was Zayed." Jill's voice grew angry. "They beat him so bad, Lei, I don't think he could see. His face was swollen. Then they stuffed sand down his throat and lit him on fire."

"What the...?"

"On fucking fire, Lei, like poof." Jill's hands shot up in the air.

Leila didn't say anything. The shocked look on her face said it all.

"The fat man was there again." Jill's teeth began to grit. "It was like he gave the order to kill Zayed. He spoke in Arabic." Jill paused, trying to summon the courage and find the strength to continue the story. "That's not the worst part, Leila. I saw David. I think the fat man was going to kill him next. I think Stan will have David tortured, beaten, and then set on fire." Jill jumped up frantically, moved fast to the desk, and smashed her arm across it. Her computer, notebook, and numbers flew across the room. Jill was hysterical now. With a sudden start, she grabbed her notebook off the floor.

"You see this," she growled as she tried to rip her notebook in half. It was too thick. "And I can't do a goddamn thing about it." In frustration, she pitched the notebook across the room. It smacked off the door and landed on the ground. Then she plopped onto the chair, wrapped her arms around her head, leaned over, pressed herself hard onto the desk, and sobbed.

Leila walked over and put her hand on Jill's shoulder. Several minutes of Jill's wailing had passed before Leila gave Jill a cappuccino. The smell of coffee interrupted Jill's outburst, and Jill lifted her head. Leila gave her a comforting look. "You okay?"

Jill looked at her, but all she could do was laugh. Snot ran from her nose as she grabbed a tissue and blew. "I guess that exorcist moment made the record books."

"Yup, your head was about to spin off." Leila sat on the other chair and put her hand on Jill's lap. "David's fine, Jill. We just heard from Nasser. He knows where David is. Besides, I don't think Stan speaks Arabic, do you?" That thought hadn't occurred to Jill because she was too busy having her nuclear meltdown. "Besides," Leila continued, "we just saw Zayed yesterday, and he didn't look like he was going anywhere anytime soon. Maybe what you saw was not a viewing but like a premonition or something like that."

"Yeah, or maybe I am just goddamn losing it!" Jill's thoughts haunted her. Maybe I lost my gift too. I lost pretty much everything after Matthew McGregor. My job at the FBI. Peace. And now David.

"What was David doing?"

"I only saw him for a second. I just saw his face. That stupid fat bastard's head was in the way. If only I could have drop-kicked his fat ass out of the way."

Leila rolled her eyes.

"He looked weathered. He looked like he hadn't slept in a week or hadn't had a shower." Jill conjured an image of David. That last day she saw him. That smile. The way he looked at her—the way he made her feel.

A warmth began to fill Jill. It consumed her soul so strongly that she felt a hint of peace for the first time since David had been missing. Jill looked over at the clock and back to Leila. Then Leila said, "Come on, Jill. Let's go meet Nasser. Let's go find David."

CHAPTER
THIRTY-SEVEN

The taxi smelled of curry and smelly feet. Jill reached over, put her hand on Leila's, and mouthed the word "Thanks." Leila smiled back. They were only ten minutes into the trip when Jill's phone rang.

"Jill, it's Eric. I wanted to call you myself. The police have Stan Brown in custody now. I just got the call. Got a pen?"

Jill motioned to Leila for a pen. "Yup," Jill said as she steadied the small paper on her lap.

"Call this number... you'll speak to Colonel Mohamed Al Jaber. He's with the Abu Dhabi police."

"Abu Dhabi police?"

"Stan checked into the airport at Abu Dhabi."

Jill recalled the giant octopus building. "Where was he going?"

"Georgia," Eric responded. "Tbilisi, to be exact."

"Georgia in the US?" Jill queried.

"No, by Russia. It's a sovereign state, former Russian, well, sort of. Anyway, Jill, don't get too excited. I know what you're thinking. But they are only detaining him for potential money laundering, and the UAE only cares if he's laundered through any of their banks. Nothing more. Mr. Jaber is expecting your call. He's agreed to speak to you.

And Jill," Eric's voice warned, "don't mention your Remote Viewing; that's enough to land you in the clink over there."

"They got Stan," Jill announced as she closed the phone. She repeated what Eric had said. "I guess he's with the Abu Dhabi Police because he was apprehended in Abu Dhabi."

"For what?" Leila asked.

"Potential money laundering. That's it. You'll never guess where Stan was flying to."

"You mentioned Georgia in the US?"

"Nope, Georgia, the country. It borders Russia," Jill said.

"Oh, God."

"I got the number to a colonel at the police department." Jill glanced at the time on the dash. "It's almost six. Let's go see Nasser and then call the colonel."

They had been sitting under the pergola for a while when Jill asked the waiter for the second time what time it was. "He's late almost by half an hour," Leila complained. One thing about Leila—she was never late.

"Chicken, in the Arab world, being on time is like forty-five minutes late. In our world, being on time is early to an Arab." But still, Jill looked nervously around, and as every minute ticked past, she fidgeted more.

"Your boot-tapping will drive me up the friggin' wall." Leila pushed hard on Jill's leg, forcing Jill to stop. The sun was almost down now, and after the last pass by the waiter, it was 7:12 p.m.

"He's not coming," Jill said, followed by, "What the..." Jill watched as three security guards approached the pergola. Jill tensed, but the officers didn't even look their way. They passed the pergola and headed down the canal to where a crowd was gathering.

"Excuse me, excuse me," Jill said as they pushed through the crowd to follow after them, but they couldn't move past the wall of tourists.

"What's going on?" Leila asked after tapping a man's shoulder who was wearing an orange golf shirt.

"Appears someone drowned or something." He sounded Spanish. Hearing this, Jill grabbed the sides of two people and plied her head through the wall of bodies. She gasped when she saw Nasser in a wet brown velvet suit. His face was blue. The three guards stood there, not doing a thing to help him.

Without hesitation, Jill pushed herself through the crowd and bent over Nasser. She put her ear to his mouth. Nothing. She put her hand on his chest. Nothing. She was about to begin resuscitation when he grabbed her arm, yanking her away from Nasser. He said something in Arabic and then, "What are you doing?"

"CPR." Jill attempted to pull her arm from his grip.

He held on tight and said, "Are you a doctor? Do you have a certificate for medical practice here?"

"What? No," Jill said, yanking her arm free. This time she pulled a little harder, and pain jabbed her side.

"Then you cannot touch him. Understand." He breathed Marlboro.

"But... but, I might be able to save him," she pressed.

"Lady." His teeth were tartared so badly his lips looked like they were getting stuck on them when he spoke. "It's against the law to practice medicine without a certificate. Do you understand?"

It was at that moment Jill wanted to knee him in the groin, twist her back towards him, and flip him onto the ground before smashing her boot into his jaw. But a single voice interrupted her vision.

"Jill!" Leila called to her. Jill looked over at Leila, and Leila shook her head no.

Well, the least she could do was spit in his face before she agreed. But she decided against that too. The security guard released Jill, and they morphed back into the crowd.

"So they're going just to let him die?" Jill reasoned.

"Yup, same thing they do in Afghanistan. No good Samaritan laws there either."

"But he was going to tell us where David is." Jill abruptly stopped and turned to go back until Leila grabbed her by the shoulder and said no.

CHAPTER THIRTY-EIGHT

17:33 Zulu Time—ABU DHABI, UNITED ARAB EMI-RATES

It was quiet at this time of night and a bit too anticlimactic for Jill as they drove towards Abu Dhabi. She had called the police station at least seven times before she got an answer.

She was told that the colonel would see her, but not until after his nap, which apparently ended at nine p.m. It was after nine o'clock now. Jill was also told that she could not speak to Stan. They didn't have visiting hours like a jail in the US. Special permission would be needed, letters signed and stamped, and reasons for visiting declared before approval. For Leila, it was just all too much bullshit, and she'd rather watch TV than be included in a handshaking introduction meeting. After all, it would be repeated the next day anyway. She'd go then. Jill felt a tinge of envy for a moment, knowing Leila was comfortably wrapped in a blanket watching National Geographic in high definition.

The drive was uneventful as she sped along the highway. Jill admired the endless rows of bright streetlights that lit up the smooth pavement mile after mile. They drove fast on the Sheikh Zayed highway, but it wasn't fast enough for some. Cruising at 160 km, the speed limit, they were still flashed by speeders in large white SUVs to move out of the way. Every time one kissed their ass, Jill thought of the Chechens.

She didn't know what to think of Nasser's drowning. Was it an accident? It was too coincidental, Jill thought. But her exhaustion was not allowing her to think straight. Then there were her viewings. How could her viewings have been so wrong? How could she allow McGregor to steal this too? Then she thought of where Stan was flying to. Georgia.

She only had about fifteen minutes to Google that before the concierge called to announce her car's arrival. Well, a car rental with a driver, not a limo. It seemed that one had to book far in advance to hire a taxi to take you to Abu Dhabi.

Georgia made sense for Grozny. The Google results produced information that gave Jill some insight into what Zayed had told her. Zayed. Was he really in her viewing? She tried calling the hospital but kept getting switched from one person to the other. None, it seemed, spoke any sort of recognizable English. She resigned herself to the fact that she would go there tomorrow and talk with him further. Find out more about Grozny.

Grozny was the capital of Chechnya and bordered Georgia. Georgia was between the Black Sea and the Caspian Sea. Wikipedia told her that in the past, the US wanted to control the three-hundred-mile gap that separated Ukraine and Kazakhstan, as it is today. The US had even set up a base in Poland to ensure close proximity in the region. Most Russian oils flowed through the Caucasus Valley and the major pipeline through Grozny. Why was he going there? Jill looked out the window and pondered.

The endless days with little sleep were beginning to take their toll on Jill. The forty-minute drive to the Abu Dhabi prison, AL MUKALIM, almost lulled her to sleep. She tried to Google the prison but only got the warning icon that blocked any computer in the UAE from viewing the website; this made her wonder if she shouldn't have come alone.

On the top of the grand white reinforced cement fence walls sat coils of barbed wire. Jill couldn't help noticing as the car pulled up to the gate. The guard came and asked her for ID. The gate lifted, and the long black Mercedes went through.

Inside the prison was a large reception area. Two men and one woman sat behind it. They were dressed in baby green uniforms with maroon berets snugly tilted on their heads. Their shoulders sported branded maroon appliqués with a single shiny gold star. The woman had a matching headscarf under the beret and was tucked tightly inside her collar. After more ID checks and stern nods, the woman officer stood up and, with a no-nonsense gesture, motioned Jill to follow her.

It was a typical interrogation room—four metal chairs and a table squashed against the double-paned glass. A man wearing the same police uniform sat at the table and yelled into a mobile phone. On the metal table sat an ashtray full of cigarette butts. He didn't acknowledge her. His arm just moved frantically in the air, shouting into the phone. Jill decided whoever he spoke to in Arabic was on the receiving end of a rant. Awkwardly, she waited in the room for quite some time before the locked door creaked open.

A tall Arab police officer walked through. He was followed by a small Indian servant carrying a tray of tiny cups and a carafe of coffee. "I took the pleasure to order you some coffee," the man's tongue rolled.

"It's Turkish, the best." He smiled wide in Jill's direction, showing his teeth.

He leaned in, poured the tar coffee into two small cups, passed one to Jill, and sat back. "I hope you found your way to the prison easily. But I'm afraid you came too soon." He leaned forward into Jill's personal space, and his expression went from host of the year to menacing disregard. "We don't like foreigners telling us how to do our jobs here. We have our way of dealing with these problems. We do not like when people attempt to make us look bad; our country looks bad. We take care of things in ways the Western world would deem harsh. It keeps crime down, and it works." The metal chair pinched on the cement as he sat back and took a gulp of his coffee.

Jill sat quietly, noticed the two shiny gold stars on the officer's appliqué, and tried to figure out this man's problem. Suddenly, she felt like she was the one being interrogated.

"I've been told you know this man, Stan." His eyes began to glare again. "How do we know you are not working with him?" His fist slammed hard on the metal table. His pinky ring gave a sharp clang when he hit the table again. Jill started to feel uneasy and wondered if it was such a brilliant idea to come along to a prison in the Middle East. Let alone being a woman.

There was a slight tremble in her voice before she held her ground. "I'm here on behalf of the US Government." Jill realized that was probably not the best thing to say, but it was too late.

"Khalas," the other police officer shouted. He had two shiny stars and a gold emblem resembling a falcon on his appliqué. He gave the subordinate a "shush" hand gesture and looked back to Jill. He introduced himself as the colonel Jill had intended to meet with and said, "The US are our friends, Habibi." He spoke sternly to the other officer. "Why do you speak to such a beautiful woman like that?" He looked back at Jill and grinned a placating smile.

A man in a dishdasha walked into the room, intruding. He spoke to the colonel, and the colonel pointed in a direction, clearly giving him a location. A little Indian servant walked back into the room carrying a filing box and placed it on the table before the colonel. Then another police officer came in and laid a file before him. The colonel flipped it open, read the page, and signed it before the officer left the room.

He then looked at Jill. "We're holding Mr. Brown as a favor to your government. We can hold him as long as we feel necessary. Well, long enough to determine if any crime has been committed in the UAE. But my preliminary report says there is no reason to keep him. The contents of his briefcase are in the box, and he had no weapons." Jill looked at the box and was about to say something when the colonel's mobile phone rang again. She looked at the other police officer, who was busy texting on his mobile phone.

A few minutes passed, and Jill's annoyance grew. Courtesy, my ass! She turned toward the hall when she heard people approaching. Two men stopped in front of the door. Stan saw her, and although Jill's stomach jumped, he didn't seem surprised. It was almost as if he knew she was coming. He stood next to the police officer—who had just left the room five minutes ago. Stan's orange coveralls bulged at his waist. His cheeks were flushed a light rose color. He looked at Jill and smirked.

Stan looked over at the subordinate officer and said, "Assalamu Alaikum." Peace be with you.

"Wa alaikom assalam." Peace be with you as well.

"Kaif haluk?" How are you?

"Zain wa anta?" Fine and you?

"Bkhair Alhamdulillah." Fine, thanks be to God.

Jill's jaw dropped. Stan could speak Arabic. Shit!

The smug look from Stan lasted for only a few seconds; it faded fast when he saw the filing box on the table. Jill thought she had read a hint of anxiety on his face before his stance shifted. He didn't have handcuffs on. That bastard's getting the VIP treatment. She looked towards the box and then back at Stan. The vile look he gave her physically changed the shape of his face. Evil flickered in his beady eyes.

Still talking loudly into the phone, the colonel looked over at Stan, scowling at Jill, and dismissed the young officer with a curt wave. It took Jill's strength not to run after him, grab him hard, and twist his goddamn head off.

"My apologies for the interruption. I have many problems that give me a headache," he explained.

Jill didn't give a shit. Then she did something she had never done before. She pulled a Leila. With a flirting smile, she tilted her head and asked, "What's in the box?" The words almost purred out of her lips.

"Not much, I have been told. Would you like to have a look?" the handsome young colonel flirted back.

The other police officer protested in Arabic. The colonel showed his subordinate the palm of his hand. Then he reached into the box, pulled out a bright yellow file folder, placed it in front of himself, and began thumbing through it. It was all show. "Looks like some drawings and a contract of some sort. I think this is normal for a businessman." His tongue curled. "We don't normally let people see this stuff, but since you are a US Marshal..." He smiled at her. "And one of such beauty. Why not!"

He closed the folder, twirled it with his finger, and pushed it before Jill. Jill looked down at the folder and could hear the colonel rummaging through the box as she flipped open the file.

She stared at the second-to-last page and blinked as if adjusting her eyes to what she was reading. The impact of it hit her hard. Her world began to quake. It felt like giant pieces of sandpaper scraping down her face to Jill. The room was spinning now. She tried to focus, tried to understand what she was reading. The impact of the deception was like being drop-kicked in the gut. She could see the colonel talking to her, but what was he saying? He was pointing to a Ziploc bag on the table.

Her ears shrilled a cacophony of bells when Jill picked it up and moved the things in the plastic with her fingers. A Rolex watch that seemed too big for any man's wrist. Keys. For what, she did not know—a ring.

Grayness crept around her eyes, attempting to shut her down. She pinched the ring in the plastic bag and looked at the inscription she had engraved inside the gold and silver inlaid circle for David: "To Eternity." Then all she could hear was someone screaming. Someone was crying, and a split second later, she realized it was her. No recognition, no sense. Dizziness. Sounds muffled. Darkness.

EPILOGUE

Four Weeks Later

15:27 Zulu Time—TUCSON, ARIZONA

It would be one of the last times for a long time that Jill would be in Arizona, or America, for that matter. She tried not to dwell on the sad beauty of Tucson as she headed toward the airport. The glass house in the Catalina Mountains sold in less than one day. The trunk of the Uber cab was filled with only insignificant attire that held no memories. It was almost 10:30 p.m. Beside her sat a briefcase, and inside were two files. One on Stan Brown, the other on David Brown. She glanced at her pouch of clay numbers and a plane ticket to Istanbul, Turkey.

A week after she was back in Tucson, Jill had received a call from Eric. Interpol had called him regarding a reference. "They want your skills, Jill, and I think you should take their offer seriously," he counseled. "You could help so many more people globally." Jill accepted the job through Interpol in New York City, knowing her first assignment would be the break she desperately needed and two months working with Europol in Istanbul—the new hub of ISIS. Jill wanted to get as far away from her past as she could. And Turkey was just the place.

Inside the file on David was a translated copy of the schematic. The original words in Chechen were names of people and their positions and what each individual's role was in the plan. According to the pages in Stan's file, David worked with Stan. His name was in bold letters below the words "Communication Tower." In her copy, she had read David's name over and over again. The only reason Jill had a translated copy was that she had a copy of the scan in a hidden file on her computer when she first sent it to Kali. No one knew she had it. Not even Eric.

Jill had explained to the colonel what she thought was in the file that night at the prison after she regained some coherency. But he just snatched up the files and the box and demanded Jill leave the prison immediately. Later she was told by Eric that the colonel needed to save face. It was an Arab thing, he said. And he was certain Stan was no longer receiving any VIP treatment. You wouldn't want to attempt to pull the wool over an Arab police colonel, definitely not in a country with strict laws. Jill wouldn't wish their interrogation techniques on anyone, and as for Stan, she didn't care anymore.

David, a traitor, how could this be? She asked herself every moment of every day since. Jill felt a nagging sense of dread about what Zayed had said just before they left the hospital. Leila and Jill talked about what he must have meant. How well do you know David? Jill sighed at this thought. How could she have been so wrong? So off? How could she have loved a man that would work with such an evil person? David hated his father. None of it made any sense; well, that was until Leila told her what she had discovered.

Sure, some things didn't make sense in the past year. But Jill excused David's absences and closed-door conversations as part of his job. With the confirmation at GSG that David was a NOC, she almost made it all add up. Jill's plan when she found David was to confront him about it all. But now that was too late. And right now, she didn't feel anything.

Leila didn't believe David was a traitor either, and the more she snooped around in the CIA for information, the more she uncovered intel about the plan. After Jill's prison visit, they spent the next week searching in the UAE for any information on what had happened to David. The hospital told them that Zayed had checked out the night before Jill's viewing in the desert. But the desert was a big place, and they were searching independently. She'd tried viewing several times more and got nowhere. Not so much as a scribble surfaced. Jill didn't know if she could ever Remote View again.

Jill and Leila pushed hard to see Stan before leaving for Brussels. They were told it was in the two governments' hands to sort out. Dribbles of information were sent from the UAE to the US regarding Stan, and Leila had said what was in the file. But that was classified. Eric had urged them to leave before anything negative happened to them.

They spent round-the-clock time in Brussels searching and reviewing anything they could get their hands on to try and determine what had changed the course of Jill's life. They found nothing.

No one knew any more details about the Star of David, or they wouldn't talk. But it was gone when Leila returned to the old church where the star once lay. "Burnt down in a fire," the old man next door had told her.

Based on Jill's viewings, these social network demonstrations called Operation Silhouette were set up as a ploy to distract the Chechen Mafia, the US, and Russia from what Jill believed to be the Ochrana group. Stan's group. Well, at least that was what Jill thought. But Leila didn't believe so.

No one believed Jill, not even Eric. But Jill was determined to find out the truth. Committed to clearing David's name and what her viewings had uncovered made even Leila think twice about her employer.

Jill sat in disbelief as Leila told her the story. "You were right, Jill; your viewings were correct." Somehow this did not give Jill any relief. "Stan cracked once he got to Guantanamo Bay. Cracked like a fat baby. He sounded pathetic, actually, from what I understand. I think the questioning by the UAE authorities wore him down before he was extradited. He'll be locked up for many years and die there, Jill."

Leila then began to tell Jill that there was a plan to execute a nuclear device and make it look like the Russians did it. "But here's the kicker," Leila chimed. "When Stan was questioned about David and his whereabouts, he said he didn't know and that David had given him his ring so no one could positively identify him during the operation. He fanatically denied killing him. Apparently, David wanted you to have the ring if anything happened to him. Sounds so sweet, doesn't it? Not! Enter Petrovich. It was his knowledge of nuclear weaponry that kept the uranium enriched. He despised the Chechen Mafia, and it was his way of payback and earning a few big bucks too."

Jill had discovered that several years ago, the Chechen Mafia had set up a demonstration planned for the media. It was designed to prove the mafia's power to the rest of the world and boast of its nuclear power. Because the then CIA director had played it down, the Chechen Mafia lost its clout. That left the mafia desperate to make a deal. The pipeline was the collateral they needed to prove to the world that they were serious players. A Saudi newspaper report speculated that the US and Russia were in a race to make a deal with the mafia. To control the oil.

Two men Stan worked with were mercenaries and part of a rogue group that had broken away from the Chechen Mafia. They met with David in Afghanistan. Apparently, there was some sort of ambush, and they fled. They lost contact with David until Dubai. It was the Chechen Mafia that had been tracking Jill. But the mercenaries were also tracking her—tracking David.

"Something's not adding up, though, Jill. I called a few higher-ups in the CIA, but no one is talking about this operation. And what's even odder is that David's name is still in our NOC database. It's almost as if David was a double agent, undercover so deep that even Stan didn't realize it."

Jill didn't know what to believe. The CIA was clearly working to suppress the details. Frank Wells from the CIA in Dubai was a good indication of that. Their hush was a telltale sign that perhaps the Saudi paper was correct.

Jill was numb with pain. Her heart no longer ached, for it was broken. She couldn't get into the tunnels. If Jill's viewings were accurate, then Zayed was now dead, and so was David. She didn't believe Stan would be gracious enough to hand her David's ring. She would never believe him. Not now, not ever.

There was no memorial service for David, for his body was never found. His colleagues had stopped calling now; even Leila had. Jill left nothing behind.

As she pulled up to the airport, there was only one thing left to do. She dropped her bags on the curb, stood, and checked the time on her phone. She looked towards the lights in the airport and saw people moving inside. Even this late at night, airports were always busy. Then something caught her attention. Something in the shadows. She could make out a figure standing there watching her. As she tried to focus her eyes on the dark figure, a large truck pulled up behind Jill. Its headlights flashed on the shadow. Jill's phone fell onto the concrete, cracking when she saw David.

www.ingramcontent.com/pod-product-compliance
Lightning Source LLC
Chambersburg PA
CBHW062029170626
46813CB00001B/339